THE WORLD'S COOLEST CULT-MOVIE CHRONICLE!

BY MARTY BAUMANN

A priceless compendium of personality profiles, interviews and reviews from the author of the Internet's most popular cult-movie resource!

WWW.BMONSTER.COM

Published by Dinoship
New York, NY

ISBN 0-9728585-4-7

All contents copyright 2004, Marty Baumann.
No reproduction of this material is permitted without permission from the author and publisher unless excerpted for review purposes.

"Warning: Those easily nauseated approach with caution!" The Werewolf vs. The Vampire Woman

THE ASTOUNDING B-MONSTER

"New thrills as the Monster stalks again!" The Ghost of Frankenstein

To the Bride of B Monster.

"Terror ... that screams from the grave!" The Undead

Contents

Foreword by Fess Parker — 7

Part 1: But, Before We Begin ... — 9

Part 2: Beauties, Beast and B Kings — 15

  James Arness: Now Here's The Thing — 17
  Charlotte Austin: The Gorilla Can't Help It — 25
  Pat Boyette: Texas Terror's Lone Star — 35
  Bruce Campbell: Army of Darkness: Militia's Intent — 43
  Robert Clarke: Here Comes the Sun Demon — 49
  Dick Contino: Daddy-O's Double Life Story — 61
  Richard Cunha: Giant Among Unknowns — 71
  Pamela Duncan: A Trance Encounter With Fame — 79
  Anne Francis: She Made Id Worth the Trip — 85
  Robert Fuller: Fuller's Brush With the Brain — 93
  Beverly Garland: Queen of the Screamers — 101
  Alex Gordon: The Fan Behind the Camera — 111
  Leo Gordon: Big As Life And Twice As Ugly — 119
  Jack Hill: Giving Birth To Spider Baby — 129
  Jimmy Hunt: Sci-Fi Fairy Tale — 137
  Ed Kemmer: Buzz Corry's Personal Space — 145
  Lori Nelson: How the Creature Finally Caught Up With Her — 153
  Fess Parker: Them's the Breaks — 161
  Rex Reason: The Voice of Reason — 175
  Ann Robinson: George Pal's World War Wonder — 179
  Herb Strock: How To Make a Monster — 185
  Del Tenney: Horror of Party Beach: A Shore Thing — 193
  Mamie Van Doren: The First Sex Kitten in Cyber Space — 201
  Yvette Vickers: Lust Among the Leeches — 211
  Mel Welles: The Little Shop's Original Proprietor — 221
  Marie Windsor: Kubrick and the Cat-Women — 227

Part 3: Beware the Baby Boomer's Wrath! — 233

"Prehistoric rebels against prehistoric beasts!" Teenage Cave Man

Acknowledgments

First and foremost, I must thank the indefatigable P.L. Joy, editor, critic, confidant and that rarest of specimens, a FEMALE who enjoys 1950s science fiction AND the Three Stooges (like some strange, hybrid creature from Greek mythology).

Special thanks to "The Author With the Atom Brain," Tom Weaver. Anything he DOESN'T know about the making of these movies probably never happened in the first place. (He might forget the five bucks he owes you, but if you want to know what Skelton Knaggs had for lunch on the third day of shooting **Dick Tracy vs. Cueball**, Tom's your man.)

Thanks to messrs. Madison and Frost and all the Dinoship worker ants.

Thanks to Bob and Kathy Burns for remembering our past and managing to fit all of it into their basement for safekeeping.

Thanks to the organizers and bestowers of The Rondo Awards.

Thanks to The Fabulous Brunas Boys.

Thanks to ALL B Monster contributors and supporters, past and future.

Thanks to all of the people listed in the table of contents.

EXTRA special thanks to Mr. Fess Parker and Mr. Jack Davis, living legends who measure up to our impossibly lofty preconceived notions of them with modesty, grace and generosity.

Thanks to everyone I've forgotten to thank. You'll be in the next book.

"The super-shock sensation of all time" House of Dracula

Foreword

Photo by Kirk Irwin

I am very pleased to be included in this book and I am happy to contribute a few words on the importance of these "B" pictures to the careers of up-and-coming young actors.

The movie **Them!**, about giant ants mutated from the atomic development in the New Mexico desert, created a science fiction cult following and played near the top of the box office list in Great Britain and many other places when it premiered in 1953.

I had a role in the film as a rancher named Alan Crotty who had been confined to a psychiatric ward after claiming he'd seen the big insects. It was a small but very important part.

Them! did big business and generated a great deal of publicity. Intrigued, Walt Disney viewed it in his studio and it led to my being cast in the role of Davy Crockett in 1954.

I enjoy many of the other early science fiction films with fervor; naturally **Them!** is one of my favorites.

These early films afforded young actors such as myself the opportunity to gain invaluable experience and exposure. I recall them fondly, and I hope you enjoy reading about them as much as we enjoyed making them.

Fess Parker

"An endless terror! A nameless horror!" Them!

"An unspeakable horror ... Destroying ... Terrifying!" The Beast With a Million Eyes

But, Before we Begin ...

Obviously the subjects herein — the films reviewed, the personalities profiled — are chosen at the B Monster's discretion. That point having been made clear, there are still a few ground rules that need establishing. And so ...

"How did it get here?" The Thing From Another World

"You'll be gripped by unholy horror when you realize what H really means!" **The H-Man**

The genre idea

First of all, this is not a book for movie experts. **The Astounding B Monster** — book or Web site — was never conceived as a definitive, "last word" reference guide. There are plenty of research hounds with faultless memories out there. Rather, it was created for the weary salesman in the stuffy office, cruising the Internet on his lunch hour. He (or she) happens upon a page and says, "Wow! I remember that movie!" There's a spark of nostalgia that makes them smile and maybe they dig a little deeper into the genre. They connect via e-mail and the questions begin pouring in. "What was the movie about the walking tree?" "Was **Monster From the Surf** the same movie as **The Beach Girls and the Monster**?" "Whatever became of Pamela Duncan?"

And the question we're most often asked: "What is a 'B' movie?" The definitive answer depends on who you ask. But the consensus is that, in the days of the double feature, the top half of the bill was "A" and the bottom half was "B." (I for one am glad they didn't refer to them numerically; *The Astounding 2 Monster* doesn't have quite the same zip.) Producers weren't apt to lavish as much time or money on the second fiddle and subsequently "B" became associated with the film's budget, which was almost always incredibly low. (In the heyday of top-40 radio a similar rationale was applied to 45 rpm records; the "A" side was the "hit," the "B" side was the throwaway.)

As exploitation cinema reached its zenith with the drive-in fare of the 1950s, more and more of these "B" budget movies could be classified as science fiction, horror or juvenile delinquent/rock 'n' roll films. (Some films fell into more than one of these categories. Some fell into all of them!) Simultaneously, the late-night "Shock Theater" offerings, composed mostly of the classic Universal monster movies of the 1930s and '40s, were popping up in television markets across the country. This became the baby boomer's horror heritage. *The Astounding B Monster* employs a very broad and flexible umbrella in an attempt to provide an edifying overview of this genre. (Some of those boomers, inspired to pursue a career in film, grew up to make their own B-movie homages. At our discretion, our coverage might extend to them, as well.)

What rankles me today are the innumerable soft-core porn makers, film school students and any Bozo with a video recorder who thinks that, just because his film has a tenuous tie to science fiction, it should be celebrated alongside **The She-Creature, Invaders From Mars** or **Frankenstein Meets the Wolf Man**. Just because you say it's a "B" movie in the best tradition of the term doesn't make it so. (Which is not to say that these amateurs won't someday turn out classics along the lines of **The Adventures of**

"If your flesh doesn't crawl, it's on too tight!" The Night Visitor

Pluto Nash, or **Leprechaun 3**).

How did we get to this point? Seeing as how the majority of the films we salute are science fiction, for the benefit of the uninitiated, we provide a genre overview which we hope will prove illuminating:

Science fiction, the most mitigated and misinterpreted film genre, has managed to snake its way into our collective consciousness despite the way it's been misunderstood and mangled by adolescent practitioners. But don't let the field's history of malignment stop you from pursuing a career in fantasy film. If you're going to create a science fiction project (and if you've yet to work on a science fiction film, be patient, there's only three guys in line ahead of you), let me lay out a few easy guidelines that will make your job much easier.

1. Know your history

Though historians are hesitant to put too fine a point on it, science fiction was invented by James Cameron some time in the mid-1980s. Sure, there was a smattering of "speculative" fiction prior to Cameron, and even a film or two that one might categorize as "non-documented scientific theory," but put every pre-Cameronian idea out of your mind as you approach the genre.

2. The future will suck

No two ways about it, we'll live in squalor with no hope. We're all doomed to a gloomy dystopia, where we'll be relegated to emotionless servitude as depicted in Cameron's triumph, **Titanic**, which featured a sleek, futuristic craft piloted by powerful, snooty people who force the less fortunate below deck, where they must chop wood and Riverdance. (Truth be told, I nodded off four hours into the film, only to be awakened by the audience chants of "ICE-BERG, ICE-BERG!")

Another excellent illustration of this noirish forecast can be seen in the film **Dark City**. That's the one with the perpetually rainy, neon-lit city run from behind the scenes by several dozen clones of **The Addams Family**'s rascally Uncle Fester. Turns out it's all some kind of intergalactic real estate scam that gets exposed by this pouty British guy. And, of course, there's **Blade Runner**, which, as I recall, has something to do with knives and running. The plot isn't important. What's important is that in the future, everyone is damp and unhappy.

This sub-sub-sub-category reached its innovative epitome with **The Matrix**, which

"They planted the living, and harvested the dead!" **Invasion of the Blood Farmers**

takes all the tired old "future dystopia" conventions and turns them on their ear by adding the crucial element of mid-air limbo dancing. (Special kudos for casting Laurence Fishburne against type as Luke Skywalker's wizened mentor, Yoda.) Again, I must stress, forget plot. Even the guys who wrote this baby don't understand it. You might argue that casting bland Keanu Reeves as the Savior of mankind was a miscalculation, but let's face it, the guy can limbo like Tommy Tune! In short, the "dystopic future" is the most popular strain of sci-fi because it is the ultimate slacker's dream: "Why should I try? The future's gonna suck anyway."

3. Dazzling dialogue

Keep in mind that no matter how breathless the action, how fast-paced the story, how perilous the situation, there's always time for the protagonist to pause and make a wisecrack. This, too, was a Cameron innovation. Before his **Terminator**, heroes never uttered wisecracks. Now, there's no escaping it: "Hasta la vista, baby," "I'll be back" and "I burned my tongue on that skim latte!" Among my favorites is Bruce Willis's line from the 16 or so **Die Hard** films, "Yipee ki yay, Mother Fletcher!" He is, of course, misquoting the oft-sung cowboy phrase "Yippee Oh Ti Yay," but the way he mangles it is adorable.

4. It's inevitable: Your robot will go haywire!

This originates, of course, with HAL, the talking computer from Stanley Kubrick's film **2001: A Space Odyssey**, and it is one of a very few sci-fi conventions James Cameron did not invent. Since its debut, EVERY robot in the movies has run amok, killing its creator and wrecking the neighbor's lawn. (Incidentally, there has been much speculation concerning the acronym HAL. Some think it stands for Human Artificial Life, others say it was chosen because H, A and L precede IBM in the alphabet. Hal was, in fact, the director's pet name for a large-mouth bass he nailed while vacationing at Lake Winnebago.)

5. Plan for sequels

They're already casting **Matrix** 4 through 9. Keanu will just be turning 60 when No. 8 wraps. And even if your film bombs, you can slap together SOMETHING with a numeral after the original name and pray to God that things pick up when it hits video stores. As an example, I cite the excellent **Species II,** starring Natasha Henstridge and George Dzundza (rhymes with Rzundza), which was the Forbes "Video Pick Of The Day" just three weeks after it shipped!

"Before - a beautiful girl, one moment later – a skeleton!" Teenagers From Outer Space

6. "It's a good popcorn movie!"

This phrase was coined, I think, by Roger Ebert to describe all the movies he's ashamed to admit he likes. For instance, anything with the name Bruckheimer attached to it is a "'good popcorn movie." Are "good popcorn movies" necessarily "good" movies? Nope. Take Bruckheimer's **Armageddon**. Watching it is a little like being strapped to a jukebox and pushed over a cliff. It must be very exciting to live in Jerry Bruckheimer's world, where the ground is always jiggling, Aerosmith is always blasting and everything is always exploding. (Interesting side note: Of all the films produced in the past 50 years, only **Judgment at Nuremberg** was NOT a "good popcorn movie.")

7. Don't get caught up in that whole "originality" thing

Heck, they can't even decide what to call this genre. Some call it "Scientifiction," others insist upon "Science Fiction." Another camp is adamant that SF is the most respectable sounding term, while the breezy "sci fi" will do just fine for others. I personally hoped that my own coinage, "Skiffy," would catch on. Look, if there's one thing James Cameron has taught us, it is this: Call it what you will, but contemporary science fiction is not about creativity. It is instead a lush, plagiaristic mosaic. A piece of this movie and a piece of that movie. A melting pot, if you will, where a savory bisque of unoriginality is forever simmering.

Are we clear? Good. Now that we've identified what genre films have become, we can focus on what they once were.

"Gruesomely stained in blood color!" **Two Thousand Maniacs**

Beauties, Beasts and B Kings

The B Monster's personal encounters with the B-movers and shakers who made the cult-movies we love. Some are, sadly, now among the late and great, others are still quite hale and hearty. All were kind and refreshingly candid.

"Drenched in crimson color!" Color Me Blood Red

"Monsters come out of screen! Invade audience!" **Monsters Crash the Pajama Party**

NOW HERE'S THE THING james ARNESS
MEETS THE B MONSTER

Jim Arness seems surprised to hear that fans, writers — even fellow cast members — have the impression that he's somehow embarrassed by his role in one of the best horror films ever made. "I never played it down at all," says Arness. **"The Thing** was a big hit and a very good film credit for me at the time." Now that that's settled ...

profile

The Thing From Another World is a textbook thriller, a blueprint, a signal film

"The most fantastic expedition ever conceived by man!" **Flight to Mars**

that, to varying degrees, informed and influenced every successful science fiction filmmaker who saw it. A more efficient and arresting movie in any genre is hard to imagine. In the title role, producer Howard Hawks cast Jim Arness, a strapping young actor with the physical presence necessary to portray a brutish, bloodthirsty "intellectual carrot" from outer space. "It gave my career the boost I thought it would," says Arness.

He's known and loved the world over as Dodge City Marshal Matt Dillon of **Gunsmoke**, one of television's best-made and longest-running Westerns. But how long has Arness been aware that there is also an intensely devoted audience to whom he'll always be known as **The Thing From Another World**? "I've been very aware of the large number of fans who remember me from that picture," he says. "Since the moment **The Thing** came out, I've received hundreds of cards and letters." When asked if there are more fans who remember his work in **Gunsmoke** than for his turn as **The Thing From Another World**, the actor readily responds, "**Gunsmoke**, without any question."

> "I NEVER PLAYED IT DOWN AT ALL. 'THE THING' WAS A BIG HIT AND A VERY GOOD FILM CREDIT FOR ME AT THE TIME."

James Arness was born in Minneapolis on May 26, 1923. He began a career in radio there in 1945. The following year, he headed west with the movies in mind. His first break was a showy role in the 1947 film **The Farmer's Daughter**. Before long, he was landing small parts in many films, primarily Westerns, including **Man From Texas, Wyoming Mail, Cavalry Scout** and, most notably, director John Ford's impeccable **Wagonmaster**. "Wow," says Arness when reminded of the film, "**Wagonmaster** goes back quite a ways." He was terrific as wild-eyed, simple-minded Floyd Cleggs of the villainous Cleggs clan. Did this role (and others as brawny, intimidating types) lead indirectly to his role as the Thing? "I really don't think that had any bearing on my future career."

"Are they human, or awesome things from another world?!" It Came From Outer Space

The Thing From Another World did. "My agent heard they were casting the part, and he took me to interview with Howard Hawks, who was producing the film." Arness acknowledges that the landmark sci-fi film marks the point when his career began to gain momentum, but did he have any apprehensions about appearing in a horror film, and would he have done it if Howard Hawks weren't involved? "I had no apprehension whatsoever," he states. "It was early in my career, and I needed the work. **The Thing** was touted as a big-budget horror film, and I knew that being in it would be a big break for me."

It should be clear to anyone who's seen Arness perform that his acting style is practical and unmannered, possessed of genuine humanity. So did he do anything special to prepare for his role as an intellectual alien monster? Did he study Karloff and classic films such as **Frankenstein** and its sequels? "I had no idea how to play the character," he answers modestly. "I just went along with the director's idea of what he wanted. It seemed to work out well."

There's one lingering question about **The Thing** that just won't go away, and no amount of documentation seems to satisfy movie "experts." Who actually directed **The Thing**? Some maintain that Howard Hawks was solely in charge, others say that Hawks' protégé Christian Nyby deserves all the credit. (Someone even advanced the theory that Orson Welles wandered by the set and pitched in.) How does Arness remember it? "Hawks was there a great deal of the time overseeing the picture, but Christian Nyby directed it. Nyby had been Hawks' longtime film editor, and he wanted to give Nyby an opportunity to direct. So Hawks produced it so Nyby could direct." Next question.

Hawks and Nyby were, in any case, very exacting about the look of the film, and the shooting schedule was a long one. Arness got to know his castmates — Kenneth Tobey, Margaret Sheridan, Robert Cornthwaite — quickly and intimately. "I have very fond memories of them," he says. "We got to know each other well during filming, and it was a long shoot. Howard Hawks wanted to make sure he got the exact shots he wanted, so all of us spent a great deal of time together."

As one might expect, the demanding schedule gave way to levity on more than one occasion. "The makeup man [Lee Greenway] and I were cooped up in the studio for days," Jim recalls, "trying to get the look of the Thing just right. We hadn't even started

---

"Maidens without men on mystery planet!" Fire Maidens From Outer Space

on the face yet. We were just trying to get the claws to look right. And, you know, those claws I wore in The Thing were huge. Well, [Greenway] says, 'Let's take a break and go get a bite to eat.' So we drove to this drive-in down on Melrose where they had curb service. The waitress came around to my side of the car to hand me the menus and I stick these two gigantic claws out the window. Well, she dropped the menus and her tray and jumped away from the car in shock! It took a few minutes for her to pull herself together and realize that it was a gag."

Arness says he had no say in the final look of the monster, minimally seen to maximum effect in the film. "It took about two hours every morning to get me made up. We would do it in the morning at the studio and then be driven to the set for filming. It wasn't particularly uncomfortable."

The trip to the set provided another opportunity to let off a little steam. "One day, we were driving from the studio down to the old L.A. Ice House where we were shooting. It was down in the old L.A. railroad yard. Well, we came to a stoplight right in the heart of downtown Los Angeles, and one of the crew says, 'Jim, why don't you hop out and get a paper?' So, I jump out of this limo in full Thing costume and makeup, and dash over to a newsstand where I grabbed a copy of *The Times* from this guy hawking his papers. Well, he just freaked out! And this crowd that had started to gather began backing away in shock! I gave the guy a nickel for the paper, hopped back in the limo and we sped off. Boy, we had a lot of fun on that picture!" So much for the myth of Jim's embarrassment.

The film's combination of nail-biting suspense, punctuated by brief, violent glimpses of Arness's monster, called for atmospheric lighting and realistic action. A standout example is the unbearably tense climactic scene in the hallway when the Thing hauls off and knocks meddling professor Robert Cornthwaite to the ground. "I may have actually hit him," says Jim, "I really don't remember." And what of memorable scenes showing Arness smashing his hand through a door, or, doubled by stuntmen such as Tom Steele, fighting off angry huskies — even being set ablaze and crashing through a window? "I do know that even though the director wanted realism in all the shots, great care was taken to ensure everyone's safety. It was an accident-free set as I remember."

It may have been a long, workmanlike, even uneventful shoot — no particularly embarrassing moments that Jim can recall — but the finished film is a benchmark that

"The first new look since the invention of the camera!" **The Angry Red Planet**

subsequent thrillers would be measured against.

Reflecting his publicity-shy nature, Arness had little to do with the hype and hullabaloo that accompanied **The Thing's** release: "I did see it in the theater, but I did not attend the premiere." Dignity and modesty are virtues that formed his iconic portrayal of Matt Dillon, the pragmatic frontier marshal who was the idol of millions. This modesty accounts for understandable curiosity on the part of his fans. There may be quite a few things you don't know about Jim Arness.

He is a decorated World War II veteran, wounded at the battle of Anzio. Throughout his film and TV career, he contributed time, a 1,400-acre ranch — even his 60-foot catamaran, 'Sea Smoke' — to charitable and non-profit organizations including the Brandis Institute and the Sea Scouts. (To this day, he devotes much of his time to helping the United Cerebral Palsy organization.)

The Dec. 6, 1958, edition of *TV Guide* with Jim and **Gunsmoke** castmates on the cover shattered all previous sales records, and in 1959 television critics voted him the No. 1 Western star. (Bear in mind, this was a very crowded field in the late 1950s.) Ten years later, he received the prestigious Golden Boot Award and in 1972 was made an honorary United States marshal. He's been awarded the Western Heritage Award by the Gene Autry Western Heritage Museum and been inducted into the Cowboy Hall of Fame.

Many forget that Arness spent the first decade of his career making a specialty of smallish roles as tough-guys in films as diverse as **Iron Man, Battleground** and **The Veils of Bagdad**. The diversity of roles and

SELECTED FILMS FEATURING JAMES ARNESS

The First Traveling Saleslady
1956
Gun the Man Down
1956
The Sea Chase
1955
Many Rivers to Cross
1955
Flame of the Islands
1955
Them!
1954
Her Twelve Men
1954
Hondo
1953
The Veils of Bagdad
1953
Island in the Sky
1953
Ride the Man Down
1953
Lone Hand
1953
Horizons West
1952
Big Jim McLain
1952
Hellgate
1952
Carbine Williams
1952
The People Against O'Hara
1951
The Thing From Another World
1951
Iron Man
1951
Belle le Grand
1951
Calvary Scout
1951
Wyoming Mail
1950
Double Crossbones
1950
Stars in my Crown
1950
Two Lost Worlds
1950
Wagonmaster
1950
Battleground
1949
Man from Texas
1947
The Farmer's Daughter
1947

"Ghouls, see if your boy fiends can take it!" The Vampire

Jim's well-known modesty gave rise to several questions over the years, and one in particular seems to plague genre-film buffs to this day. There seems to be some confusion among sci-fi fans and researchers over whether or not Arness played one of the mutants in the original **Invaders From Mars**. Can he set the record straight? "Yes I can," says Jim. "I did not appear in that film."

Jim's first real leading role was in **Two Lost Worlds** (1950), a low-budget oddity that finds Arness shipwrecked on a volcanic island populated with stock footage dinosaurs. Arness recalls the film, as well as co-star Laura Elliott (aka Kasey Rogers), with affection. "It was a fantastic film to work on. Boris Petroff produced it, and it was the first leading part I had." Roles in **Double Crossbones, Stars in My Crown** and **Belle le Grand** soon followed.

> "They were the best years I spent in Hollywood. Working with John Wayne, you became a part of his family."

In 1952, Jim came to the attention of John Wayne, who took an immediate liking to him. Under contract to Wayne's Batjac production company, Arness made four films opposite Duke. "They were the best years I spent in Hollywood," says Arness. "Working with John Wayne, you became a part of his family. This working relationship extended into personal life. He had a cadre of friends he hung out with, and I was included in that group. There was always an open invitation to drop in on him and just hang out. It was like being with Robin Hood and his Merry Men." Wayne was instrumental in helping Arness land the role of Marshal Matt Dillon. When the **Gunsmoke** series transitioned from radio to television, CBS wanted Wayne for the part. He declined, suggesting Arness as the ideal candidate. "He was one of a kind; there will never be another guy like him." Arness claims he had reservations about moving to television. Nevertheless, he made the move and stayed for 20 years.

"What supernatural force made them want to kill?" Shadow of the Cat

In 1954, Jim co-starred in another trendsetting sci-fi film. Arguably the best of the big bug pictures (movie screens were soon to swarm with them), **Them!** featured Jim as a rough-and-ready monster hunter. The film's mystery-charged, suspense-building scenario set it apart from other flat-out fright films of the day, and **Them!** did monster business at the box office. "It was a very fun set to be on," says Jim, recalling co-stars Edmund Gwenn, James Whitmore and Joan Weldon. "All of the cast members were so much fun [to be around]."

Jim's last feature film credit was **The First Traveling Saleslady**, released in 1956, and he focused on television work thereafter. **Gunsmoke** was an unqualified critical and popular success, its quality remaining remarkably consistent for two decades. Notwithstanding, although it was still highly rated, CBS bowed to advertising demographics and canceled the series in 1975. Arness has starred in several telefilms since then, including successful revivals of **Gunsmoke**. He and his wife, Janet, live in the L.A. area and stay in close touch with three sons, three grandchildren and Jim's brother, actor Peter Graves. He continues his charity work and has completed two volumes of memoirs. The official James Arness Web site, www.jamesarness.com, provides readers with a biography, photo gallery and an opportunity to e-mail Jim. Letters continue to pour in from **Thing** fans — and, of course, **Gunsmoke** fans. He's not ready to clear out of Dodge just yet.

"Color by Spectrum X, a new dimension in terror!" Horror of the Blood Monsters

"Strange things walk among the living to quench their vile desires!" *Unearthly Stranger*

THE GORILLA CAN'T HELP IT *charlotte* AUSTIN
MEETS THE B MONSTER

Maybe the last thing Charlotte Austin would want to be remembered as is "Queen of the Gorillas." That was the working title of the film for which she may be best known, **The Bride and the Beast**. Exploitation filmmaker Adrian Weiss commissioned

profile

Hollywood fringe-dweller Ed Wood to script the low-budget shocker, in which Charlotte plays a newlywed whose simian genes beckon

"Be sure you can take this tremendous adventure into terror!" The Revenge of Frankenstein

her to return to the jungle and abandon her understandably confused husband. But there's more to Charlotte Austin than her brief film career would lead you to believe.

She was named for the North Carolina city in which she was born, the daughter of Gene Austin, one of popular music's most unjustly underrated entertainers. Gene Austin's recordings gave rise to the "crooning" craze that made stars of Crosby, Sinatra, Dick Haymes and many others. He also co-wrote or introduced numerous songs that have become pop music standards, **My Blue Heaven** and **Lonesome Road** among them. (Gene Austin died in 1972.)

But the daughter of one of the century's most influential pop music innovators shied away from a promising musical career and, through a series of chance encounters, found herself appearing in a handful of cult films including **Gorilla at Large, Frankenstein 1970** and **The Bride and the Beast**, all of which qualify as "must-see" viewing for anyone interested in low-budget horror.

And while she didn't pursue it as a career, her father's passion for music is nevertheless very much a part of Charlotte, who is equally zealous where politics and civil injustice are concerned. She remembers becoming infuriated by Richard Nixon while watching the Kennedy-Nixon debates with her close friend, Marlon Brando. As a young woman, she circulated a petition for gun control, at one point finding herself surrounded by pro-gun truckers who tore her petition to shreds. She and a fellow petitioner were later arrested. Her twin passions for music and the rights of the underdog in the judicial and political scheme of things have led her to write **Scared White**, an uncompromising musical satire of the O.J. Simpson trial.

B MONSTER: What's the status of the musical?

CHARLOTTE AUSTIN: It sort of came to a grinding halt for a while, but I'm just now starting to write some additional material — sort of from the jury's point of view. I've made some wonderful friends in the black community that are just fantastic, and I'm seeing other sides of the story.

Q: What makes you so passionate about the project?

"You'll scream yourself into a state of shock!" Horror of the Blood Monsters

CHARLOTTE: I'm passionate because I've always felt a connection with the black community — with anyone who's endured any kind of suffering. To me, the O.J. story was one more knife in their back. They were fooled into believing that this man was part of their community, and he's not. The [not guilty verdict] was a crumb they were tossed, but it's not from the same cake. It wasn't payback for anything because he is not black, and has never claimed to be. He envisions himself as part of white corporate America. He is not representative of them. He is not the man to be paid back for years of suffering. He never identified with [other blacks], was not a part of the community and did nothing for them. He had the ability to do something for them, but he's very carefully chosen not to be a part of his own heritage.

In the prologue to the play, he's contemplating how to get off. There's a voice, like the voice of God, that asks, "How do you plead?" And he answers, "I plead 100% black," and the lights go out. He's going to pretend to be black for the next nine months to save his ass. And that just infuriates me.

Q: What's the general reaction when you approach people with the idea?

CHARLOTTE: Positive. I really haven't gotten any negative response. I have a very dear friend who is black who thinks he's innocent and I say, "I can show you scientific proof that he's guilty." But these are very clever people, Johnnie Cochran and that whole crew. Extremely manipulative and clever. I wrote a song that's sung to Cochran by one of the jurors: "A Rogue Can Steal the Sweetening Out of Gingerbread (Without Breaking the Crust)" — and [Johnnie Cochran] is a rogue.

My family was very bigoted and I was always fighting with them because it's something that's totally against my nature. I just can't bear injustice. I'll go down fighting for something if I think it's right.

Q: Has anyone expressed interest in backing the show?

CHARLOTTE: I sent the script and the CD to the New York Theater and my friend, the actor-director Max Showalter, told them about it. [Cult-film fans will remember Showalter as Casey Adams, a stage name he adopted when appearing in films such as **Indestructible Man**.] He got so excited. But I haven't heard a word from them. I really

---

"See natives eaten alive by giant vultures!" Beast of Blood

need an agent and I need to make a concerted effort to find one.

Q: Your father's name pops up in Peter Guralnick's two-volume biography of Elvis Presley. What's the connection between Gene Austin and Col. Tom Parker?

CHARLOTTE: My dad did this incredible tent show called Broadway Rhapsody. It was just unbelievable. I was on the road with him when I was five years old. Tom Parker was a partner in the show. He did the bookings and managed him. We had a memorial for my father years ago and played all these incredible outtakes from things he had recorded that were never released. Tom called us to reminisce, because he couldn't be there.

Q: It seems that few people today realize how influential your father was.

CHARLOTTE: He was the first of the "crooners." He was in at the inception of the record business. This was in the early 1920s. He was only 22 or 23 years old when he wrote **Lonesome Road**. There's a Swedish doctor who's done a discography. I was astounded at the massive amount of work that my father did and the number of recordings he made. There's a man in Georgia who has a collection of every single thing he ever recorded. Every video, every television and radio appearance, every film — all of it. Tony Bennett called him the "granddaddy of all pop singers," which he was. He was huge. I remember when I was a little girl, wherever we went, people knew him.

Q: Why isn't your father credited with co-authoring Duke Ellington's classic **Mood Indigo**?

CHARLOTTE: My dad heard the music at a club in Harlem and said to Duke Ellington, "I know you're writing with Vernon Duke, but I have an idea for some lyrics." They went back to Duke's apartment at Sutton Place and wrote the lyrics for **Mood Indigo**. Irving Mills was his music publisher at the time and said, "Gene, it doesn't look good. You're doing so much recording that it's not a good idea to have your name on the music AND you're singing the song." That's contrary to what's being done today. So my dad sold him the lyric for $15, and Irving Mills put his name on it.

Q: Was your father disappointed that you didn't pursue a career in music?

"Space-brain invades a human body with its destructive evil power!" The Brain From Planet Arous

CHARLOTTE: Dad begged me all my life to sing and I wouldn't because I didn't want to live the life he lived. I didn't want to go out on the road. That was his greatest frustration. When I had my daughter he said, "I think you finally found your happiness. But I gotta tell you something — you're the best goddamned singer I ever heard." My biggest fear was that I loved music so much that it was going to eat me alive. Because I would eat, sleep, drink music and nothing else, and it would kill me. I know how I am. I'm very passionate about it. I was afraid that I'd never have any other kind of life than music. Music is consuming.

> "MARK NEWMAN CORNERED ME AND SAID, 'I'M TAKING YOU TO 20TH CENTURY FOX TOMORROW.' I SAID, 'NO, NO, I DON'T WANT TO.' HE SAID, 'I THINK YOU'VE GOT SOMETHING, KID.'"

Q: How did your film career begin?

CHARLOTTE: My best friend was getting married, and I was a bridesmaid at the wedding. I was only 16. She was marrying Richard Newman, who was the nephew of all the Newmans who were at Fox. Lionel Newman, Alfred Newman, Mark Newman — I met the whole family. And Mark Newman, who was an agent, cornered me and said, "I'm taking you to 20th Century-Fox tomorrow." I said, "No, no, I don't want to." He said, "I think you've got something, kid." I didn't want to go but I went to the studio. I had never acted. I worked with a strange drama coach for about three months, did a screen test and that was it, they signed me.

Q: What's your first screen credit?

"A Psychedelic trip into the 5th dimension!" Curse of the Doll People

CHARLOTTE: It may have been **The Farmer Takes a Wife**. I probably had one line in it. And I did a picture on loan to Columbia that was called **Rainbow 'Round My Shoulder**. My studio wouldn't let them buy my contract. I wish they had because they were saying things like, "She's a young Rita Hayworth," who was then about to leave Columbia. But my studio wouldn't give up my contract.

Q: Around that time, you appeared in a 3-D thriller called **Gorilla at Large**, which still turns up on cable quite often. What do you recall about making it?

CHARLOTTE: Anne Bancroft, Cameron Mitchell and Raymond Burr were in it. Lee Marvin had one line. Everyone that was in it was under contract to Fox. I played Cameron Mitchell's girlfriend. We all tried our best. Everyone must have been broke at the time to agree to do it.

Q: You appeared in your share of "A" films, such as **Daddy Long Legs**. How did the experience differ from, say, a "B" picture such as **Gorilla at Large**?

CHARLOTTE: It was nice to be in a good picture, a good musical. I would rather have done more of those. I'd rather be in something wonderful and have less to do than have more to do in something bad. Those pictures were wonderful and expensive. The sets and costumes were beautiful. We were all spoiled rotten. They were wonderful to do.

Q: Soon after, you appeared in a Western called **Pawnee,** playing the part of Dancing Fawn.

CHARLOTTE: Yes, I finally got to play an Indian. My father had always told me that Sacajawea, who led the Lewis and Clark expedition, was my great, great, great grandmother. Actually, Paramount did a movie about her and Donna Reed played Sacajawea [**The Far Horizons**.] I was so hurt that they didn't even give me a chance at the part.

Q: Around that time you appeared in **The Man Who Turned To Stone**, which featured an interesting cast. What do you recall of them?

CHARLOTTE: There was Victor Jory, Ann Doran and William Hudson was my love

"A helicopter's churning blades whirl inches from your head!" It Came From Outer Space

interest. And Frederick Ledebur, the German Count, played **The Man Who Turned To Stone**. He didn't have any dialogue, but he was a lovely man. What I remember best about that was sitting in a tub of ice-cold water with electrodes on my head for hours and hours. I was like a prune by the time we got done. I was shriveled. And I'll always remember — maddeningly — doing a close-up with Victor Jory. He would be looking past me, not AT me. He could not look me in the eye. It drove me absolutely crazy. I kept turning around to see what he was looking at.

Q: Another late-show staple in which you starred was **Frankenstein 1970**, with Boris Karloff.

CHARLOTTE: **Frankenstein 1970** I barely remember. It was directed by Howard Koch, that darling man. We called him "The Velvet Whip." When we finished the picture, I got a riding crop and covered it in black velvet and gave it to him as a gift. He really was a wonderful man. He had been an assistant director on some of the pictures I'd done at Fox.

Q: What memories of Karloff?

CHARLOTTE: He kept very much to himself. Very gentle and very quiet and very reserved. He really didn't mingle with anyone, but was just a lovely gentleman. It must have killed him to do that film. It was NOT a good movie. And Don "Red" Barry was in it. By the time he did this movie, he had converted and become a Christian. In fact, he took me to church one morning. It was at Graumann's Chinese Theater. They had this big revival. Mickey Rooney was there and nearly broke my hand shaking it. He was one of the Deacons. It was unbelievable.

Making **Frankenstein 1970** was fun because it was shot at Warner Bros., which was right across the street from the house I grew up in. The backlot was on California Street in Burbank. It was a lovely, quiet little street. They had a victory garden there on the backlot during the war. So it was fun just walking across the street and doing this movie.

Norbert Schiller [who played Shuter in the film] was a wonderful German actor. A very sensitive, fragile man. He spent the night at my mother's house [during shooting]. He didn't have a place to stay and I said, "You can stay with my mother." I remember her

"He turned the greatest show on earth into a ..." Circus of Horrors

getting up and cooking breakfast for him. We had to go right back to work at 5 o'clock every morning.

The first night of shooting, Jana Lund had to run into an icy pond of water as she was being chased by Frankenstein. It was winter so it was freezing. We were all bundled up, but I remember her teeth chattering. She was blue and they kept giving her brandy to drink every time they'd pull her out of the water. She was absolutely freezing to death. We did some stupid things in those days.

> "'GORILLA AT LARGE' WAS RIDICULOUS — BUT IT WASN'T AS BAD AS 'THE BRIDE AND THE BEAST.' NOTHING CAN TOP THAT! NOTHING!"

Q: Have you seen any of these films since you made them?

CHARLOTTE: I've never seen them since. Never, ever.

Q: Not even **The Bride and the Beast**?

CHARLOTTE: **Gorilla at Large** was ridiculous — but it wasn't as bad as **The Bride and the Beast**. Nothing can top that! Nothing!

Q: How bad was it?

CHARLOTTE: I remember coming to work on **The Bride and the Beast**, really very sick, and having to work anyway. Lance Fuller had pneumonia. And he couldn't talk because he had laryngitis on top of it. [Producer] Adrian Weiss said, "That's okay. Just go ahead and say the lines and we'll dub them in later!" He was talking but nothing was coming out. He was just mouthing the words.

That was the nuttiest, craziest film. I've never worked on anything like that. That whole

[Weiss] family was like that. I should make a movie on the making of that movie because it was hysterically funny. Ed Wood was nothing compared to this.

When I first met these people in some little office on Fairfax, Adrian Weiss presented it as a film that they just had to make because they had so many stock shots from a gorilla movie. And stock shots from an old Sabu movie. So they decided they couldn't let that go to waste and they wrote this insane, unbelievable script around that.

At one point in the film I was being chased by a tiger's head on a stick because that scene was in the Sabu movie. They put me in the same clothes as the woman who was running for her life in the Sabu movie. It was unbelievable.

Lance and I broke up laughing so badly one night that we couldn't shoot for an hour and a half. We were in a truck, supposedly traversing the African veldt. The stock shots of zebras and giraffes and rhinos and elephants would be added later. I happened to look out the side of this fake truck we were in, and there was a round barrel with twigs stapled to it. It was turning around and around, and I saw at the bottom two little feet running on a treadmill turning this barrel. It was one of the Weiss family. They had stuck in a cousin or an uncle or something to run this treadmill to make it look like we were moving. I turned to Lance and we just fell apart. We couldn't work. These feet were running, running, running — like a gerbil — to move this barrel with twigs nailed to it.

Q: Did you meet Ed Wood?

CHARLOTTE: No. I don't remember meeting him at all — but I thought that whoever wrote this monstrosity ought to be hung.

FILMS FEATURING CHARLOTTE AUSTIN

Frankenstein 1970
1958
The Bride and the Beast
1958
Pawnee
1957
The Man Who Turned to Stone
1957
How to Be Very, Very Popular
1955
Daddy Long Legs
1955
Gorilla at Large
1954
There's No Business Like Show Business
1954
Desirée
1954
How to Marry a Millionaire (TV series)
1953
The Farmer Takes a Wife
1953
Rainbow 'Round My Shoulder
1952
Monkey Business
1952
Les Miserables
1952
Belles on Their Toes
1952

"You'll see it tear a city apart!" **The Beast From 20,000 Fathoms**

Q: Would you say that that was the film that convinced you to stop making movies?

CHARLOTTE: Yes, I would say that. I had just bought my house when I got the script. I remember feeling physically sick when I read it. Then I got control of myself and said, "Now, Charlotte, you have to make your house payments." And I did it. I reached a point where I realized that I wouldn't associate with these people on a social level, what am I doing working with them? Today, I'm more tolerant.

There were a lot of opportunities I let go after that. I remember somebody arranged a meeting with Elia Kazan — it may have been Marlon [Brando]. Kazan was doing **Cat on A Hot Tin Roof**. I met with him and kept saying, "But, I don't want to be an actress. I'm not interested. Why are you pursuing this?" He said, "I've got girls on their knees begging me for this part!" I told him, "I just don't want to be an actress."

Q: Have you kept in touch with anyone from the old days?

CHARLOTTE: Marlon and I have been friends since I was 19. We still are. Friends and fighters — for causes AND with each other. The people I've kept in touch with are people I've known right from the beginning — Max Showalter, Richard Allen, Merry Anders and Marlon. We're still close.

Q: What's kept you motivated through the years — through the cheap movies, the social causes and the trying times — through the hassles of trying to get your show produced?

CHARLOTTE: I learned very early on, through my father, that the show must go on. And it has really carried me through a lot of things. I just don't give up that easily. A lot of musicians and groups, especially during the hard-rock era, would sell a million dollars' worth of tickets and, at the last minute, one of them would O.D. or catch cold — and they'd cancel the entire concert. We wouldn't have dreamt of doing that, no matter what condition, no matter how sick. You came to work. There were no excuses.

"Every horror you've seen on the screen grows pale beside the horror of ..." **The Black Scorpion**

TEXAS TERROR'S LONE STAR pat BOYETTE MEETS THE B MONSTER

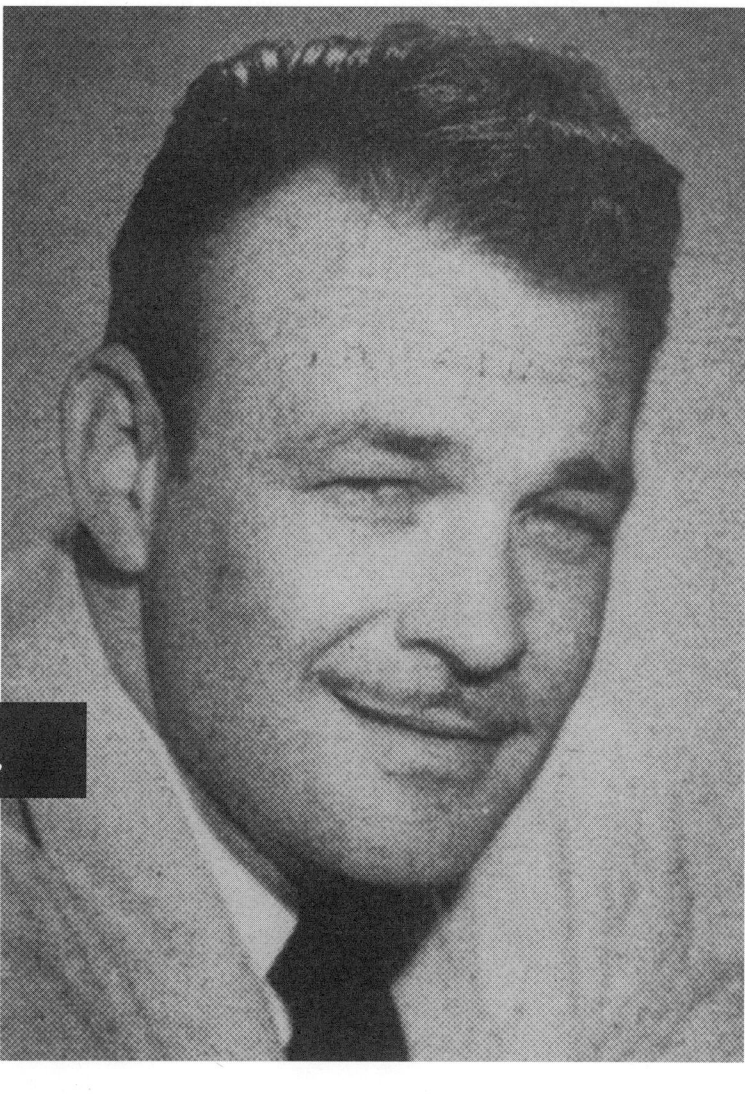

Author, producer, director, historian, television and radio broadcaster, painter, comic book artist; Pat Boyette is a pop-culture Renaissance man. Yet for such a talented guy, he's about as unpretentious a fellow as you'd ever want to meet. It's more than likely that the devoted clique of fans

profile

familiar with his prolific stint drawing a variety of comic titles in the 1960s and '70s have no knowledge of

"An orgy of looting and lust!" Panic in Year Zero!

the cult films, most memorably **The Dungeon of Harrow**, for which he may be best known. "Making those films were the happiest moments of my life," he says, quietly beginning the tale of how movies came to dominate his fondest memories.

"In my mind, what I have always been is a television anchor man," Boyette clarifies. "That's how I spent my life. Radio and television were my loves. WOAI was one of the most influential 50,000-watt radio stations in the country. I started off there in my teens, editing the 10 o'clock news. I loved the business so much that I put in 60 and 70 hours a week. At that time, television was still the thing that loomed in the future. That was still Buck Rogers."

Boyette was taken with the infant medium, and nostalgically recalls his introduction to it. "I'll never forget the night I was walking down St. Mary's Street in San Antonio," he begins, his voice softening with nostalgia. "It was just at twilight and all the lights were on in the buildings. I passed this oyster bar and there was a strange, flickering, blue light coming out of it. I looked inside and saw a television screen for the first time. I said, 'My God, that is for me.' Within a few weeks, I got my first job in television. I went to work as chief announcer and news director for KENS in San Antonio."

As the medium matured, Boyette demonstrated a tenacious professionalism. "I absolutely cannot stand to start a project that I can't finish," he states, explaining his determination to master the varied tasks that presented themselves. "Most guys, somewhere along the line, will give up. But I can't do that. I have to finish. That's why I've never missed a deadline on a comic strip. Push, push, push." It wasn't long before Boyette trained this tenacity on the film business, where such qualities would be sorely tested.

"I'd been in love with motion picture-making for a long time," Boyette recalls. "When television came in, suddenly there was going to be a big market for films. I thought, 'This is the thing to do. You can make some schlock and get by with it at this early stage.' Not that you purposely go out to make schlock. But the fact is, with limited resources, that's the best you can hope for."

Much has been made of the French "auteur" theory — the reasoning that a film's director, consciously or not, imbues the property with his own unmistakable, personal

"See giant tarantulas eat men alive!" **Women of the Prehistoric Planet**

> "I WROTE IT, EDITED IT AND SCORED IT ... I PUT SOME NAMES IN THERE THAT I MADE UP SO IT WOULDN'T LOOK LIKE ONE GUY."

vision. Does this reasoning apply as well to B-level curiosities such as Boyette's home-grown, cult-film classic **The Dungeon of Harrow**? "I wrote it, edited it and scored it," he laughs. "I put some names in there that I made up so it wouldn't look like one guy." His determination to learn every aspect of movie-making — from financing to finished film — qualifies Boyette as a B movie "auteur."

Pat recalls a visit he made to a Hollywood television studio just prior to embarking on his film career. He would soon come to know firsthand the aggravations encountered by the writers he met that day. "I'll never forget the first time I walked in on the stage of **Perry Mason**," he laughs. "Andrew McLaglen was directing this episode. There was some guy pacing up and down between the sets saying, 'They're ruining it! They're ruining my script!' I guess it always has been and always will be that way. When you've got more than one cook on the broth, it's going to be some kind of chili you get."

Boyette calls San Antonio, Texas, home. "I never found a place I liked better," he declares. "I loved every rock and every bit of history that went with it." (When we last spoke, he'd recently completed a volume concerning Texas history, focusing on the Alamo.) In the 1950s, he established his credentials as a respected TV anchor man and news producer. Eventually, his ability to anticipate the path that the growing medium would follow prompted the young broadcaster to begin an invigorating, though brief, film career. He surmised that TV stations would soon be paying good money for inexpensive late show features to fill out rapidly expanding schedules. Admiring the work of maverick B movie-makers, particularly Roger Corman, Boyette determined that

"Diabolical power that made him the most feared man in the universe!" **The Brain From Planet Arous**

horror films were an accessible venue.

Boyette possessed the acumen, and even accumulated the necessary equipment to make a film. "I collected motion picture equipment," he recalls. "I had a complete studio." But a crucial ingredient was lacking. "Getting financing is quite a different operation," he states. "For the simple reason that people in my area thought I was crazy to make a movie, never mind getting their financial support."

Fortunately for Pat, San Antonio quartered its share of aspiring actors. "This kid, Russ Harvey, had this guy who believed that Russ Harvey could be a star. So he put up some of the front money for this damn thing. The only problem was that Russ had done very little acting. But because he carried the title of producer, he was also going to be casting director."

When it came to casting the deranged nobleman, Boyette needed an actor capable of offsetting Russ Harvey's conspicuous lack of experience. "I'm a great fan of British comedies," Boyette relates. "I think the Brits are the greatest actors there are. One guy in **Dungeon of Harrow**, Bill McNulty, who was a Brit, was so far superior to the rest of the cast. If I'd had the quality of Bill McNulty throughout that film, it would have been a different story."

Another stroke of luck was the casting of B Western veteran Lee Morgan as the bedraggled ship's captain. "Lee was a guy that was always just passing through," Boyette recalls. "The last Hollywood film he was in was **Sierra Baron** [1958]."

Maurice Harris, who portrayed the demented Count's indentured manservant, evidently found no sacrifice too great in the advancement of his film career. "He was a basketball player with one of the subsidiary teams of the Harlem Globetrotters," Boyette recalls. " He had just gotten married and that was how he spent his honeymoon."

In fact, Harris went to the mat, quite literally, to ensure the film's realism. Boyette describes a pivotal scene wherein Harris is knocked unconscious by the film's heroine. "I asked [art director] Don Russell to paint this Styrofoam to make it look like a board," he laughs. "So he coated it in plaster of Paris and painted it. That thing was just like a rock. When she hit that guy in the head, it knocked all his makeup off and really bloodied him

"See strong men forced to satisfy a passion no human knows!" The Wasp Woman

> "I'D WORK ALL DAY BUILDING THE SETS, GO HOME AT NIGHT AND WRITE THE SCRIPT A DAY AHEAD OF TIME, AND WE'D SHOOT IT THE NEXT DAY. WE MADE THOSE THINGS AND WE MADE 'EM FAST, PAL."

up. Next time you see the film, watch for that."

Boyette was pressed to innovate in order to disguise the lack of funding, constructing miniatures between script revisions and hammering together sets himself. But he was having the time of his life, happily employing every familiar convention of Gothic horror. Boyette acknowledges that the subject matter greatly resembled the comic stories he later produced for Warren Publishing's line of horror magazines (*Creepy, Eerie,* etc.), involving as it does the lone survivors of a cleverly staged shipwreck (actors treading a rickety, rocking sound stage) and a forlorn island castle (2 1/2-inch, hand-painted miniatures fashioned by Pat himself). with a grotesque prisoner locked in its dungeon. Boyette also narrates the film but, contrary to B film lore, does not appear on screen.

Dungeon of Harrow wrapped quickly. "Less than 14 days," says Pat. "And that included building the sets. I'd work all day building the sets, go home at night and write the script a day ahead of time, and we'd shoot it the next day. We made those things and we made 'em fast, pal." But the crass meddling of backers and distributors, anathema to any independent filmmaker, was inescapable. "The film was supposed to run 71 minutes," Boyette grumbles. "When we got it finished, the guy that was going to distribute the film wanted 91 minutes. I had to go from clapstick to clapstick. That thing

---

"See the doll messengers of death!" Curse of the Doll People

should have been tightened up all the way through. When I was editing, it made my head ache to sit there and leave stuff in that I wanted to cut out."

Several sleepless nights later, **The Dungeon of Harrow** was finally complete, but Pat was thoroughly disillusioned by the intrusive backers and distributors. Following a war drama called **No Man's Land** (1962), he began work on a second thriller called **The Weird Ones**, a film that met with a fate not uncommon to the work of maverick filmmakers. "**The Weird Ones** got taken away from me," Boyette recalls. "It got butchered and turned into a porno movie, practically. I haven't seen it and I don't want to see it because I would be absolutely infuriated."

Soon after, one of Boyette's scripts, **The Girls From Thunder Strip**, was picked up by another renegade filmmaker, David Hewitt (**The Wizard of Mars, The Mighty Gorga**). "It takes place in the Georgia uplands during the hippie invasion," Boyette remembers. "All these hippie motorcycle riders come into the South where they run across these gals who are running stills. It was a pretty good film with Jody McCrea." But once more, Pat found that there was no safeguarding his vision. "Hewitt had a guy who was a pretty good actor," he laughs, "but he thought he was a better ad-libber than he was. He started ad-libbing script that nobody had written and it didn't turn out that well. Like living room comedians at a party — boy they are funny. But you put them on a stage and say, 'Okay, now be funny for me,' nothing happens. That's the way it was with this guy."

Though tampering of this nature tried his patience, nothing compared to the financial headaches involved in B movie making. "When you go into making a film, you want it to be the best you can," Pat states. "What you do is take every dollar you've got and put it on the screen. That leaves you with no money to have pre-screenings or publicity — all those things that are so damn vital to successfully marketing a film. By the time you go to a distributor with your product, you're flat broke, you need money and he knows you need money. And he can write incredible contracts that favor him so he's in beautiful shape. It's not a pleasant experience. I realized that there was no way that I could beat the marketing. There was no way I could get my money out. That's what discouraged me from making any more films."

It wasn't long before the aggravation of marketing personal films surmounted the

"The most gruesome day in the calendar!" Black Sabbath

> "IT GOT BUTCHERED AND TURNED INTO A PORNO MOVIE, PRACTICALLY. I HAVEN'T SEEN IT AND I DON'T WANT TO SEE IT BECAUSE I WOULD BE ABSOLUTELY INFURIATED."

simple joy that Boyette derived from making them. Following **The Weird Ones** and **No Man's Land** (both 1962), Boyette interpreted the signs and philosophically shifted gears. "I had most of the equipment — cameras, everything — stored in my house," he sighs. "My house caught fire one night and burned it all up. As I stood in the front yard wearing only my shorts, I looked down and saw the clapsticks. I reached down, picked them up and, threw them on the fire. I said, 'It's over. I don't have to worry about it any more.'"

Likewise, broadcasting had begun to lose its charm. "Television was really wearing on me. I'd been in the game a long time and I was getting tired of the discipline it required of me. I was waiting to go on one night. I looked over at the monitor and said to myself, 'I don't have to watch myself grow old.'"

Boyette again marshaled his tenacious creativity and focused his talents in a new, artistic direction. "The next day a friend of mine came to my house," he recalls. "I was feeling real low and so was he. He was an account executive at a newspaper who was a pretty damn good artist. I said, 'Do you want to draw comic books?'" The pair thumbed through a Charlton comic that was lying nearby, and placed a call to their offices. They were assured that Charlton purchased freelance art. The phone call solidified his decision. As quickly as he'd closed the curtain on his previous career, a new door of opportunity opened, and Pat Boyette prepared to master another medium.

"Can anything escape its venomed terror?" Tarantula

Regrets never seem to crop up in the course of a conversation with Pat Boyette, and he asks no one to pardon the shortcomings of his films. "You can sit around and say 'if, if, if,' and make all kinds of excuses," he growls, "but what you do is what you do. And that's what we did." What he did was produce a grim little shocker that entertains in spite of — maybe *because* of — the conspicuous lack of funding.. "You know that bloody film is still running today," he laughs. "It's been a real money maker for somebody. Not me, but somebody!"

Pat Boyette was battling cancer when we last spoke. He'd recently finished a punishing round of chemotherapy and was holding his own. He never seemed frightened and never felt sorry for himself. "My bags are packed," he joked philosophically. He passed away in January 2000.

"Human or inhuman? No woman is safe!" The Man Who Turned to Stone

ARMY OF DARKNESS: MILITIA'S INTENT
bruce CAMPBELL
MEETS THE B MONSTER

profile

Of the torrent of celluloid inspired by the success of George Romero's quick-buck watershed **Night of the Living Dead**, only the **Evil Dead** films of director Sam Raimi have successfully tapped into the wellspring of black humor which is a latent but indispensable ingredient of any good horror film. Raimi added innovation to inspiration by tempering Romero's gore with tension-

"You are in the future before it happens!" The Time Travelers

puncturing humor. At the center of Raimi's saga is a likable schlub named Ash. As portrayed by Bruce Campbell, the vain and undaunted Ash finds his frazzled patience tested time and again by all manner of ghoulish, supernatural phenomena. (At one point in **Evil Dead II**, Ash replaces his severed hand with a chainsaw which he proceeds to wield with wild-eyed glee.)

Raimi's **Dead** cycle is capped by 1993's **Army of Darkness**, which features broader slapstick, name actors, better production values and significantly more Ash, with Campbell pulling out every comedic stop, wooing Embeth Davidtz and doing battle with a Harryhausen-esque army of the living dead.

Search through Yahoo's listings and you'll find at least half a dozen Web sites devoted to Campbell. Dig a little deeper and you'll unearth an additional dozen or so sites devoted to the **Evil Dead** films. Campbell is beloved across the World Wide Web. The versatile actor established a horror foothold as Ash in Raimi's trilogy, and is now among the hardest working players on the scene.

B MONSTER: I've heard from readers in Japan who tell me you're known over there as **Captain Supermarket**. Were you aware of this? Any reaction?

BRUCE CAMPBELL: Yes, I know all about it. It's not uncommon for titles of movies to change when they enter foreign markets. A film we did called **Crimewave** is called **The Two Craziest Killers in the World** in Italy and **Death on the Grille** in France. Go figure.

Q: What's the significance of the Shemp credit that pops up in your collaborations with Sam Raimi?

BRUCE: We were all big fans of the Three Stooges growing up — Sam Raimi, filmmaker friend Scott Spiegel and myself.

In learning more about the Stooges, we found that when they made their films (or "shorts" - 20 minutes in length), they not only made one at a time, but two or three - thereby capitalizing on standing sets from the big, Columbia "A" pictures currently in production. This allowed them, for example, to use a large castle set (and shoot a pie

"Turning men and women white with the awesome, horrible way it kills!!" **The Lost Missile**

> "WE THEN BEGAN TO USE THE TERM 'FAKE SHEMP' FOR ANY ACTOR WHO DIDN'T HAVE ANY LINES, OR WAS DOUBLING FOR ANOTHER ACTOR."

fight or something) before it was torn down. As a result, they were always shooting pieces of shorts as well as complete ones.

Well, one fateful day, Shemp (the really ugly one with the long, stringy black hair) was incapacitated by a heart attack, and the rest of the Stooges, distraught as they were, had to finish a number of shorts. So, they brought in a "Fake Shemp." The doubles they used were often the wrong height/weight and lacked in the true Shemp mannerisms. Even in high school (in the mid-'70s), distracted by commercials, eating bowls of Captain Crunch, we could tell whenever the obviously fake Shemp made his appearances — which is in about three or four shorts — and we were amused to no end.

We then began to use the term "Fake Shemp" for any actor (in our early Super-8 flicks) who didn't have any lines, or was doubling for another actor (which happened a lot when you couldn't pay an actor to stay around), or who was just way in the background doing ridiculous things.

So, in the first **Evil Dead** film, we decided to designate Fake Shemps as an official credit category. The names listed were people who we shot "parts" of - a hand, a foot, someone under heavy make-up, etc. It seemed to be handy, since films (particularly low-budget ones) are usually pieced together in many different ways over a long period of time.

The term has since expanded in our vocabulary to include a number of fun uses:

"Shempish" - anything that is cheesy or second-rate - "Man, throw that shirt out, it looks really Shempish."

"Shemping" - doing nothing of any great importance - "I have no plans Saturday night, I'm just Shemping..."

"Shemp Alert" - sighting of a Shemp - either being "Shempish," or just "Shemping."

Q: You were slated to write, direct and star in a film called **The Man With The Screaming Brain**. What's the status of that project and are there other personal films you're working on?

BRUCE: **The Man With The Screaming Brain** is an on-again, off-again hobby of mine. It's almost been made several times, but for whatever reasons, it fell through. It's sort of a modern-day **Frankenstein**. I am contracted to direct a film called **The Night Man**. It's a story about a night janitor at a high school who accidentally kills a student, his descent into madness, and his violent attempts to cover up his crime.

Q: Do you have a list of favorite actors, past or present, whose work inspires you and do you find yourself emulating them in your performances?

BRUCE: Jennifer Jason Leigh, she's professional, smart and very friendly. I'm also a big fan of Robert Duvall because he makes acting look easy. I don't really emulate anyone.

Q: If someone gave you a zillion bucks to make any movie you want, what would it be?

BRUCE: One with a story about people, based on a factual incident. I find truth much stranger than fiction, as they say ...

Q: Have B horror type films always been a love of yours or are those types of films just another gig for you?

BRUCE: I'd have to say it's just another gig. I do have a certain fondness for the genre — after all, that's where it began for me. When we made the first **Evil Dead**, we had made the decision to shoot a horror film because at the time it was a very marketable and successful genre. Granted, because of that and **Evil Dead II**, I ended up doing several

"A blood-sucking mummy ... a seductive cat-goddess!" **Pharaoh's Curse**

> "I'D HAVE TO SAY IT'S JUST ANOTHER GIG. I DO HAVE A CERTAIN FONDNESS FOR THE GENRE — AFTER ALL, THAT'S WHERE IT BEGAN FOR ME."

genre pictures. Now, I'm trying to do as many different types of roles and receive as much exposure as I can. Don't get me wrong, I will do another genre film as long as and only if it's a good script.

Q: It's been pointed out that Ash is sort of Raimi's (and the audience's) punching bag. Why do you think people like to see this guy get beat up?

BRUCE: He's basically an idiot, and he asks for everything he gets. Also, Ash represents everything that people would like to see happen to a "hero."

Q: Did you sustain any injuries in the course of making those films?

BRUCE: Let's see, three films over the course of twelve years ... well, I got a nasty cut on the face (required stitching), various bruises, scratches, lacerations — that and the mental anguish.

Q: Do you have a favorite among your own films or performances?

BRUCE: I like to think I was bearable in the two-parter I did for **Homicide** and the pilot episode for **Brisco County Jr.**

Q: At this point in your career, which project do fans seem to best remember you for and is it the work you want to be remembered for?

BRUCE: I always find it funny when I'm signing autographs to see a six-year-old and his mom ask me to sign a picture of Brisco right after a mid-20s guy dressed all in black

"Terror on the African voodoo coast!" Zombies of Mora Tau

asks me to autograph his chainsaw. It seems to be half and half between **Brisco** and **Evil Dead**. I have no complaints about being known for Brisco and Ash. I'm proud of the work I did with those characters.

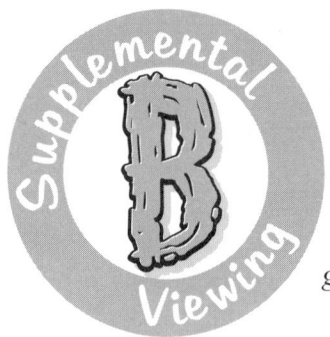

The slashing and gore of modern horror films is used most often to disguise a conspicuous lack of intrinsic merit. Graphic and grisly horror films can, however, be intelligently rendered with coherent storytelling and genuine innovation as in the following examples:

Night of the Living Dead (1968)
George Romero's trendsetting "B" ushered in a new wave of graphic horror that has yet to crest. Lingering shots of zombies slurping up human innards, and stark simplistic black-and-white photography enhance this tale of a sequestered band surviving a mass zombie onslaught.

The Evil Dead (1982)
An unstoppable industry buzz (helped along by Stephen King) turned this innovative cheapie into an internationally recognized cult gem overnight. Director Sam Raimi scraped and scrimped to complete this flick, filled with budget-conscious innovations and boundless energy.

The Evil Dead II: Dead By Dawn (1987)
Not so much a sequel as a freewheeling remake with a more accommodating budget. Arguably the best of the **Evil Dead** trilogy, it features a refreshing dose of genre-tweaking comedy. Gags notwithstanding, the film delivers its shocks with unerring skill.

Dead Alive (1992)
Peter **Lord of the Rings** Jackson staged this hyper-kinetic gross-out, filled with mind-blowing effects and over-the-top gore. Jackson displays a remarkable — some might say disturbing — knack for delivering chuckles and shudders simultaneously.

"It will shock your senses and chill your brain!" **The Vampire's Coffin**

HERE COMES THE SUN DEMON robert CLARKE
MEETS THE B MONSTER

B-movie veteran Robert Clarke has performed with an impressive roster of film stars that spans every genre and budget: Gable, Karloff, Lugosi, Chaney, Carradine, Price, John Wayne, Randolph Scott. He also appeared in a handful of the most memorable sci-fi films of the 1950s.

profile

Few B-movie actors have credentials that compare. "I'd wanted to be in movies since I was 12 years old and saw Tom Mix and Douglas

"Half-man, half-beast but all monster!" Half Human

Fairbanks Sr. and Buck Jones — and later, Gable and Robert Taylor," he says. Clarke left his native Oklahoma and headed for Hollywood in 1943. It wasn't long before producers at RKO took notice of the 24-year-old's boyish virility and smooth delivery. "I went under contract the same month and year as Bob Mitchum. And of course, we all know what he's accomplished."

Clarke landed his first role in **The Falcon in Hollywood** by marching into the office of producer Maurice Geraghty and declaring that he'd like to play the part of the assistant director. "I was hopeful and full of piss and vinegar," he laughs. Geraghty gently explained that the aspiring actor's youthful appearance might be a disadvantage, but offered to speak to production chief Sid Rogell on his behalf. Clarke got the role.

The actor found himself hustling through six films over the course of the following year before supporting Conway once more in **Criminal Court**. "Tom Conway had replaced his brother, George Sanders, as The Falcon," Clarke recalls. "This was one of the first pictures that Tom did. A very pleasant man. Nice, easygoing — and had not as much of the English accent as George Sanders. Tom was kind of more down to earth. He wasn't as aloof as Sanders appeared to be. Tom, poor fellow, died a pauper, I remember seeing it in the paper. He'd been in the hospital and was emaciated. Very, very sad for a man who had accomplished quite a bit in the inexpensive, B-budget type of films."

Clarke was befriended by several aspiring young thespians, all of them as anxious for experience and exposure as he was. "I became good friends with Barbara Hale, Bill Williams and later, on the Tim Holt Westerns, Dick Martin, who was a sidekick to Tim Holt. We were very, very close friends. Dick just passed away a few years ago."

The road to Clarke's inexorable identification with genre films had a bumpy start. He'd landed a smallish part in a Val Lewton-produced thriller, **The Body Snatcher**, which would feature two of his screen idols, Boris Karloff and Bela Lugosi. The young director of the film was Robert Wise. "I arrived at the set late. The lights were all set up. They were all ready to rehearse. Wise's first words with me were, 'Bobby, this is bad.' And I said, 'I know it, I know it. I'm sorry. But it was raining and I couldn't find a place to park.' Here I am getting these few lines and I'm screwing up right at the beginning. Hurriedly, I got into the wardrobe and got to the set — again, late — and everybody was standing around. You can imagine how I felt. I was so screwed up, I didn't say my lines.

"Half corpse ... all killer!" A Taste of Hell

> "I WAS SO DISORGANIZED AT THAT MOMENT THAT HENRY DANIELL JUST SWEPT RIGHT THROUGH THE SCENE AND I DIDN'T GET TO SAY MY LINES."

I was so disorganized at that moment that Henry Daniell just swept right through the scene and I didn't get to say my lines. Bob Wise stopped and said, 'Wait, wait. Bobby has a line in there. Let's take it again.'"

Clarke's encounter with his screen hero Lugosi was despiriting. "If you recall that scene with Henry Daniell, Russ Wade, Bill Williams and Carl Kent ... it is the only photograph that I have [of myself] with Bela Lugosi. He was very, very ill. He was barely conversant with any of us. They'd block the scene, whatever it was, and he'd go back to his dressing room and lie down. None of us had hardly any conversation with him. With Karloff, it was quite different."

Following **The Body Snatcher**, Clarke was seen to good advantage in one of the more stylish Lewton thrillers, **Bedlam**. Not only was his role a showy one, but he once more shared a sound stage with an actor he'll always regard with great admiration. "Mr. Karloff — and that's what I always called him — was absolutely, without question the kindest, gentlest — the antithesis of everything he was on the screen. He was superb. And yes, very, very helpful. Mr. Karloff would often be sitting in his dressing room and I'd ask him what were, to me, interesting questions about his career."

Clarke still treasures a memento from Karloff that bears a message indicating the magnanimous actor's great modesty. "I was later in a picture with him that wasn't too good called **Dick Tracy Meets Gruesome**. It was at the end of that picture that they had what they call a wrap party. Hardly a party on this occasion. A bare, empty stage at the

---

"Half angel, half monster, all woman!" Night Tide

RKO studios, somebody had brought a couple of plates of cold cuts and such. Kind of shabby is what I'm trying to say. Mr. Karloff was standing there with 8 x 10s, signed to anyone who would like to have one. And on mine he said to me — and of course I treasure it so greatly — 'To Bob Clarke. Be as lucky as I am.'"

Throughout the late '40s, Clarke found himself cast in a string of B Westerns, some with matinee idol Tim Holt, that were not without their travails. "You ought to try riding a horse behind a camera truck going 40 miles an hour, keeping your hat on, keeping a gun in your hand, firing it — and every time you fire it, the horse gets scared and throws his head and almost throws you in the ditch. It's not easy."

In the 1950s, Clarke performed in a spate of genre films (some of which chagrined him greatly at the time) for which he's remembered by a devoted generation of fans. The **Man From Planet X** is undoubtedly the best of these. Its follow-up from the same production team, **Captive Women**, pales in comparison, as it lacks the storytelling verve of journeyman director Edgar G. Ulmer, so vital to the success of **Planet X**.

The Man From Planet X, the very first film about a visitor from space, was also one of the best. Made on a shoestring in less than a week, it is one of the era's most enterprising science fiction films. Its damp and disturbing Scottish setting is almost enhanced by the lack of budget, as the filmmakers were forced to disguise every scene with impressionistic landscaping and dry-ice fog. The pall that permeates the film's every frame is both functional and artistic. The shadows enrich the movie's atmosphere while masking its cheapness. Additionally, the cast of future B film veterans conveys the story with credibility and refreshing subtlety.

At the urging of Malvin Wald, a writer and business partner of Ida Lupino, Clarke was one of over 100 actors to audition for **Planet X**. He and Margaret Field were chosen by producers Aubrey Wisberg and Jack Pollexfen from this sea of hopefuls.

If ever there was a film that demonstrated what could be accomplished on a minimal budget, **Man From Planet X** is that example. As Clarke relates, "Jack Pollexfen told me that the total price, negative cost for **The Man From Planet X** was $41,000. That's all. We got — Margaret Field, that's Sally Field's mom, and William Schallert and I — we got the Screen Actors Guild minimum for a week, $175. NOW, the daily rate is $540 just

"The grave can't hold it! Nothing human can stop it!" The Thing That Couldn't Die

for one day's work. We did the picture in a week — and we had some overtime. My check came to $208 for the whole picture. And there were no residuals at that time. That was 1951. I've mentioned this at some of the seminars and these conventions and their mouths drop open. But quite frankly, if I'd had the $200, I would have paid them to let me do the part.

"[Pollexfen] had 25% ownership of the picture," Clarke continues, "and that was the springboard for him to do 29 pictures. That got Aubrey and Jack a three-picture production contract with RKO studios and I was in two of the films, **Captive Women** and **Sword of Venus**, which was a **Count of Monte Cristo**-type story. And my salary went up from $175 to $350 a week ... and we still made the picture in 10 days. So you see, I was really getting rich. I figured I could never make a living in this business at that rate. My total income for the year wouldn't even be $3,000. That's why I [eventually] went into the life insurance business with Gale Storm's husband."

> "WE DID THE PICTURE IN A WEEK — AND WE HAD SOME OVERTIME. MY CHECK CAME TO $208 FOR THE WHOLE PICTURE."

Who played **The Man From Planet X**? That question has been put to Bob Clarke many times: "They did not give screen credit to the man who played **The Man From Planet X**, thinking that that would fool the public into thinking that it was really a man from another world ... which I thought was very, very unfair. People have asked me, 'Who was it?' I have no idea. I couldn't remember his name if my life depended on it. [Ed. The actor, we've since learned, was Pat Goldin.] He was always itching in that leotard outfit. He was always uncomfortable with the headpiece. And he wasn't making much. I think he was making whatever extras got or maybe a little more. But he wasn't making what we made — the huge sum of $175."

"Man at grips with jaguar fury!" *Curucu, Beast of the Amazon*

Was it worth it? Ultimately, yes according to Clarke. But as he remembers, the set was not completely free of tension. "After about five days of the six-day schedule, I was so drained at one point, I was having difficulty with my lines. Bill Schallert and I were up on a precipice — a set originally made for **Joan of Arc** in which Ingrid Bergman starred — doing a scene. I couldn't get the lines out and I was frustrated, stressed out — and Edgar said something that didn't help. As I told his daughter Arianne, 'I'm sorry that I said [in my autobiography] that Edgar was a pain in the ass but he was!' And she said that at times, 'My father was very tempestuous. He was very temperamental.' Ulmer was very creative and he had one focus ... he didn't want to have any argument. He was the boss on the set. But, I was probably as big a pain to him as at times he was," Clarke admits. "But he was the genius behind the look of that picture — the atmosphere, the fog, the paintings of the broch [castle], the glass shots — he painted them himself. He was a tremendously talented man."

> "ULMER WAS VERY CREATIVE AND HE HAD ONE FOCUS ... HE DIDN'T WANT TO HAVE ANY ARGUMENT."

The Man From Planet X remains one of Bob Clarke's personal favorites. The film was screened recently at the newly renovated Orpheum Theater in Los Angeles with Clarke and Arianne Ulmer in attendance. "To see it on a big screen once again ... it really held up," he says with a smile. "It really was a big thrill. I think it will last a long, long time."

With the brief resurgence of costume action films in the mid-1950s, Clarke appeared in several discount swashbucklers, even playing Robin Hood in one feature. In **The Black Pirates**, Clarke co-starred with yet another horror film icon, Lon Chaney Jr. "We were in San Salvador doing **The Black Pirates** in 1954," he recalls. "Every day at noon the rains would come ... they would send us back to the town ... and Chaney would pull out the bottle of bourbon and say 'Any of you fellas want a pop?' He spoke of his father, Chaney senior as the 'good actor.'"

"Wherever you sit it watches you and makes you part of the show!" **The Hypnotic Eye**

A trusted mutual friend once related to Clarke an anecdote revealing Chaney's eccentricities. "He and Lon would go hunting together, fishing, that sort of thing. Chaney had a ranch down near San Diego. [Lon had this] strange idea about going hungry. Between L.A. and his ranch he had lockers. Food lockers. Storage freezers stocked with fish and beef and game he'd killed as a hunter. I don't know how many — four or five I guess, and he had these in areas where, if he were in that area, he knew he could get something to eat. If that's not freaky ... "

It was inevitable that Clarke, moving undaunted from one B picture to the next, would cross the path of cheap-jack filmmaker Jerry Warren. "Oh god. A screaming idiot!" Clarke scowls. Clarke cites **The Incredible Petrified World**, a turgid hash of ideas about undersea exploration co-starring John Carradine and Phyllis Coates, as perhaps the best picture Warren ever made. This may be true, but it's one of the WORST pictures Bob Clarke ever made, as is Warren's later **Frankenstein Island**. Experiences like those with Warren and novice filmmaker Ronnie Ashcroft, the man who gave the world **The Astounding She-Monster**, inspired the actor to undertake his best-known film, **The Hideous Sun Demon**.

Clarke realizes, with appreciation, that he is identified more with **Sun Demon** than any other film in which he appeared. "I'm known as the Sun Demon," he laughs. "At Forrest Ackerman's 80th birthday they announced me — they said, 'Now we'll hear from Robert Clarke, The Sun Demon.'"

Though the film is certainly not up to the standards of **Man From Planet X, Bedlam, Beyond the Time Barrier** or **The Body Snatcher** to name just a few, "it's interesting," Clarke says, "that the following of that film — which I don't think is as good as **Planet X** nor as well made as **Time Barrier** — the **Sun Demon** has a following."

After his star turn in director Ashcroft's sci-fi cheapie **The Astounding She-Monster**, Clarke realized that there were drive-in dollars to be made with minimal investment. Instinct told him that an actor of his experience could turn out a film at least as good as **She-Monster**. His instinct was correct. "Because **Astounding She-Monster** was so bad, I said, 'God I can make a better film than that.' It inspired me to do **Sun Demon**."

But as a novice indy filmmaker, Clarke learned several lessons the hard way. "When

"He builds a bonfire of human souls!" The Mad Doctor

Alyce and I were first married, I took our last $5,000 and started making this movie. Does that sound like Ed Wood? I had taken a course in film writing down at USC at the suggestion of Ida Lupino's partner in her Filmmakers company, Malvin Wald. And I met some guys that were department students, and I cajoled and promoted them into the idea of making this movie." Banking on the audience's familiarity with Stevenson's classic **Dr. Jekyll and Mr. Hyde**, Clarke and his accomplices updated the time-worn theme, and turned out an enterprising, entertaining B picture..

Clarke correctly surmised that there would be no need to press the story beyond its simple bounds. A nuclear accident exposes a dedicated doctor to radioactive toxins. When caught in direct sunlight, he's transformed into a vicious, bipedal reptile. It's not a cautionary tale regarding toxic hazards, nor a chronicling of man's desire to sublimate his animal inclinations. But it works as a rousing thriller, as well as campy escapism.

"We made the movie without a release," Clarke recalls, "and when the time came to show the movie, my brother was manager of a radio/TV station in Amarillo, Texas. He said, 'Bob, I've lined up a guy who has a drive-in down here and will offer you, if you will, a chance to premiere your picture here with a lot of publicity.' And we did and it came off great. That gave me something to come back to L.A. with. [I could] say, 'We've made this much money, close to $1,000 a night for five nights.'"

Clarke was already wearing three cumbersome hats — producer, director, star — and sought help in

SELECTED FILMS FEATURING ROBERT CLARKE

Haunting Fear
1990
Alienator
1989
Frankenstein Island
1981
Zebra in the Kitchen
1965
Terror of the Bloodhunters
1962
The Hideous Sun Demon
1959
The Astounding She-Monster
1957
The Incredible Petrified World
1957
My Man Godfrey
1957
King of the Carnival
1955
Sword of Venus
1953
Captive Women
1952
The Man From Planet X
1951
Pistol Harvest
1951
Tales of Robin Hood
1951
Riders of the Range
1950
Ladies of the Chorus
1949
Return of the Bad Men
1948
Dick Tracy Meets Gruesome
1947
Bedlam
1946
Criminal Court
1946
Genius at Work
1946
San Quentin
1946
Sunset Pass
1946
The Body Snatcher
1945
The Enchanted Cottage
1945
Those Endearing Young Charms
1945
The Falcon in Hollywood
1944

"A fiendish experiment performed with sadistic horror!" Teenage Zombies

handling the distribution of his film. "I went to AIP and showed it at Jim Nicholson's home," he remembers. "He said, 'I'll call Sam Arkoff and tell him to see it.' And he did. [Arkoff] said, 'Well, we've got to be careful when we get to that scene at the beach where you stop with the girl and go for a swim ... her boobs jiggle real obviously — we're gonna have to cut that out.' Oh, times have changed."

> "SHAME ON THEM FOR WHAT THEY'D DONE TO ME, BUT SHAME ON ME FOR LETTING THEM. AND SHAME ON ME IF I EVER LET IT HAPPEN AGAIN."

After some hemming and hawing, the cigar-chomping Arkoff seemed ready to deal. According to Clarke, "He finally asked, 'What do you want?' I said, 'I want to make another picture.' 'Well, we got too many producers now, but we'll distribute it for you.' And it was very well-known that they never paid well for the pictures they distributed, they kept [the money]. So I didn't go with them. I went with a new company called Miller Consolidated Films."

Miller agreed to distribute **Sun Demon** as part of a double-bill. Its co-feature would be **A Date With Death**, starring Gerald Mohr and Liz Renay. In exchange, Clarke absorbed the cost of 100 prints of the film to be distributed around the country. In addition, Clarke took on a supporting role in **A Date With Death**. Owing to an expensive and ill-fated promotional scheme suggested by a Miller consultant, the legendary exploitation showman Kroger Babb, Miller went belly up almost overnight. Bob Clarke lost his shirt. Compounding his personal disappointment, Clarke realized years later that Miller had been selling off the **Sun Demon** prints Clarke had paid for in order to recoup their own losses.

"The ultimate in diabolism! Can you stand pure terror?" Die Monster Die!

Clarke recalls the **Sun Demon** experience with understandably mixed feelings. "Shame on them for what they'd done to me," he says, "but shame on me for letting them. And shame on me if I ever let it happen again." He's long since sold the film rights to collector/entrepreneur Wade Williams, and a new generation has discovered the **Sun Demon**, allowing him to profit at last from his original financial and emotional investment.

Today, Robert Clarke is a retired a bank officer. He's produced **To "B" or not to "B"**, an engaging autobiography co-written with Tom Weaver, and found devoted audiences at film convention appearances around the country. **Sun Demon** and **The Man From Planet X** live on in the memories of genre-film devotees. All things considered, Bob Clarke has lived out Karloff's admonition to 'be as lucky as I am.'

A handful of actors qualify as genre film icons; John Agar, Richard Denning, Jeff Morrow, Richard Carlson and, indisputably, Robert Clarke. This sampling of Clarke's sci fi and horror film credits runs the gamut from excellent to execrable:

THE BODY SNATCHER (1945)
Producer Val Lewton and director Robert Wise wring class "A" quality from a class "B" budget. This moody filming of Robert Louis Stevenson's tale of grave robbers supplying fresh cadavers to an unscrupulous medico (Henry Daniell) features one of Boris Karloff's very best performances.

BEDLAM (1946)
The notorious lunatic asylum is the setting for what is perhaps Lewton's most unusual and sophisticated film. Once more Karloff, in an insidious performance as the callous asylum master, dominates the proceedings, abetted by strong supporting portrayals, including that of a young Robert Clarke as a craven inmate with a canine complex.

THE INCREDIBLE PETRIFIED WORLD (1957)
From the sublime to whatever the opposite of sublime is. Tightwad auteur Jerry Warren

"You'll be rocked out of your seat — shocked out of your skin!" **Beginning of the End**

hired Clarke and Phyllis Coates to bring a whiff of professionalism to this ultra-cheap film about underwater exploration. Something about the briny deep brings out the bellicose in John Carradine.

Frankenstein Island (1981)

The final film from junk-movie mogul Jerry Warren, in which a hot air balloon sets down on an isolated island where the work of the world's most famous monster maker is being carried on by SHEILA Frankenstein. Give Warren credit for one thing: somehow, he managed to charm respectable actors into appearing in his films for peanuts, in this case, Clarke, Cameron Mitchell, Andrew Duggan and Steve Brodie. Warren regular Katherine Victor (**Teenage Zombies, The Wild World of Batwoman**) portrays Sheila and there's a brief cameo by John Carradine as the spririt of Daddy Frankenstein.

"The screen's 300,000 volt shocker!" Indestructible Man

"Wild and wicked, living with no tomorrow!" **Motorcycle Gang**

DADDY-O'S DOUBLE LIFE STORY
dick CONTINO
MEETS THE B MONSTER

To one audience, Dick Contino will always be "The Valentino of the Accordion;" his chiseled features, easygoing stage presence and peerless mastery of the instrument as entrancing today as they were 50 years ago. To another, he's a sardonic, hard-bitten crime-fiction

profile

hero, the former star of a string of B pictures reincarnated as a film noir phantom haunting Hollywood's underworld. Fans of his

"Revved-up youth in souped-up cars!" Hot Rod Rumble

films see him bridging the attitude gap between rock 'n' roll delinquency and the "Beat Generation." Indeed, his words often flow in a Kerouac-like stream (which I've done my best not to inhibit).

Contino maintains a busy schedule of concerts and club gigs. He continues to parlay the adulation that he first enjoyed more than 50 years ago. What keeps him vital? "I hate that old cliche, 'It's a state of mind,' but it is. It's where you are in consciousness. Where you are in awareness." An upcoming tour with singer Julius LaRosa includes stops in "Buffalo, Toronto, Montreal, Rochester, Utica. There's a thing planned for me in Chicago to celebrate my 50th year as a professional in the business since I first introduced **Lady of Spain** on **The Horace Heidt Show**. I'm looking forward to that. It's been a nice ride, y'know."

The ride began on bandleader Heidt's radio program in the late 1940s. In a Heidt-sponsored talent search, Contino smoked the competition week after week with a blistering rendition of **Lady of Spain**, a song that went on to become as closely identified with the accordion as mustard is with hot dogs. Overnight, a squealing brigade of bobby-soxers realized that the accordion was cool. Contino made it cool. Five hundred Dick Contino fan clubs covered the nation and Dick was pulling down $4,000 a week for club dates and radio appearances.

Many of those same fans that comprised the original Contino constituency maintain an allegiance today, and their devotion is evident in "some very exciting compliments," Contino says. "Like the younger people say, 'I've heard about you ever since I was a little boy.' Like maybe their parents or their teacher might say 'Dick Contino blah, blah, blah.' It's the kind of a thing that has helped me, and yet I play mainly concerts and Italian festas. I haven't really done a young people's gig as a result of the resurgence. And yet I feel capable of playing other types of music besides what I have been doing for so many years."

But by way of an unlikely avenue, Contino seems destined to reach a younger audience. "The thing that's probably most exciting is sort of off the wall in a sense; about three or four years ago a guy named James Ellroy — y'know? James wrote the story on me, **Dick Contino's Blues**. Well, he's written a sequel to that and it's going to be [serialized in issues] of *GQ*. It's called **Hollywood Shakedown**. He's got me the central

"Dig the playgirl sensation of the nation!" Twist All Night

figure again. I talked to the editor at *GQ* — she said, 'It's ten times more exciting than **Dick Contino's Blues**. I said, 'I don't think that's possible,' 'cause I really enjoyed **Dick Contino's Blues**."

Ellroy, a hard-boiled crime-fiction writer with a devoted cult following, had stumbled upon Contino's film **Daddy-O** while still a young man. The movie's rough-hewn combination of hot rods, thugs and rock 'n' roll made an indelible impression. Years later, Ellroy mined the latent memories and churned out a gritty and engaging pulp gem starring Dick Contino with the lensing of **Daddy-O** serving as a noirish backdrop. "The guy's a real good friend," Contino says. "I love the guy. It's one of those chemistry things."

It's likely that Ellroy, whose tumultuous youth fuels much of his dark fiction, identified strongly with the heavy dues Contino was forced to pay at a critical juncture in his career. The height of the Korean conflict coincided with the zenith of Contino's show business success. The world was snugly in his back pocket when a draft notice arrived. It triggered a long-dormant phobia that Contino was suddenly forced to come to grips with. He failed to report and was officially described as AWOL. He begged for time to combat his fears and was instead branded a "draft dodger" and sentenced like any other criminal. In time, he served honorably and was officially pardoned by President Truman. But when he returned to the stage, the applause was peppered with cat calls and whispers. "At the Mocambo I really bombed out because of the Army beef," Contino remembers. "Many times when that stupid line would be thrown at me about 'draft dodger,' I'd think violently. Although not quite so violently as the quote [Ellroy] has me telling the guy in the story. But I'm sure I thought something like that. (The Dick Contino of Ellroy's novella advises a heckling veteran to engage in intercourse with relatives and domestic animals.) "[Ellroy] knows my personality. There's just sort of an underline, sort of an edge away from actuality." As Ellroy ruefully conveyed to his subject, 'You just gotta promise me that if anybody asks you, you've got to say 'Yes, it's all true.'"

"He's a funny guy, man," Contino laughs. "He'll call me up and say, 'Hey Dick. It's Dog.' He doesn't like to be called James. 'They gave me $10,000. I'm gonna send you $3,333.33.' I've never signed a contract with the guy. For **Dick Contino's Blues** he sent me $15,000. There are no demands on each other. Just a real good chemistry. He says, 'It's gonna turn your whole career around. Even if it doesn't, it's a great ride.'

"The intimate story of today's shook-up girls!" *Life Begins at 17*

> "I DON'T HAVE ANY FALSE HOPES ABOUT ANYTHING. I'M THE TYPE OF GUY THAT BUILDS MY CORRAL AROUND MYSELF. I TAKE CARE OF MYSELF".

"After he did the initial thing in *GQ* he decided to move it into this other thing. He said, 'I'd like to do this novella thing. Kind of mix up a few things here and there.' I said, 'Sure. Go ahead. Turn on the burners.' Usually, y'know, a personality or whatever would say, 'Hey, I didn't quite say it that way or do it that way, y'know.' I thought, 'Ah, I'm not going to mess with it. Do something really different. Turn on the burners!"

So, how true to life is the two-fisted, tough-talking Dick Contino of Ellroy's fiction? Did he actually employ a burning mattress to send a serial killer plummeting to his doom in Hollywood's Bronson Canyon? "No, I didn't really do that. I wish I had. But I did stop Spade Cooley from committing suicide. There are a lot of things that are very true in there. It's a funny thing, a lot of it is very authentic and a lot of it is — if I didn't actually do this or that I sure thought about it. In fact, a guy named John L. Smith out here, at the [*Las Vegas*] *Review-Journal*, up until then, for whatever reasons, they just hadn't found any reason to write about me. Maybe one or two lines in a hundred years. But when the Ellroy thing came out, he called me up and says, 'Hey, I gotta interview you.' There was this huge thing, 'Who is the real Dick Contino?' When we're doing the interview he says, 'Ellroy's story is done so well, I don't want to know what is fact and what is fiction.'

It's done so well that, after 40 years, Hollywood is once more interested in Dick Contino. Ellroy's novella was optioned but has yet to find the proper backing. "Jeff Stein and this other guy came up with some money on that but it didn't quite materialize. I flew into L.A. three or four times — to meet money people and stuff. They were really

"Sucker-bait in the underworld's hottest, dirtiest racket!" Hot Cars

hot to trot. But Ellroy believes that this next one might really put it over the top. What makes it nice is that I don't have any false hopes about anything. I'm the type of guy that builds my corral around myself. I take care of myself. I work out every day. I've developed a good strong mental attitude — emotional feelings. If anything comes along, I'll take it, I can enjoy it. If it doesn't, I can't rely on that to make me that much happier. It's a very healthy thing. Really, truly. Like I told him, I says, 'Really, Dog. Even if nothing happens, man, it's a great ride."

Contino's unconditional faith in his "biographer" reflects his roll-with-the-punches philosophy concerning all things. "I hadn't read [**Hollywood Shakedown**] but I signed the release without even reading it. I don't give a shit what he says. I know the guy and I believe in him. After you've paid a few dues, y'know, sometimes you do build up a sense of invincibility. Like, c'mon, I gave you all this time to destroy me, man, and you didn't destroy me — the elements, so to speak. So, c'mon. Let's have some fun. What do I care?"

Contino's breezy fatalism and affable nature are decidedly non-Hollywood attributes. Little wonder that he was never comfortable with Tinsel Town's fickle machinations. With just four features to his credit, he split for Vegas and settled into a smoother groove. "My whole principle is that I'm sort of a cautious optimist in a sense. I never try to make things happen, yet I don't sit back and expect people to knock the door down. I try to be in a position to develop a receptive attitude to a rhythm. To things that kind of come out of the ether. That could come through somebody else as well as myself. Contact for the good of the whole is made, as opposed to 'How can I benefit? What can I do?' and screw everything else. It's like it's supposed to be a rhythm. A rhythm. I'm one of those type of people. I'm a Joel Goldsmith student of The Infinite Way. I have been secretly for many years. It's not an organization. It's just developing a state of consciousness — a deeper sense of awareness.

"I'm not a theologian. I don't believe in a God so much as a God principle. And I believe that if I can just tap that — if I can somehow get in rhythm with that which makes apples only come from apple trees and the sun always rise and set on time — the planets and things. A rhythm. A rhythm. Like begetting like. It gives me a great sense of peace. So I just try to tap into that as opposed to the mind of man that says, 'I've got to have this because ... I must have despite this and in spite of that.' Through trial and error.

"Excitement cuts like a switch blade knife!" Girls on the Loose

Through experiences. Through payin' some dues, it gives me the best peace. It's not a passive thing. It's like a very alert kind of passive thing. There is a rhythm. And if I can just tap into it, something will happen. Maybe I'm the instrument for somebody else as well. The principle of oneness, so to speak. That's it. That's how I enjoy life, mostly. I can enjoy the simple things or I can go to the Hilton hotel in Rome, y'know, and enjoy it with the best of them. But I don't have to have them. That's the best way, I find.

"I lost my wife 15 years ago. But this girl I met now, she's 35 years old. I said, 'Y'know, I'm almost twice your age.' She said, 'I'll be honest with you, that's part of the attraction.' So I'm very, very fortunate. I'm not boasting. I'm very fortunate. I feel great. All the parts are working like they did when I was 25 years old."

Contino maintains an enviable peace of mind that isn't dependent on public approval or a Hollywood handshake. "I'm comfortable. I'm healthy. I'm able to enjoy some good meals and some great company. What comes can be beautiful, but if it doesn't, f—k it."

Dick is likewise philosophical about his film career. He had a ball and who cares where the chips fell? But what was it about **Daddy-O** that hit Ellroy where he lived? What accounts for its cult status? "That thing was like a class Z picture," Contino laughs. Good, bad, what difference does it make? Some films just seem to flicker on stubbornly in our memories. Any movie combining hot rods, gangsters, shapely chicks and rollicking rockabilly is bound to have staying power. It certainly isn't a great film. But it oozes the ambience of a late-'50s counter culture, encapsulating all that we choose to remember as cool from that era. The fact that it entertains in spite of its impoverished look is one reason genre film nuts admire it. At its center is Dick Contino, sneering and singing his way through a muddled plot about a taciturn rocker involved with drug running. But **Daddy-O** is beloved less for its execution than for what it represents: jumpin' rock tunes, swinging beer joints and late night drag races through Griffith Park.

"That was something else, wasn't it? **Daddy-O**, man," Dick muses through the same blinding smile he wore as Phil "Daddy-O" Sandifer 40 years ago. "The songs. I love the songs," he says. "Isn't that funny? The guy that wrote the music is — y'know — what's his name? John Williams. **Rock Candy Baby. Angel Act**. And what was the other one. God, a couple of nice ones in there. **Wait'll I Get You Home!** Lou Place, man, was the director. This was, like, my first movie, y'know? I hadn't done anything. In the studio,

"The tense, taut story of the big city's delinquent daughters!" Girls in the Night

I'm doing the pre-recording — singing the song. And I get to the end of **Wait'll I Get You Home**, and I finish it and I go, 'Hah!'"

Contino's enthusiasm startled the director during the song's on-set playback. "All of a sudden we're doin' the song and Lou hears this 'Hah!' and he says, 'What the f—k was that?' I says, 'Well, I don't know ... ' He says, 'What are we supposed to do with that?' I says, 'Well, maybe after I kiss her [in the scene] I'll turn around and go 'Hah!' He says, "That's great!'"

> "'ALL THEY'LL PAY IS A THOUSAND DOLLARS, BUT YOU'RE DADDY-O.' I SAID, 'I DON'T CARE WHAT IT PAYS. I'LL PAY THEM. LET'S HAVE SOME FUN.'"

Daddy-O wrapped quickly and was marketed to drive-ins on a double bill with **Road Racers**, a marginally slicker film with far less to recommend it. To the dismay of Place and Contino, **Daddy-O** did very little for their film careers. "Man! Six weeks later we're both literally in the unemployment line in L.A., man," laughs Contino. "I got in the unemployment line and I see Lou Place right behind me. I says, 'Hey Lou, what a career, huh?' That was kind of a funny scene. Lou actually finished the movie on his home camera because they ran out of money."

Daddy-O originated as a showcase for producer Elmer Rhoden's paramour, Sandra Giles, a mainstay of West Coast tire commercials. "The guy — what the hell was his name? Elmer, Elmer something — the producer, he wanted a vehicle for Sandra Giles. That was his girl. He came up with the money. It was like $100,000, which was nothing. But I guess it's a lot of money for a throwaway picture. So a guy named Howard Wormser, who I'd known on **The Horace Heidt Show**, he said 'I can get you this. All they'll pay is a thousand dollars, but you're Daddy-O.' I said, 'I don't care what it pays.

"Terror flares in the slum shadows of the city!" Key Witness

I'll pay them. Let's have some fun.' I really loved it. It only took a couple of weeks. But it was fun, man."

One cult film myth surrounding the making of **Daddy-O** turns out to be true. "I did my own driving," says Contino. It's actually Dick at the wheel when that '50 Ford becomes airborne avoiding a cop roadblock.

Some 35 years later when the pundits at **Mystery Science Theater 3000** aimed their barbs at **Daddy-O**, Contino was genuinely amused. "I enjoy things like that, y'know, where they pick on you that way. Y'know, where he wore his pants up to his chest and things like that?"

The movie's dismal box office performance didn't stop Contino from landing small roles as teen toughs. "I did a couple things after that like **Girls Town** with Mamie Van Doren and Mel Torme, man, who was like, the other gang leader — 'You cats wanna rumble?' What was the other one? **Beat Generation** — [producer] Albert Zugsmith had a thing about Mamie's boobs — but Mamie was a really sweet girl.

"There was another one called **The Big Night** with the guy who used to do the washing machine commercials. Nice guy. He was a seasoned actor and he really helped me a lot. I can picture his face. Can't think of his name. Maytag. On the Maytag commercials. Jesse White, man! Jesse White. What a beautiful guy he was. Man, he helped me a lot. Jesse and Venetia Stevenson were in it. I played a terrible guy, holding guys under oil pumps. When they finish me at the end of the picture, the cops are all circled around me, y'know, pumping lead into me. One of the blanks, a piece of cardboard, hit me in the chest. I thought 'Jesus Christ,' an actual bullet. They had to stop the scene 'cause I thought I'd really gotten hit."

Contino considers a live production of **Night Song** for TV's **Lux Theater** to be his best acting. The film was a remake of a 1947 feature detailing the emotional travails of a blind pianist with Contino opposite Barbara Rush in roles originated by Dana Andrews and Merle Oberon.

Contino's voice gets softer as he recalls his 26-year marriage to beautiful starlet Leigh Snowden. She'd originally been noticed in a dazzling cameo in **Kiss Me Deadly**, going

"What they did to men was nothing compared to what they did to each other!" **Three Bad Sisters**

on to appear in films such as **I've Lived Before, The Creature Walks Among Us** and the juvenile delinquent classic **Hot Rod Rumble**. The latter film featured unknown Richard Hartunian, who died soon after its completion, in a role that nearly went to Contino.

He met Snowden on a blind date. "Back then I was dating just about anyone I wanted to in Hollywood. Wherever I would go, it was acknowledged that they would write about me. So even if the girl wasn't quite that interested, we'd date because, if nothing else, it would be a good political date. Places like Mocambo, Ciro's, Crescendo, The Ambassador in the Coconut Grove. There was a woman by the name of Rae Lynn at the *Movie Stars Parade Magazine*. I'd flip through the pages and if I'd see anything that looked pretty I'd say, 'Yes, Rae. I want to date her.' But it was always with a sense of wonderful humility. Never presumptuous just like, 'I'd sure like to date this girl.' She'd say, 'Yeah, I can set it up. We'll make it a date layout.' Sometimes I'd get laid. Other times I wouldn't. It was a lot of fun just to flip through the pages. Well, to make a long story shorter, what happened was, Tony Curtis and Janet Leigh, man, they were still married, they had sent out a telegram they had sent probably to a hundred million people. 'We're throwing a party for Rory Calhoun.' He'd made this appearance on — what the f—k was the name of that? **Playhouse 90**. So 'we're going to be throwing a party for him. You're cordially invited. Bring a date.'

"So I called up Rae. I says, 'Rae, I know a lot of girls, but do you know anybody that's really pretty and got some sort of, y'know, class? Not that the others don't, but something really nice?' 'There's a girl just got in town, walked across the stage on **The Jack Benny Show** and stopped the show cold. That's how pretty she is. No particular asset. Just a beautiful girl.' I says 'Give me her phone number.' She said 'No. Let me see if she'd want to date you.' She called her and said 'Yeah, she'll date you. Here's her number.' I called her up. I went to pick her up. I swear to God, I heard her voice upstairs. She said, 'Come on in, door's open,' with that Tennessee accent. I swear to God I was looking all over for a picture. I thought, 'If this girl doesn't look quite right, I'm outta here.' Well I'll tell you what. She walked down those stairs, about 118 pounds, this black dress wrapped around her. I saw those ankles as she's coming down the steps — it was just like a gradual thing until I saw her face and I went, 'Oh shit.' And that's how it happened. We got married. After 26 years, she developed cancer and I lost her. She had two kids when we met and we had three. My daughter is living here with me presently and she has a little girl. It's my first blood granddaughter. I'm really enjoying all that."

These days, how does Dick Contino, the master accordionist who makes feminine hearts flutter at Italian festas across the country reconcile his alternate fame as a two-fisted hot rodder? "The 'snowbirds' remember me for the accordion," he says, invoking the endearment he uses to identify his legion of graying fans. "But strange thing, man. We did a book tour with the release of **Dick Contino's Blues** and I didn't try to be [Ellroy's] character at all. Ellroy's always written about dead people or fictitious people. But I was, like, his one live person. And the places we went were jammed. They were there because of **Dick Contino's Blues**. In England and in Germany and in France, the book was called **Dick Contino's Blues** but they chose to call it **Hollywood Nocturnes** here in this country. We went on this book tour. I had my son Pete on drums and I brought the accordion. And the places, all of them, were packed. Ellroy would read the whole first chapter, and then he'd say, 'Okay, now I want you to meet Dick Contino.' Well, I didn't get up and try to be that character. I just got up and I did my act. I just talked with everybody like we're talking now and it really clicked. A lot of people have come up to me saying they hadn't heard of me as an accordionist, but they loved the character. A guy in Australia says, 'You're like a cult figure here. The people love **Dick Contino's Blues**.' He was talking to Ellroy about maybe the two of us going over there. I'd love to go." Contino concedes that he is probably best known for **Lady of Spain** and similar anthems, but is quick to add, "I think that maybe something could come out of the **Dick Contino's Blues** series. It could produce an entirely different thing, y'know?"

As a recent tour was taking shape, one promoter excitedly told Contino, "'You'd be amazed at the number of people that are so anxious to see you. It's like a cult thing. They ask, 'Is he really coming?'" Dick is clearly enjoying the second "career" as a fiction hero ("It's a nice ride, y'know?"), but he makes it plain that, "the thing I enjoy most — that I've been hearing a lot lately — is that I've touched the lives of a lot of people with the accordion. I'll hear somebody say, 'Because of you I started on the accordion ... ' Or maybe we're doing a show somewhere and somebody will come up and they look like they're older than I am and say, 'Since I was a little kid you inspired me.' That touches me mostly. Like you've had something to do with somebody's life. This isn't bullshit. I'm telling you the honest to God truth." Maybe the ride is just beginning.

"Why do teenagers try to find out what it's all about too soon?!" **Look In Any Window**

BACK TO THE SUTURE
richard CUNHA
MEETS THE B MONSTER

You might not recognize the name at first glance, but if you grew up watching late-show horror pictures in the 1960s, odds are you've seen the work of director Richard Cunha. The handful of horror films he directed in the late 1950s are exquisite examples of maverick,

profile

low-budget filmmaking. From the marauding 500-year-old conquistador of **Giant From the Unknown**, to the Nazi scientists and mutant

"Goddess of love in a city of sin!" **Fabulous Fabiola**

native girls of **She Demons**, to the rock men, juvenile delinquents and giant spiders of **Missile to the Moon**, if it was exploitable, Cunha had it covered. With **Frankenstein's Daughter**, Cunha and partner Marc Frederic appropriated a name with built-in cachet and ran with it, fashioning a film that cult-movie lovers can't seem to forget.

B MONSTER: Of all your films, readers seem to ask us about **Frankenstein's Daughter** most often. Care to hazard a guess as to why that might be the one they remember best?

> "WE WERE LUCKY, I GUESS, THAT THEY DIDN'T SAY 'FRANKENSTEIN'S MOTHER-IN-LAW.'"

DICK CUNHA: I guess that the name Frankenstein has been well exploited and indicates in one word that there is horror connected with it. I think people remember the title and not necessarily the film.

Q: Did you come up with the idea for the film?

DICK: Producer Marc Frederic and I were given the title **Frankenstein's Daughter** by the distributors and told to develop a story to fit that title. We were lucky, I guess, that they didn't say "Frankenstein's Mother-in-Law."

Q: How was the cast chosen?

DICK: With the finished script in hand, we paged through the Screen Actors Guild Directory and selected faces that we thought would fit the parts. We were careful to select choices that we thought we could afford. The caliber of the agent was also a consideration. We got the word out that we were casting a low-budget film, please apply if interested. We were required to submit our final choices to the distributor for approval, as they wanted "names" that would help sell the picture. Our budget was low and fixed so this was always a tough job. In our favor, we already had the name Frankenstein for them to sell. As I recall, Sally Todd had some recent screen credits, and the name Harold Lloyd worked. Also we hired Robert Dix because his dad Richard Dix was a marquee name. We made it clear to the agents that we had x dollars for the cast and that was it, period, so there was never ever squabbling over salary.

Q: John Ashley was something of a teen star at the time. Was he happy to be involved?

DICK: We were lucky to get John Ashley, as his agent felt he needed experience and exposure. He read enough of the script to know that he liked the part. He worked hard and was very professional. Everyone had fun working on the show.

Q: Was Sandra Knight married to Jack Nicholson when the film was being shot?

DICK: I don't recall that Sandra was married at that time.

Q: I thought Donald Murphy had an oily, unctuous quality that should have carried him to more prominent bad-guy roles. Was he your first choice for that part?

DICK: If I recall, Donald Murphy had just come to Hollywood from New York, and when he read for me, I knew he was the man. My producer, Marc Frederic, wanted a bigger name for the part, but although we looked hard, Murphy was locked in from day one as far as I was concerned.

Q: What became of Donald Murphy, Sandra Knight and Sally Todd?

DICK: I have no idea what happened to Murphy, Knight and Sally. Maybe the movie done' em in. (Only foolin'.)

Q: Felix Locher was getting on in years by that time. Was he sharp and eager to work?

DICK: Felix Locher was a dream to work with and always came up with something to improve his character. I have to mention Wolfe Barzell, who also was no spring chicken. He was very important to the story and had lots of dialogue. At the end of one of his big scenes, the cast and crew applauded his performance, a very unusual occurrence during our kind of speed filming.

Q: On films such as **Frankenstein's Daughter**, did the actors resent being stuck in a low-budget film, or were they happy to have work? In other words, was it a "happy set"?

DICK: No one was ever stuck in our films. We were very careful to lay out the ground rules before filming started for both cast and crew. The crew was hand-picked and we had all worked together before and knew what to expect. The cast pitched in and moved furniture, cleared props and helped in every way they could to keep the company on schedule. We made these films in six 10-hour days and had lots of fun doing it.

> "THE CAST PITCHED IN AND MOVED FURNITURE, CLEARED PROPS ... WE MADE THESE FILMS IN SIX 10-HOUR DAYS AND HAD LOTS OF FUN DOING IT."

Q: Where did you find the Page Cavanaugh Trio, who'd done a number of Hollywood gigs with Sinatra?

DICK: I believe a friend of the producer, who represented them, offered them so that they could get exposure. The deal was set prior to writing the script, so they were committed from the beginning. Page furnished the music as part of the deal.

Q: I love the songs — particularly **Daddy Bird** — but why is Harold Lloyd Jr.'s singing so out of sync?

DICK: I don't recall Harold Lloyd Jr.'s being out of sync during his singing. I have a print of the picture and will check it out. He was singing to playback and the lyrics were so fast that he didn't quite hit them right on the head, but I don't remember ever hearing a complaint before.

Q: John Ashley was known as a singer. Why didn't he sing the tunes? Did he want to?

"Special Singing Guest Star Neil Sedaka!" Sting of Death

DICK: If John Ashley was a singer I didn't know it, and besides, there was no room for a song from him. Part of Harold Lloyd's deal was that he would sing in the film.

Q: Who owned the place where those party scenes were shot?

DICK: The party scenes and the pool were filmed at producer Marc Frederic's home in West Los Angeles.

Q: The story has been told and retold, elaborated on and exaggerated. Please set the record straight: What was the deal with Harry Thomas' misguided makeup?

DICK: Holy Samoly! That story got screwed up from the beginning. Harry Thomas did a fabulous job creating the monster about two hours before his (her) first scene. As critical as the creature was to the film, for some unknown reason, we never gave a thought to what "she" should look like. As hard as that is to believe, it is true. It would take a miracle to make Sally Todd ugly as a monster, so we hired lovable Harry Wilson to play the role. We had no money for a day's prep by Harry Thomas to create a lady monster out of Wilson, so part of his daily make-up chores was to create **Frankenstein's Daughter** one morning before the monster was to appear on stage. (Not necessarily the first day of filming.) I haven't the foggiest idea what I expected, but between setups a few minutes before the creature was to be filmed, someone went ta-da and out came the monster.

Q: Be honest — what was your reaction when you first saw the monster?

DICK: I blinked my eyes and was in complete shock. I may have cried. I don't know what I expected, but that wasn't it. Harry Thomas had done a fabulous job with what he had in the time that he had. We just hadn't given the Daughter of Frankenstein enough preparation, time or thought. What the hell does the daughter of Frankenstein made from a squashed Sally Todd look like? I thought to myself, 'Not like this,' but the show must go on so we put her in front of the camera and kept filming. Never was any blame put on Thomas for his creation. The fault was entirely on poor preproduction planning. I remember the crew applauding when Harry proudly presented his creation.

Q: Any particular embarrassing occurrences during filming that you'd care to relate?

"One man's lust made men into beasts!" Circus of Horrors

DICK: No, not embarrassing, but a credit to Harry Thomas. When he created the creature that Sandra Knight played, he made her up without permitting her to see what was going on until he had finished. When she saw herself in the mirror for the first time she actually went into shock. She was so horrified at how she looked that she got hysterical and cried and it took some 20 expensive minutes and the company first aid person to calm her down before filming could continue.

Q: Were you drawn to horror pictures in general, or were your films strictly a business proposition?

DICK: No, I wasn't a horror films fan. I had made some 200 half-hour films for television featuring a cowboy singer and another series with Bob Steele the legendary Western movie hero. I spent a season in Africa filming an adventure travel program.

Q: I get the impression that you don't particularly like **Frankenstein's Daughter**. Is that true?

DICK: I don't mean to give the impression that I do not care for the film. It was less interesting to me and not as much fun to make. It was more like work. It was not a tongue-in-cheek project like **She Demons** and **Missile to the Moon**. I am very proud that we were able to complete it for $60,000.

Q: Where would you rank **Frankenstein's Daughter** among your films?

DICK: **Frankenstein's Daughter** was just another day's work.

Q: Are you nostalgic for your horror movie-making days, or is it something you'd just as soon forget?

DICK: The production of these exploitation films involved a little over a year of my career. I had good fun doing this and learned a great deal. I moved on and got reinvolved in the production of TV commercials, which was more gratifying and allowed me to focus my creative talents in a more limited area. One minute of commercial time costs more than the cost of our feature films. I was fortunate to work as a director/cameraman at the commercial division of Columbia Pictures for the next 20 years until I retired in

"The party picture that takes off where the others pooped out!" Pajama Party

1980. I enjoyed and will never forget any phases of my career in the film business. I grew up with a passion to take pictures and still do on our RV trips around the country.

The directing career of Richard Cunha may have been brief, but he left us with a handful of precious, no-budget cinematic gems. What his body of work may have lacked in intrinsic merit was more than compensated for by his enthusiasm and productivity. In just three years he turned out five films which are essential B-movie viewing.

Cunha was later to serve as principal photographer on another enjoyable low-cost cult film, **Bloodlust** *(1961), a rather tepid retelling of the classic* **The Most Dangerous Game**. *It featured Robert (***The Brady Bunch***) Reed and an enjoyable, hammy performance by Wilton Graff as the manhunter. Following his late-'50s spurt of creativity, Cunha moved into television commercial production even as his films were beginning to haunt the late show. He was never to direct another feature. Berate his films or adore them, but an overview of Cunha's canon is necessary to understanding what makes a film truly "B."*

Frankenstein's Daughter (1958)

According to Cunha, makeup man Harry Thomas, working with NO budget, had all of two hours to transform a male actor into **Frankenstein's DAUGHTER!** A dab of lipstick was smeared across the mangled "female's" putty-plastered kisser. Pressed for time, Cunha had little choice but to "roll 'em!" One of the film's highlights is Harold Lloyd Jr. singing **Daddy Bird**, poolside, backed by the swingin' Page Cavanaugh Trio.

Giant From the Unknown (1958)

Ex-wrestler Buddy Baer plays a malicious conquistador resurrected by a bolt of lightning after a 500-year snooze. Capable Ed Kemmer, Commander Buzz Corry of **Space Patrol** fame, is the archaeologist/hero. Applying the greasepaint to Baer's face was Jack Pierce, who created Karloff's **Frankenstein** and **Mummy** makeup, Chaney's **Wolf Man** and just about every other classic Universal monster.

"Suspense that will rock and shock you with its impact!" The Glass Web

SHE DEMONS (1958)
Debatably Cunha's best film in which super-pinup Irish McCalla, TV's **Sheena, Queen of the Jungle**, finds herself stranded on an island crawling with mutant-breeding Nazis. Rudolph Anders is the demented doc doing the breeding. Washed up with her is Victor Sen Yung, Charlie Chan's No. 2 son, soon to become Ponderosa chef Hop Sing.

MISSILE TO THE MOON (1959)
When Cunha needed a second feature to co-bill with **Frankenstein's Daughter**, he was told (for some unfathomable reason) to remake the 3-D schlock classic **Cat-Women of the Moon**. Highlights are the flabby suited rock men and the same giant spider doll that found its way into any number of B-grade shock films.

THE GIRL IN ROOM 13 (1961)
Cunha's final film as a director was lensed in Brazil and stars an aging Brian Donlevy as a taciturn private dick. Tacky and muddled with amateurish performances, the ambient sound of the outdoor scenes — honking horns and rustling leaves — nearly drowns out the dialogue.

"An avalanche of grisly horror!" **Fangs of the Living Dead**

A TRANCE ENCOUNTER WITH FAME
pamela DUNCAN
MEETS THE B MONSTER

Actress Pamela Duncan will always be remembered by cult-film fans for the pair of classic, low-budget horror movies in which she starred. **The Undead** and **Attack of the Crab Monsters** are regarded today as two of director Roger Corman's very best efforts, and Duncan

profile

recalls working for the controversial filmmaker fondly. "He treated me as though I was something fragile," she remembers. The B

"Terrorizes city, attacks women, annihilates men!" Snow Creature

Monster tag-teamed with peerless film historian Tom Weaver to chronicle Duncan's bright but abbreviated B-movie career.

Duncan was born and raised in Brooklyn and became interested in an acting career while still in school. "I would bring my high heels and a little jacket and put them in a subway locker," she laughs. "I would cut school, and put on the high heels and go on interviews for acting jobs." At about the same time, she embarked on a short-lived marriage. "I met a young man in the service and we got married. He asked me to go back to school to get my degree so that I could work while he finished his medical studies. I was making my living at the theatrical profession while I was still going to school, and one thing led to another."

It was on a trip to the West Coast to greet her husband's ship that Pamela learned "he wanted the marriage dissolved because he didn't like being married and wanted to stay in the service. I was in Hollywood working at that time and I didn't know what to do with myself," she recalls. "One day, I stopped to get my hair done at a place called Helen Hunt's Salon, and Helen happened to be there that day. She was Columbia Pictures' hairdresser-stylist. And she brought me in to meet the casting people at Columbia. I had gone west to meet my husband's ship and instead I met the casting director of a studio." The meeting led to appearances in the screen tests of many Hollywood hopefuls. "I would do the screen tests, hoping that someone would notice me, too. The notice didn't happen, but the paychecks did."

Eventually someone did notice, and Duncan landed her first film role opposite Whip Wilson in a low-budget Western called **Lawless Cowboys**. As she was learning firsthand the rigors of B-movie making, Duncan furthered her acting education via the fast-paced creative frenzy that was early TV — and learned a bit about the acting temperament in the bargain. "I remember Jack Palance was on a series called **Martin Kane**," she remembers. "He was the guest star, the heavy. After we changed costumes between scenes, he was waiting in the wings for his cue to go on. The stage manager tapped him on the shoulder and Palance turned around and said through gritted teeth, 'Don't cue me. I'll go when it's time to go.' And he went out and he did his usual good job. But it was a startling thing, to have the stage director [told off] by an actor!"

In New York, Duncan appeared in a slew of Army Signal Corp. films while

"Incredible revelations from the blackest chapters of unholy medicine!" The Man Who Turned to Stone

simultaneously working in a pair of pioneering science fiction television programs. "I was in **Captain Video**," she says, "and another 'space cadet' show called **Rocky Jones, Space Ranger**. On one episode, the script called for the bad guys to put me in a closet. When they finished the show, nobody remembered to get me out of the closet!" Duncan has happy memories of the programs, despite the relatively primitive conditions. "**Captain Video** was shot at Wanamaker's Department Store, in the piano section," she laughs. "We would rehearse in the ladies' room because there were chairs and mirrors in there."

Though she'd appeared in numerous television performances, the actress was nevertheless amazed when producer Roger Corman called her from out of the blue and offered her the plum lead in his upcoming shocker **The Undead**. The whirlwind, six-day shoot went smoothly, and the film has since accrued a reputation for its delivery of moody thrills on a modest budget, centering on Duncan's solid portrayal of the reincarnated hooker, Diana Love.

Not unlike the character she portrayed, Pamela Duncan was resurrected and celebrated, years after **The Undead**'s completion, by B-movie buffs who "rediscovered" her on the late, late show. **The Undead**, a shadowy mix of medieval sorcery and modern psychology is arguably one of Corman's best, and Duncan is convincing as the hypnotically regressed streetwalker. "I think that film was underrated," she says. "The title made you think there were zombies in it. Actually, it was the Bridey Murphy story."

Capitalizing on the public's sudden interest in reincarnation, brought on by the sensational Bridey Murphy case, Corman needed a leading lady who could deliver credible performances as both a streetwise prostitute and a medieval maiden. "He called me and offered me the role," Duncan recalls. "I don't know what made him think of me, except that he must have seen me in something; I was on TV a lot. Things like that just happened in my career. Somebody sees something and likes you, and then he hires you."

The Undead was the first movie Roger Corman produced using money out of his own pocket. "That makes me feel proud," Duncan declares, "that he picked ME out, without auditioning or anything. He just said, 'I want you for this film.'" The film hinges on Duncan's credible performance as the hooker who relives her medieval existence as a doomed maiden via the hypnotic inducement of a psychiatrist, encountering dwarves,

"The first satellite that returned to earth ... and the hell it brought with it!" **The Flame Barrier**

> "I THINK THAT FILM WAS UNDERRATED. THE TITLE MADE YOU THINK THERE WERE ZOMBIES IN IT."

demons, magic spells, superstitious villagers and wily witches. The film is one of Corman's most ambitious and satisfying efforts.

Duncan realized that her live TV experience had been excellent training for working at Corman's accelerated pace. "Roger Corman's movies were six-day wonders," she laughs. "He shot the Crusades on a 60-foot sound stage, with horses and the knights with their maces and the rest of the weaponry! He was a good director — business-like. He directed according to what he felt. And since he was also the producer, that was what he shot."

Many of his actors remember Corman as a difficult director, unsympathetic to their needs. Pam Duncan recalls a different experience. "He accepted what you brought him," she states. "My long speech at the end of **The Undead** was very reminiscent of Hamlet's 'to be or not to be.' Should I go to the guillotine and give [my future incarnations] their lives? I remember he was sitting with his head down, listening as I worked. And when I finished, he said quietly, 'Cut and print.' He didn't want to redo anything." Told of actor Richard Devon's claim that Corman displayed a ferocious temper when things went awry, she is dismissive. "I think he was overstating it — unless he had some discrepancy with Roger — in which case, that's any director's prerogative. But I don't remember his scolding anybody. On a six-day schedule, I don't think there'd be time!"

As shooting began under the film's announced title, **The Trance of Diana Love**, Duncan was impressed by what Corman could accomplish on such a minuscule budget. "It was a sound stage, with beehive smoker pots. It was the Crusades, shot in six days! We shot some of it at the Witch's Cottage in Beverly Hills, diagonally across the street from Jack Haley's home. It's a cottage, covered with vines and plants. It looks like it's in a forest. An old-type building. That was [actress] Dorothy Neumann's home [in the film], the Witch's Cottage."

"Shown uncut! Every terror exactly as filmed!" The Black Scorpion

Duncan says that she barely had a chance to strike up an acquaintance with her co-stars. "There was no time for anecdotes on those pictures," she laughs. "Richard Garland was a quiet person. He was going through a divorce at that time from Beverly Garland. Dorothy Neumann was a very nice lady. Allison Hayes played the 'cat woman' — the witch who turns herself into a cat. She was engaged to a director at that time. Later she did the **50 Foot Woman**. And Billy Barty is unique. I don't think there are many actors that give him competition for the roles he plays!"

Corman always said that filming **The Undead** was great fun. Duncan is quick to agree — with certain reservations. "I had rather a skeptical moment or two which had to do with the axe man," she laughs. "He kept lifting this axe up over his head, getting ready for the blow, and the blood was running down the handle — his hand could have slipped off. It was a real axe."

Duncan had enough confidence in Corman to work with him a second time. "I would have liked to have kept on doing films for him," she declares. But while filming **Attack of the Crab Monsters**, she stopped short of stepping into a tank filled with live sharks. "They said, 'Don't worry about it. The sharks won't attack you.' I said, 'You tell that to the sharks! I'm not about to go swimming with sharks!'" Likewise, the hefty scuba gear proved more than the actress could handle. In a key underwater scene, she was submerged by prop men who had forgotten to turn on her air valve. "It was men's equipment — too big for me, and I couldn't reach the valve. So I went shooting back up to the surface, and that was the scene! Roger said, 'Go down! Go down! I need the shot!' And I had the courage to say, 'You just got it!' Corman had me taken to a swimming pool to try on the underwater gear," she adds. "I couldn't handle it, even in a swimming pool! One of the boys who had a part as a Navy crewman

> "THEY SAID, 'DON'T WORRY ABOUT IT. THE SHARKS WON'T ATTACK YOU.' I SAID, 'YOU TELL THAT TO THE SHARKS!'"

"A tide of terror floods the screen!" Zombies of Mora Tau

was about my height and weight — and he had good legs! So he was 'padded out,' and he did all the doubling for me underwater."

Following the completion of these low-budget shockers, Duncan worked sporadically, popping up in small roles in larger-budgeted films — **Don't Give Up the Ship** and **Summer and Smoke** among them. "Now you're talking about production moneys in the millions," she says. "There's a big jump between **Crab Monsters** and a major movie! But I was mingling with the top directors and the top producers, and a break could come out of that. That's your compensation for taking a smaller role. But they would always give you billing and they would always pay you your salary. I got a thousand a week at that time."

But just as she was poised to enjoy a satisfying career as a serious actress, her West Hollywood home was badly damaged in a mudslide with Duncan inside at the time. Subsequent lawsuits and legal action left her little time to pursue an acting career. Returning to New York, she took on stage work and appeared in a few commercials.

Though she rarely screens her own movies today, Duncan says that "When I saw **The Undead** recently, I thought it was well done. In fact, I enjoyed seeing both of them, **Crab Monsters** and **The Undead**. I can see where **The Undead** would become a cult film."

What if fate had dealt her a more favorable hand? What if she'd landed that one, conspicuous breakthrough role? Would she have been uncomfortable with the burdens and scrutiny of stardom? "Oh, of course *not*," she states. "That's what you're working toward, that one big break." The lucky break that might have secured lasting success for Pamela Duncan never materialized, and she slipped quietly from the Hollywood scene. Though she has many happy memories of her filmmaking days, she doesn't appear to be yearning to get back in the game. In fact, she doesn't seem to care much for modern films and the direction they've taken. "I wouldn't say I don't like them," she laughs. "I struggle to UNDERSTAND them!"

"Freezing horror as a living nightmare strikes from the depths of the ocean!" The Phantom From 10,000 Leagues

SHE MADE "ID" WORTH THE TRIP
anne FRANCIS
MEETS THE B MONSTER

Browsing though a memorabilia shop, I came across an old copy of *Sweet 16*. Along with a brief biography, there was a photo of a stunning, 16-year-old Anne Francis on the cover. Unfortunately, I couldn't afford the book. It's as collectible as the **Forbidden**

profile

Planet posters and **Honey West** dolls that deep-pocketed collectors snatch up on eBay every day. Upon meeting Anne Francis

"Shuddery things from beyond the stars, here to breed with human women!" I Married a Monster From Outer Space

in person, I was struck by the fact she still possesses the same vitality and arresting sex appeal that could be seen in that teenage face.

As the star of **Forbidden Planet**, easily one of the most influential science fiction pictures ever, Anne is in constant demand at film conventions across the country. Based loosely on Shakespeare's **The Tempest**, the film features stunning effects (even by today's standards), a terrific cast, the marauding monster from the "Id" and, of course, science-fiction icon Robby, the Robot. But Anne is far from overshadowed by the impressive sets and pioneering gadgetry, and is easily the movie's most eye-catching visual. Today, she's patient, sweet and candid with every fan she meets at signings and film cons, and maintains a steady schedule of movie and television work, with appearances in popular TV fare as varied as **Murder, She Wrote, Home Improvement** and **The Drew Carey Show**. The real-life **Honey West** seems as vital and popular as ever.

B MONSTER: Was that *Sweet 16* magazine piece a part of the movie star-grooming process that existed in those days?

ANNE FRANCIS: I don't remember the *Sweet 16* magazine or cover. I remember there was a magazine called *Seventeen*. I believe it still exists. I do remember a layout, though, that was done the first time I was with MGM as a young teenager. My mom was with me then. They borrowed a black cocker spaniel from the apartment manager and palmed him off as mine in the pictures. I did have a black cocker spaniel at home back in New York that I missed very much. I was glad when they let me leave after a year with only two days work in a film with Mickey Rooney called **Summer Holiday**. All I did was ride back and forth on the trolley from Santa Monica to Culver City to go to the little school house on the lot. MGM did not do any buildup with me the first time I was under contract to them.

Q: Were there any actors or directors who were particularly helpful when you were getting started?

ANNE: I started as a kid in New York. I was six when I started modeling, and seven when I went to work on a children's show called **Coast to Coast on a Bus**, at NBC. Actually, I learned by hard knocks. If you didn't perform the way they wanted, your lines

"Terror stalks! Half monster, half man!" Giant From the Unknown

were given to another kid. Earning a few dollars a week was important in those days to help put food on the table. My dad lost his business as an aftermath of the Depression, which is why we moved from the country to the city. He took a job as a salesman in Macy's basement, and my working helped with the finances. Families pulled together in whatever way they could to make ends meet. I still think twice before throwing out a sliver of soap! I have one in my shower right now. So, no, there were no actors or directors who helped me out when I was getting started.

Q: Which part do you consider your "breakthrough" role?

ANNE: My breakthrough role came many years later when I was in my late teens. It was a film called **So Young, So Bad**. It was shot all over the New York City streets. I was also hosting a variety show at the time called **The Bonnie Maid Versatile Variety Show**. I did skits with the MC, and commercials for Bonnie Maid tile and linoleum, and I wore Scotch kilts. Anyway, the film was rigorous for all of us. Paul Henreid played a psychiatrist at a reform school for young women, and I played a teenage prostitute with a baby. Anne Jackson and Rita Moreno (then Rosita Moreno) were in the film as well.

Q: **The Rocket Man** is an interesting little film with a good cast. How did that come about? Did you have to deal with Lenny Bruce, who co-wrote the picture, in any way?

ANNE: It came about because I was under contract at the time, and [the studio] said I was going to do it! I was most fond of Lenny. He was a real pussy cat, and wanted me to go out with him. I told him I would be terrified to do so, and that was that!

Q: Your role in **Blackboard Jungle**, considered controversial stuff at the time, was significant. Any memories of Richard Brooks, Glenn Ford or other cast members?

ANNE: Richard Brooks was a soft-spoken man who could suddenly, out of nowhere, yell at a crew member. He was definitely a perfectionist, with an editor's eye. I admired that talent. However, his impatience could be most unsettling. I grew up in a family that stressed (there's a key word!) perfectionism. Glenn was fun and loved to tease. I was most impressed by Sidney Poitier's work. What an actor he is. I do wish he would grace the screen again. Wouldn't he and Denzel Washington be a fantastic team in a movie today?

"From out of space came hordes of green monsters!" **Invaders From Mars**

Q: I know that you consider your part in **Girl of the Night** among your favorite roles. Can you explain why this one is special to you?

ANNE: **Girl of the Night** is special to me because it was such a demanding role. It really was a tour de force, and a wonderful chance to run the gamut. The fact that it was the story of a prostitute under analysis was rather risqué, I guess, at the time, though there were no licentious scenes in the picture. I don't think there was a love scene, really. However, the studio (Warners) soft-peddled it and it opened without any fanfare, though I was pleased with what reviews we had.

Q: I've heard you say that one of your favorite directors was William Conrad. Why is that, and how does he compare with "big-name" directors (William Wyler, John Sturges, Raoul Walsh) you've worked with?

ANNE: Bill Conrad could invent on the spot, whatever the location. He would use the window of a car or a limb of a tree in the most artistic way. I remember one day when I had an hysterical scene. The film was called **Brainstorm** — not the same story that Natalie Wood did later — and Bill instructed me as to the sound and pitch he wanted my crying to end on. He had come from radio originally, and was most sensitive to sound, as am I. He knew exactly the tone he wanted to segue from one scene to the next, and we did it!

William Wyler was a taskmaster. He often ended up using the first instinct that the actor had, after trying many other interpretations. As you know, he was legendary for many takes.

John Sturges was a quiet and thorough man, having done his camera homework on paper long before his arrival on set. He and Ferris Webster (the editor) were a fine team on **Bad Day at Black Rock**. Such wonderful visuals, and dramatic cuts. John had been an editor before he was a director, so he really knew what could be done in the editing room. Raoul Walsh was a darling, shy "man's man." When the camera rolled, he would turn his back and walk away, often rolling a cigarette as he listened to the scene play out. He would then ask the actor, "How was it for you?" and if they were comfortable, and it had sounded right to him, he'd yell "print."

"Yesterday they were cold and dead. Today, they're hot and bothered!" Dracula vs. Frankenstein

Q: Who would you list among your favorite leading men?

ANNE: Les Nielsen, because he was such a fine actor, and I had a tremendous crush on him! He was most generous at work with fellow performers. Burt Reynolds, because he was so much fun and didn't take himself too seriously. Marty Sheen and Robert Ryan because of a wonderful self-possessed essence, a certain dignity that was an inherent part of their nature — a "fineness." Jimmy Cagney had that too. Tim Allen, because there is so much more there than the terrific talent that meets the eye. Have you read his books? They're wonderful. That's quite a diverse bunch to pull out of my brain in one fell swoop at this moment.

Q: Now, the money questions: What's your most embarrassing show business memory?

ANNE: My most embarrassing moment was as a teenager in a play called, **My Sister Eileen**. I was on stage at the Robin Hood Theater in Arden, Delaware, doing summer stock. I was in a slip, and one of the straps had broken, and I didn't know it until I left the stage. Of course, I was wearing a bra underneath, but for a teenager that was mortifying! At least it was then. Perhaps not today!

Q: Who was the biggest jerk you ever worked with?

ANNE: Now, Marty. You know I would never name the biggest jerk I ever worked with! But I do remember one fellow who was rather spastic when it came to action. He was a "he-man" type, and in a slapping scene he got me in the Adam's apple! Boy that smarted!

SELECTED FILMS FEATURING ANNE FRANCIS

Lover's Knot
1996
The Double 0 Kid
1993
Little Vegas
1990
Return
1985
Agatha
1979
Survival
1976
Pancho Villa
1972
The Love God?
1969
Funny Girl
1968
Brainstorm
1965
The Satan Bug
1965
Honey West (TV)
1965
The Crowded Sky
1960
Girl of the Night
1960
Don't Go Near the Water
1957
The Rack
1956
Forbidden Planet
1956
The Great American Pastime
1956
Blackboard Jungle
1955
Battle Cry
1955
Bad Day at Black Rock
1955
Susan Slept Here
1954
The Rocket Man
1954
Rogue Cop
1954
A Lion Is in the Streets
1953
Dreamboat
1952
The Whistle at Eaton Falls
1951
So Young, So Bad
1950
Summer Holiday
1948
Portrait of Jennie
1948

"See and talk to the Living Head in person!" **The Living Head**

Q: Do you ever get sick of talking about **Forbidden Planet**?

ANNE: Not so far, but try me!

Q: This may seem an obvious question, but does it surprise you that after almost 45 years, **Forbidden Planet** is still considered one of THE best science fiction films ever made?

ANNE: Forty-five years, Marty. You must be kidding. I'm not that old. Actually, at the time, I don't think I gave its longevity any thought. But, today, I see the good work that the Disney artisans did, and the film stands up well alongside all the effects that the studios can throw on the screen today. Quite amazing, I'd say. I understand there's serious talk of a remake. That should be interesting.

Q: What did you think of the film when you first saw it?

ANNE: I was pleased when I first saw it because we were all acting against visuals that weren't there. "The Monster from the Id," and all the special effects. It really was fun to see the whole thing put together.

Q: You had great parts in **Bad Day at Black Rock** and **Blackboard Jungle** under your belt when you did **Forbidden Planet**. Was doing a sci-fi film a step down in your eyes?

ANNE: I really didn't know anything about the sci-fi genre. I still am not a sci-fi person, though I have seen strange things in the heavens down here in the desert! I just took it as another acting assignment. I think we all did.

Q: Other than the notorious drunken robot, Robby, any memories of castmates in particular?

ANNE: Yes. For many years, I wondered who had left a single rose on the windshield of my car for me to find each evening when I left. Such a romantic thing to do. I found out who it was many years later when Warren Stevens flew me to Santa Barbara on a luncheon date in his plane. A kind, gentle person, Warren.

"The monster created by atoms gone wild!" **The Fly**

Q: I've heard you mention that you had quite a crush on Leslie Nielsen at the time. What do you think of the direction his career has taken?

ANNE: I think that Les in one of the most underrated actors in the business, and I guess he always will be. I hate to say that, but he will be most remembered for his later antics, though he came from some fine performances in the theater and live TV in New York. However, Les loves to make people laugh, so I'm sure it's okay with him. Recently, I caught up with him at the McCallum Theater down here doing **Darrow** (a one-man play about Clarence Darrow, the great attorney) and he was wonderful. He was delighted that he had just been asked to do the English provinces with the show. He is a special person with a gorgeous wife who is completely devoted to him.

> "HONEY WAS A ROLE MODEL FOR A LOT OF YOUNG WOMEN AND GIRLS IN THE '60S. I HAVE HEARD SO FROM MANY. BUT APPARENTLY SHE LEFT HER MARK ON SOME YOUNG MEN AS WELL."

Q: Would you say that fans remember you more for your role as Altaira in **Forbidden Planet** or **Honey West**?

ANNE: More for **Honey West**.

Q: **Charlie's Angels** always struck me as **Honey West** times three, and I think you could make a case that **Honey West** was the first sexy, strong, positive female role (with the accent on the sexy part, of course) in television history. Would you agree?

ANNE: Honey was a role model for a lot of young women and girls in the '60s. I have heard so from many. But apparently she left her mark on some young men as well. I went in for an interview with Oliver Stone for project a few years ago, and he met me with a big grin and threw out his arms to embrace me, shouting "Honey West!"

Q: There has long been talk of a **Honey West** feature film. Do you think it should be remade? Who would you cast as Honey?

ANNE: I can't imagine the "Honey" we did being in a film today. The "Honey" books presented a much more bawdy and lustful creature who rolled in the hay quite a bit. That would probably be the "Honey" of choice today, rather than the tongue-in-cheek lady I enjoyed playing. The Honey I knew loved fun and adventure, but she wasn't licentious. I would choose Meg Ryan, whom I think is delightful, and also a very fine actress. There was some talk a long time ago that Madonna wanted to do "Honey." Probably too much time has gone by now. I don't know if [producer-actor] Danny DeVito has dibs on the property any more.

Q: Have you ever taken offense at being called a "babe," a "sex kitten" or "TV's Private Eyeful?"

ANNE: "Private Eyeful" is a fun title for Honey. I don't think I've ever been called a "sex kitten" or a "babe," though. That's never been my image. Come to think of it, I'm not sure what my image is, but I know "sex kitten" or "babe" isn't it!

"They dared enter the cave of death!" The Unknown Terror

FULLER'S BRUSH WITH THE BRAIN
robert FULLER
MEETS THE B MONSTER

Science fiction fans will never forget his death by telepathic ray in the bowels of Bronson Canyon, dispatched by a bobbing, glowing brain with eyes. That role in **The Brain From Planet Arous**, opposite John Agar, was a big break for former

profile

stuntman/extra Robert Fuller, one that carried him, not only to film fame, but to lasting prominence in prime-time TV on such series as **Wagon Train**,

"What weird accident of science created it?" Tarantula

Laramie and **Emergency!** As the actor explains, it was a career path that started, logically enough, on Hollywood Boulevard.

"I was assistant manager of Graumann's Chinese Theater. I started out there as the doorman wearing a Chinese outfit. I was there maybe six months when the assistant manager left and they gave me the job. I was 17 years old. I wore a suit and tie in the daytime and a tuxedo at night. I was in charge of all the usherettes. We had 20 usherettes on staff in 1951. It was a great job. I had a good time. I met a bunch of kids around my age who'd come to the movies. They worked as extras in the business. They convinced me that I should get into the extra's guild because it paid more money. I was making 50 bucks a week as assistant manager. Extra work, in those days, paid $12.05 a day plus adjustments and meal penalties and so on. I could make 30-40 bucks a day. I went down and interviewed quite a few times and finally got in. The first picture I worked on was **Above and Beyond** with Eleanor Parker and Robert Taylor."

It might surprise those who think of Fuller as a cowpoke or paramedic that he won his first break in pictures as a dancer. "I had a background as a dancer because my parents had a dancing school down in Key West, where I'm from. I could hoof a little bit. I could fake it, let's put it that way. Somebody said, 'Why don't you go on some of these dance interviews.' Those guys were making 150 bucks a week and more. And if you got involved in a musical you could work up to two or three months. The first one I went out on I got. It was a picture called **I Love Melvin** with Debbie Reynolds and Donald O'Connor. All the dancers stood in a line. The ones that the dance director knew he would pick out because they had worked for him for a hundred years. Anybody new would have to do something. When he got to me he said, 'I've never seen you around.' I said, 'No, I'm new in the business.'

"'And you can dance?'

"'Oh, yeah, sure, I'm a dancer.'

"'Let me see you do a time step.' So, I got up and I did a time step.

"'How's your ballet?'

"'Well, not very good but I can ...'

"'Let me see you do a pirouette or something.' So I did a couple of pirouettes for him.

"After the audition he came back to me and said, 'Look, I'd love to use you but I have an allegiance to these other people and I've got it pretty much filled up.' Just as we were leaving, his assistant came up to him and said, 'You forgot about the acrobatic number. We need five people for the acrobatic number.'

"He turned to me and said, 'You don't by any chance do acrobatics, do you?' Which I did. I said, 'Yes.'

"'What do you do?'

"'I can do anything you want.'

"'Let me see you do a back handspring.' So I did a back handspring."

Bob was told his scenes would be shot in a month or so. He went home, the phone rang. A part had opened up. He reported the next day and proceeded to work in every dance number in the picture. "Debbie Reynolds was a sweetheart. She knew that I was terribly in love with her in those days. I had a big, big crush on her. We're still great friends today. But that's how it started. I danced in a lot of pictures. Then I got drafted ... the Korean War was on and I spent 17 months in Korea. When I came home, I couldn't dance at all any more after climbing up and down all those mountains.

"So I immediately started studying acting with Richard Boone, before he did **Have Gun, Will Travel**, and I started doing some extra work to pay for that. I did a little stunt work. I doubled Jerry Lewis and Steve McQueen. Dick sent me back to New York to study with Sandy Meisner at the Neighborhood Playhouse because that's where he had graduated from. I was back there in late 1955.

"When I got back home, **Teenage Thunder** came about." Fuller explains how he and his longtime buddy, actor/stuntman Chuck Courtney, schemed to win Fuller a part in the juvenile delinquent exploitation quickie. "My very best friend, Chuck Courtney, who

---

"A cult of undead creatures seek fresh warm human blood!" The Vampire People

starred in **Teenage Thunder**, was, at the time, doing a TV series called **The Lone Ranger**; he played Dan Reid, the Lone Ranger's nephew. Chuck had been signed to do this picture, and the part of the heavy was open. Paul Helmick, who was directing, was leaning toward an actor named Eddie Byrnes — remember Kookie? Edd was starting to make a little splash about that time. I went in and I read for Paul two or three times and, apparently, Eddie did too. I guess they started to lean a little more toward Eddie, and Chuck came up with the idea of us doing one of the scenes in the movie — it was the scene where I pull into the gas station in a hot rod, Chuck is working there and he's going to clean my windshield, and we get into a big fight; I jump out of the car and we do a whole number — a little dialogue and a fight scene. So Chuck said, 'I've got an idea. I'm going to have Paul Helmick come over to my house. I want you to park down the block, and at exactly 10 o'clock I'm going to have Paul come to the house. I'm going to tell him that I want to talk to him about the script. I'll be out on the lawn. As soon as he gets to the door, you pull up in your car, hit the brakes, and we'll do that scene.' I sat down the block for about 20 minutes, and I see Paul Helmick pull up and park across the street. He gets out and sees Chuck on the lawn. At that point I put it in gear, scratched the gravel and sped up there, and Chuck and I played the scene and Paul just stood there, dumbfounded. After it was all over, we were laying on the ground and he said, 'That's it! All right! You've got the damn part!'"

Fuller made a convincing teenage thug, taunting Courtney's character into harrowing drag races and games of "chicken." He certainly impressed the producers. "What happened was, Joy Houck — Howco International was the company that was doing it — put both Chuck and I under contract for two pictures. I did **Teenage Thunder** and **The Brain From Planet Arous** with John Agar, and Chuck did **Teenage Thunder** and **Teenage Monster**. We each did our two pictures and went on from there."

Guiding **Teenage Thunder, Brain From Planet Arous** and **Teenage Monster** to completion was B-movie impresario Jacques Marquette, who, teaming with **Brain** director Nathan Juran (aka Nathan Hertz), also gave the world **Attack of the 50 Foot Woman**. "Jacques Marquette was the cameraman and one of the money people involved with it. Jacques later did the camera work on a good Western that I did called **The Gatling Gun**. In fact, he was instrumental in getting me in to meet the director to get the part." Fuller has no explanation, incidentally, for director Juran's alias. "He did that quite often. I had heard that he directed under two or three other names, as well."

"Please keep the climax a secret!" **Frenzy**

Did the up-and-coming actor have any apprehensions about co-starring in his next picture with a papier mache brain? "No, not at all. I was a young actor, starting out. I was happy to have a picture to do. I liked the part. It was a real good part. John Agar was very famous at that time. Joyce [Meadows] was a very pretty young actress. I was very excited about doing it. All that cave stuff in Bronson Canyon. I was working and it was great."

> "IT LOOKED LIKE A HUGE BRAIN MADE OUT OF STYROFOAM ... BUT ONCE THEY GOT THE LIGHTS AND THE SPECIAL EFFECTS GOING, IT LOOKED PRETTY GOOD."

Bob says there are two questions he's asked most often about **Brain From Planet Arous**. First, what was his initial reaction upon first seeing the eponymous, bulbous prop on the set. He admits it required a bit of movie magic to become frightening. "When you saw it in person it wasn't convincing. It looked like a huge brain made out of Styrofoam. It wasn't Styrofoam — they didn't have Styrofoam in those days. I don't know what the hell it was. Just sitting on the sound stage not doing anything, it wasn't convincing. But once they got the lights and the special effects going, it looked pretty good."

The other question invariably pertains to John Agar. "He was really a gentleman and a nice, nice man," says Bob. "People always ask about John. They're fascinated. He was quite a star in 1940s and '50s.

Fuller notes with nostalgia how those original locations have changed over the years: "Nowadays, you'd have to be careful where you point your camera in Bronson Canyon

"Science fiction's strangest story of the weird child-demons!" *Village of the Damned*

because you'd see high-rises and homes and what have you. Back then, Bronson Canyon was huge and the only access to it was a dirt road. They did several kinds of movies there, you name it. Similarly, we shot a lot of the Westerns like **Laramie** and **Wagon Train** out in Thousand Oaks, which was just prairie and oak trees in those days. Today, there are hundreds of condominiums. Most of the interiors [for **Brain**] were rented sound stages or practical locations like somebody's house. The lab was a rented sound stage somewhere in the Valley. The house with the backyard where we had the barbecue was just a house that we rented."

Brain, of course, went on to become a cult classic, a favorite of Baby Boomers who came of age watching it on the late show. But was the film a financial success when initially released? "I'm sure that it was. I know **Teenage Thunder** certainly was. We made that picture for $46,000. Shot it in seven days, and before it was out a year it grossed a million dollars. I have no doubt that **The Brain** did close to that. Those exploitation films in those days were made very, very inexpensively. You're talking under $100,000 making back a million over a two-year period — that was big gravy in those days.

> "YOU'RE TALKING UNDER $100,000 MAKING BACK A MILLION OVER A TWO-YEAR PERIOD — THAT WAS BIG GRAVY IN THOSE DAYS."

"From there on I just got very lucky and started working. At that time, there were something like 30 Westerns in prime time. Chuck had taught me how to ride a horse and draw a gun, so I was really right for them — and I did damn near every one of them until Universal decided they wanted to put me in a series.

"But I haven't really been nailed in one medium or the other. Some of the first work I

"The tortured ghost who claimed vengeance in the bride's bedroom!" **The Screaming Skull**

ever did was in television. Then came **Teenage Thunder** and **The Brain From Planet Arous**. And then I REALLY got involved in television. All through 1957 and '58 I was doing guest star shots on every show in town. 1959 was when they offered me **Laramie**. I did that for four seasons and then went right into **Wagon Train** for three. And then I went back to doing movies. I did several here and in Europe and then Jack Webb decided he wanted me to do **Emergency!** That was in '71. I have a huge number of fans who think of me as Dr. Brackett. But if they're 10 years older they think of me as Jess Harper or Cooper Smith. It's a mix. And it's a good mix.

Bob seems completely at ease discussing the old days, realizing that films like **Brain** were springboards to the prominence he continues to enjoy. And 40 years after **Teenage Thunder**, Chuck Courtney was still his best buddy. "Chuck had a stroke about eight years ago. He's not paralyzed. He gets around. In fact, we were just at Keely Smith's big opening at the House of Blues the other night. He can't talk; it affected his speech very badly. But hell, he was dancing and having a great time." [Ed. Chuck Courtney has since passed away.]

In recent years Fuller has continued to do guest spots on various TV series as well as some voiceover work. "I'll probably do some more episodic work for another year or so. Then I'll retire and go back to Florida and go bass fishing." Whether they know him as **Laramie**'s Jess Harper, Cooper Smith of **Wagon Train**, Kelly Brackett of **Emergency!** or as the victim of an evil alien brain, Fuller is always happy to meet and greet his fans at personal appearances. "We're having a huge **Emergency!** convention this month. There are people from all over the world coming to it. **Emergency!** was a very, very popular show." Likewise, he enjoys reminiscing with former genre film co-stars such as John Agar. "I've always gotten along great with John. I saw him just

SELECTED FILMS FEATURING ROBERT FULLER

Maverick
1994
The Program
1993
Repossessed
1990
Bonanza: The Next Generation
1988
Megaforce (TV)
1982
Separate Ways
1981
Disaster on the Coastliner
1979
Donner Pass: The Road to Survival
1978
Mustang Country
1976
The Gatling Gun
1973
Emergency! (TV)
1971
The Hard Ride
1970
Mittsommernacht
1970
Whatever Happened to Aunt Alice?
1969
Kommando Sinai
1968
Incident at Phantom Hill
1966
Return of the Seven
1966
Wagon Train (TV series)
1963
Laramie (TV series)
1959
The Brain From Planet Arous
1957
Teenage Thunder
1957
Strange Intruder
1955

"Sickening horror to make your stomach turn and flesh crawl!" Frankenstein's Bloody Terror

recently at the Beverly Garland Hotel. [Ed. John Agar has also since passed away.] I see John and Joyce Meadows quite often around Hollywood or at the signings that we do. It's always a pleasure and we think back and say, 'My God, it was a long time ago.'"

QUEEN OF THE SCREAMERS beverly GARLAND
MEETS THE B MONSTER

When searching for adjectives to describe Beverly Garland, "spirited" is among the first that comes to mind — as is "candid." The two qualities in tandem make her a film historian's dream come true. A passing glance at her film credits reveals an impressive

profile

diversity. Yet she's the first to admit that B-movie fans recall the string of low-budget fantasy films she made for director Roger Corman most vividly.

"Temptation and terror in the savage land of wild desire!" *Naked Paradise*

Garland seems to be at peace with her standing as a cult-film icon. With two children and a thriving hotel business to sustain her, she reflects with few regrets on her past. "My career just kind of unfolded wherever it unfolded," she says. "I've enjoyed every bloody minute of it."

B MONSTER: Honestly, don't you ever get sick of the fans and their questions?

BEVERLY GARLAND: You know I really don't because what's happened is — we did those movies for $500, or whatever the hell we did them for — certainly not a lot of money — and we never really thought they'd amount to anything. You know, you came home and you thought 'Well, that's the end of that.' I got my money and I can pay my rent, never dreaming in a million years that 25 years — 30 years — however many years later that anybody would call you and ask about them. Half the time you did them and absolutely forgot about them. And people ask me questions about some of this stuff and I really can't remember half the time because I didn't pay any attention. I did the gig and I went home and that was that. Goodbye. And now people ask me [questions], I go, 'Gee I don't know. Let's see if I can remember anything.'

Q: Your very first role was in the classic film noir **D.O.A.** What do you recall about breaking into the business in such a highly regarded film?

> "WE DID THOSE MOVIES FOR $500, OR WHATEVER THE HELL WE DID THEM FOR — CERTAINLY NOT A LOT OF MONEY — AND WE NEVER REALLY THOUGHT THEY'D AMOUNT TO ANYTHING."

"In breathtakingly beautiful Eastman color!" Swamp Women

BEVERLY: I remember that it was fabulous to do and that it was a very prestigious picture and nominated for an award and Eddie O'Brien was just the best — an actor's actor. The one thing about him was that he really gave you a lot. I had such a good time. It was a thrill for me because I hadn't done a movie and here I was playing practically a second lead. Luther Adler was in it — just the sweetest guy in the world. I was awed by everybody. It was kind of an interesting way to finally get into this business.

Q: Your most memorable characters are strident and tenacious and energetic.

BEVERLY: Well, I'm a very energetic person. They didn't hire a centerfold stripper to do these parts. They hired an actress. And that's what they got. And that's why it holds up.

Q: Do you recall a picture called **Stark Fear**?

BEVERLY: Oh yeooh my God! I wish I didn't. It was probably — no it wasn't PROBABLY — it WAS the worst picture I have ever done. It was awful. The director really ended up not knowing what he was doing. Skip Homeier ended up finishing out the direction of that thing. It was just a disaster. A disaster! I think it played in L.A. and I went to see it. I think it opened on a Tuesday and on Thursday they said, "It's gone." Because nobody came. They did this from a college and the man that directed was from the dramatic department and they got the money together to do a movie and they were all so excited. And they came and asked Skip and I and Ken [Tobey], "Would you do it?" The script wasn't bad. It was kind of an interesting script. But it just doesn't make it. It doesn't work.

Q: Why do you think audiences are drawn to a cult film like **Pretty Poison**?

BEVERLY: I think that's probably one of the best pieces of work I've done. I loved it. I'm sorry I wasn't in the picture more. I loved the story. The story was wonderful. Noel Black was an incredible director. I thought he did a terrific job. Everybody in that movie was absolutely perfect. It's a lovely movie. Lovely, lovely. It was before its time and got a tremendous write-up in *Time* magazine and should have been nominated for an award. I don't think a lot of people at that time understood it. I love that ending, where she gets away with it all. I think that's just the best. For years nobody knew [about the film]. You'd say **Pretty Poison** and they'd go, "What?" Finally people got it. Like **Fargo**, you

---

"Like nothing your eyes have ever seen before!" Curucu, Beast of the Amazon

know? "Have you seen **Fargo**? Well, have *you* seen **Pretty Poison**?" Look how far it's come.

Q: Do you have a favorite leading man?

BEVERLY: The man that I worked with that I loved most of all was David Niven. He funny and he was wonderful and he was charming — I just thought he was the best thing that ever happened. I did a couple of television shows with him but no movies. But I loved him. He was just great.

Q: Were there any real jerks you'd like to talk about?

BEVERLY: There are so many jerks that I can't really begin to tell you all about them. Better not to mention any names than to mention them all. [laughing]

Q: Do you prefer film work or television?

BEVERLY: I prefer movies. They're the best. You have more time. You develop it. You get out there and you really have the time to think — to do. Television is fast and the directors are like — they direct traffic. "Stand here, do that, don't let the door, turn here, go to the left." That's not a director to me.

Q: How did you find your way into the hotel business?

BEVERLY: My husband is a builder and a developer and he bought seven acres from Gene Autry and at the time he was going to build an apartment house on it. Somebody came and told him that it would be wise to build a hotel. He said, "Oh no. I don't know anything about running a hotel." And the person said, "All you have to do is hire a manager, collect your coupons, go to Europe and live happily ever after." Fillmore came home and told me that and I believed him. And I said. "Let's not pass go or collect $200. Let's just do that." And we didn't. And here we are 27 years later. We started with 150 rooms and we now have 265 and a conference center and it's been a very interesting way of life. And now Ray Courts comes out four or five times a year with his Hollywood Collectibles show. [Ms. Garland's husband is now deceased.]

"It must eat you to live!" **The Spider**

Q: That seems like a perfect match of function and location.

BEVERLY: It is a perfect match because I've done all these horror films. I'm the queen of the screamers, so why not have it at my hotel? I did all these horror films because I could scream better than anybody.

Q: Would you do that kind of film today?

BEVERLY: It probably wouldn't be that kind of film today. Today there would be the sexy girl and the *Penthouse* centerfold. I don't know whether I would. That's not what I want to do. In those days, it was great. But I don't think I'm gonna do that today. I'm not interested.

Q Is there one film you're asked about more than any other?

BEVERLY: **Not Of This Earth** or **It Conquered the World** — what was the one with the carrot? Oh my god! I don't know why anybody likes that film. You know I guess I dislike it because it was so dumb. Half the time we were in that house talking to that terrible machine and then talking among ourselves and then we finally got out of the bloody house and went to the place where the monster was. Geez — the original bore. I guess people either like the carrot or thought the idea was great. I don't know. Those little things that flew around. That was something at least. But that was a picture that everybody talks about. It's never been my favorite movie. But anyway, I guess I'm glad I did it. I've been very blessed that I did all those movies. People remember them and I guess today — the way films are made today, with the amount of visual things done on the computer — these were the very beginning of the special effects but so terribly crude. But that's what gives them their tremendous charm, and people just get such a kick out of seeing the carrot. Today, it's way beyond all that. That's what makes me sort of special, I think.

Q: You are aware that they remade **Not Of This Earth**?

BEVERLY: Bad, bad, bad, bad. I didn't want to see it. So what? Who cares? I heard it was awful. It's ridiculous that they had to remake it. They remade a lot of stuff and I just think it's too bad because it never turns out as well. They're so busy with the sex and ...

"She had to kill the thing her husband had become!" **The Fly**

what a bore! Who cares?! I guess people care out there. I guess that's what they want. I don't know. But that's what they're getting.

Q: Another of the Corman pictures, **Swamp Women**, must have been a difficult shoot.

BEVERLY: **Swamp Women** was — uh — it was fun. Good old Roger Corman with his poor boy sandwiches. And everything you had to do. You worked — oh my God — incredible hours. We stayed in this abandoned hotel. I guess it was abandoned because it was an absolute wreck and of course Roger got it for nothing. And we got in the water with all these icky things in the water. And of course it was supposed to be very sexy because we cut off our Levis. In those days, kiddo, a two-piece bathing suit was oh so risqué. I had a scene in **Not Of This Earth** where I either put on my hose or took off my hose or some damn thing. Oh my god, that was sexy and I had a two-piece bathing suit. When I first did **The Bing Crosby Show**, I did a series with him, and we had these twin beds that were, you know, his was against the wall and mine was parallel. How did they ever get together in this bedroom? So ridiculous. But that's how it was. I never did think that sex was that big of a deal. Apparently, I'm wrong because that's what everybody does today. They can't wait to show you having a conversation while your husband is taking his shoes off and you're sitting on the john. It's stuff that I just don't go for. You don't need it. It's stupidity in my book. Why can't you just wash your hands or take your makeup off? Why do you have to sit on the john? I don't get it. I just come from another era, I guess, and I liked it better then than I do today. I think today they just leave nothing to the imagination. And I

SELECTED FILMS FEATURING BEVERLY GARLAND

Hellfire
1995
Finding the Way Home
1991
The World's Oldest Living Bridesmaid
1990
This Girl for Hire
1983
Gamble on Love
1982
It's My Turn
1980
Roller Boogie
1979
Airport 1975
1974
The Mad Room
1969
Pretty Poison
1968
Twice-Told Tales
1963
Stark Fear
1961
The Alligator People
1959
Chicago Confidential
1957
Naked Paradise
1957
Not of This Earth
1957
Curucu, Beast of the Amazon
1956
Gunslinger
1956
It Conquered the World
1956
The Desperate Hours
1955
New Orleans Uncensored
1955
Swamp Women
1955
The Desperado
1954
The Miami Story
1954
The Rocket Man
1954
The Glass Web
1953
The Neanderthal Man
1953
Problem Girls
1953
D.O.A.
1949

"See strangest of all rites in the temple of love!" Fire Maidens of Outer Space

think children are seeing everything on television and everything on the Internet and they don't read. When you read a book, there's a whole wonderful thing of creating who you are because you have to use your imagination. We don't have that anymore. Children are getting so they don't use their imagination. They don't sit and play outside and build castles and have little cars and go through the roads and be pretend people. They play all these games on television. That's using your imagination? I don't think so.

Q: Do you think you're better remembered for films like **The Alligator People** or for your work in **My Three Sons**?

BEVERLY: I think I'm better remembered for **My Three Sons**. Everybody remembers **My Three Sons**. And then they go, "Oh yes, and you were in **It Conquered the World** and blah, blah, blah, blah, blah." But **My Three Sons** was big and Fred MacMurray was a big, big star. And this television show represents many, many years and I think people remember me for that more than anything I've ever done — which is almost too bad because I really started off on stage and I started as a very serious actress and a dramatic actress and I really am a dramatic actress and a very good dramatic actress. And then I got into this semi-comedy rabble babble, whatever the hell that is. I really don't think that **My Three Sons** was very funny but it was billed as a comic show. It was light, airy and had no substance at all. And there I am. And I got so much into comedy that still, that's what people have me do. And I'm good at comedy, too. But I missed the dramatic acting.

The Corman stuff was really more dramatic. That's really what's funny. I mean its funny today because it's so ridiculous. But at the time, it was very serious! And I also think that **It Conquered the World, Not Of This Earth, The Alligator People** — all that stuff that I did — we were just actors really, really doing our best. None of us overacted. I'm not saying we weren't good. We didn't do it tongue-in-cheek. We really did it. We really meant it. That's why **The Alligator People** stands up so well. Because you believe this girl. You don't laugh at her. You really don't laugh at her. And it could have been played so you go, "Come on!" But you don't do that. And that's why it hangs in there. That's why Gunslinger hangs in there, and **Not Of This Earth** and **It Conquered the World**.

Q: Did you think those films were a ridiculous waste of time when you were making them, or did you always deliver the best performnace possible?

"The creature that undrapes the passions of the living!" Curse of the Living Corpse

BEVERLY: Oh my God! We gave our all. We never thought about it being ridiculous. Never, never, never. We were serious, good actors, and we played it seriously.

Q: What's kept you busy lately?

BEVERLY: Every now and then I play Lois Lane's mother [on TV's **Lois and Clark**]. I just did **Diagnosis Murder** with Mike Connors. Of course I still call him Touch. Everybody asks, 'Who is Touch Connors?' I knew him when he was "Touch" Connors.

Q: Will you be working with Roger again any time soon?

BEVERLY: He keeps claiming he's going to hire me again but if he doesn't hurry up I'll be dead. He's got a studio in Ireland. That's where I want to go. We'll see what happens.

Beverly Garland delivered memorable performances as feisty, independent women in some of Roger Corman's best known movies, but his aren't the only horrors on her resumé. She appeared in a fistful of shockers helmed by directors both obscure and renowned:

The Neanderthal Man (1953)
Professor Robert Shayne's experiments in regression get a little out of hand. His serum causes his savage animal instincts to erupt, resulting in the inflexible rubber mask he (or a stuntman) wears through much of the film. Directed by E.A. DuPont, Beverly has a smallish role as the town barmaid, accosted by shaggy Shayne at a picnic.

Curucu, Beast of the Amazon (1956)
Bev and John Bromfield, fresh from **Revenge of the Creature**, stalk an Amazon plantation in search of the bird-beaked beast. In a most disappointing B film twist, director Curt Siodmak's mossy menace is revealed as nothing more than a costumed native, attempting to frighten away the white colonists.

"See women stalked and captured for breeding with Yeti monsters!" **Man Beast**

The Alligator People (1959)
Under hypnotic inducement, Garland spills this story of hubby Richard **Rocky Jones** Crane's mysterious disappearance. Crane turns up in his bayou boyhood home where, in a bog-based laboratory, Dr. George Macready's experiments with alligator enzymes have resulted in the scaly folk of the title. One of veteran director Roy Del Ruth's last pictures, it features Lon Chaney in a juicy part as a drunken, licentious, hook-handed gator hater.

Stark Fear (1961)
Guileless pros Garland and Ken Tobey troop through this meretricious but interesting thriller. Skip Homeier, who portrays Bev's boozy loser of a husband, assumed the director's chair partway through filming. Made on location in Oklahoma with minimal funding, **Stark Fear** has the look of a film made on location in Oklahoma with minimal funding.

"Every chilling moment a shock-test for your scare-endurance!" The Abominable Snowman of the Himalayas

THE ASTOUNDING B MONSTER

"Here is horror that can happen NOW ... TO YOU!" Creature With the Atom Brain

THE FAN BEHIND THE CAMERA alex GORDON
MEETS THE B MONSTER

He's a producer, screenwriter, publicist and film preservationist. But more importantly, Alex Gordon is a fan. His legendary B-movie productions, his years as cowboy hero Gene Autry's publicist, and his tireless work in film restoration reflect the fact that his love for movies is unabashed.

profile

Growing up in Hampstead, London, Alex was hooked early on. "My brother and I and Bill Everson [the

"Scream at the ghastly fly-monster as he keeps a love tryst!" **The Fly**

noted film historian] used to go to all the matinees and see all the Westerns. I guess that stuck with me." Following service in the second World War, Alex and his brother Richard, later an esteemed B-movie producer in his own right, headed for the States with film careers in mind. "We arrived in New York in 1947," Gordon remembers. "I moved to Hollywood permanently in 1952."

Hoping for a job in publicity, Gordon stumbled up a rocky path on his way to becoming a film producer. "When I first came to Hollywood I had two things with me," he recalls, "A script for **Atomic Monster**, which became **Bride of the Monster**, and an outline for what became **Jail Bait**. I read in *The L.A. Times* that a man named Johnny Carpenter, who had made a few low-budget Westerns, had made his last one, **Son of the Renegade**, for $17,500. I looked up Carpenter, who was one of those people who could charm the fruit off the trees. He said, 'Why don't we make a picture together. It won't cost more than $17,500.' So I contacted my brother Richard, who had Gordon Films in New York and was representing producers and selling pictures for foreign distribution. He arranged the financing. Carpenter then introduced me to Eddie Wood, saying, 'He's my assistant director and he's working on the script with me.' Even though the picture came in in the scheduled 10 days, it went way, way over budget, and ended up costing $67,000 instead of $17,500. I nearly had a heart attack. Where was this money going to come from? The investors foreclosed on the picture and I needed a lawyer. That's how I found Sam Arkoff. He had represented Carpenter before and wanted to get into the movie business. It took Arkoff two years to get that picture out of hock. Eventually everybody got paid back, but it took a long time. That was my baptism of fire."

Often questioned about his association with Ed Wood, Alex is frankly tired of discussing incidents that occurred only in Tim Burton's biopic, not in reality. "I was so disgusted with what I heard about that film, I decided not to see it," he said. "I was too upset about the way they showed Bela Lugosi using such bad language and talking so disparagingly about Boris Karloff — none of which is true. And his relationship with Eddie Wood was completely distorted. The writers admitted that they hadn't contacted anybody to check their facts. They just dreamed it up based on what they'd heard and read. Having said that, my brother Richard thought that Martin Landau was very good in his portrayal of Lugosi, forgetting the bad language and the incidents that were untrue."

Teaming with Sam Arkoff and James Nicholson of American International Pictures,

"Shock by incredible shock this ravaging death overruns the earth!" Cosmic Monsters

Gordon did the lion's share of work on the pictures he produced, assembling casts, handling publicity and even writing ad copy. Many of his genre films — **The She-Creature, Day the World Ended** and **Voodoo Woman** particularly — are relished by film buffs for the veteran casts that could only have been assembled by a true movie fan. "First of all," Alex explained, "I always admired these players and enjoyed seeing them when I was a kid. I was so pleased that they were still around and available to work that I not only enjoyed having them in the pictures, but I could discuss the old days with them, and certain roles they had played. In a way, I was paying them back for all the enjoyment they had given me through the years. That was particularly true of the Western stars, as I was using people like Johnny Mack Brown, Bob Steele, Tim McCoy and Rod Cameron — even supporting players and stuntmen like Dave Sharpe, Tom Steele and Dale Van Sickel — and Edmund Cobb, who was in the very first picture I ever saw — a silent picture called **The Courage of Collins**. And of course he was amazed that I had seen that picture and, in fact, had a copy of it."

> "THE VETERAN ACTORS WERE VERY PROFESSIONAL AND DELIGHTFUL TO WORK WITH. THE YOUNG PEOPLE SOMETIMES FELT LIKE THEY WERE DOING YOU A FAVOR."

While many younger players thought of horror pictures as a blemish on a promising career, Gordon discovered that the seasoned actors who performed in his pictures dismissed the negative connotations. "The veteran actors were, first of all, delighted to be working. People like Chester Morris and Tom Conway and so many others were very professional and delightful to work with. They knew their lines, they never flubbed, they were cooperative, they were always there and eager to work. They were enthusiastic

"She's a doll, she's a dish, she's a delinquent!" **Teenage Bad Girl**

about the pictures. The young people sometimes felt like they were doing you a favor. They were goofing off and you had to call them [to the set] two or three times. But for the most part I was pretty lucky; there were only two people who really gave me problems: One was William Lundigan who turned out to be, unfortunately, an alcoholic. He was completely unreliable. He was never ready, never knew his lines or even where he was. When I used a double in an underwater suit for him while filming **The Underwater City** — you couldn't tell who it was anyway — he called the Screen Actors Guild down on me. The other was Arthur Franz, who was rather neurotic and insisted on things like seeing his rushes [on **The Atomic Submarine**]."

But, by and large, Alex recalls happy associations with the actors he'd enjoyed watching in his youth. "The ones I approached were, for the most part, delighted to appear in the science fiction pictures," he said. "The only ones who balked at appearing in the horror pictures were Peter Lorre and John Carradine. At that point in the game, they'd had enough and they didn't want to do any more of those."

Alex is responsible for an unparalleled list of fondly remembered B films. Produced in the heyday of the exploitation double feature, Gordon's titles stood out amid the motley crowd of threadbare productions being churned out by independent filmmakers. Pictures such as **Dragstrip Girl, Apache Woman, The Atomic Submarine** and **Runaway Daughters** leap to mind, as all bear the Gordon hallmarks: seasoned players blending with up-and-comers, snappy pacing and clear-eyed, no-frills direction.

What titles does Alex himself recall with fondness? Which players left a distinct impression on the young producer? "**Day the World Ended** was fine," he recalls. "Richard Denning was just an absolute delight to work with in all the pictures he did for us. And Mike Connors — at that time Touch Connors — was a good friend of ours and also a pleasure to work with. Raymond Hatton was in it and we also had Adele Jergens, who was a real trooper. Lori Nelson was a little down on the low-budget thing and still had major company ideas. But she was very nice, very attractive and didn't give us any problems at all. And I'm very fond of [director] Roger Corman. I think he's a fine director, fine producer. Particularly good at production and exploitation. It's not like he's Steven Spielberg when it comes to being a director, but for his purposes he's very, very good. He knows what he wants and he brings it in on sensible budgets. I have the highest admiration for Roger."

"A creature to freeze your blood! A story to chill your soul!" **I Bury the Living**

The stunningly prolific Edward L. Cahn helmed Gordon's jungle horror opus **Voodoo Woman**. "It was so fast — six days," Alex remembers. "While I had some good people in it, we didn't really have a chance to do much with it because we only had two weeks preparation. We really had to go like hell. We couldn't afford to shoot second takes. It was kind of a condensed picture. But the players I enjoyed."

> "I TRIED TO GET JOHN CARRADINE WHO WAS IN A HIGH AND MIGHTY MOOD. HE'D JUST DONE 'THE TEN COMMANDMENTS' FOR CECIL B. DEMILLE. HE WASN'T GOING TO DO ANY NINE-DAY PICTURE."

Gordon considered character actor George Zucco, who was then in declining health, for the lead role as a demented doctor. "I went to Zucco's agent who told me that, unfortunately, he couldn't remember lines and couldn't work anymore, but that if I would agree to at least talk to him about it — offer him the part — that would give him a real boost. I met with him and chatted for about an hour about all his old pictures. He told me that he greatly appreciated still being wanted, but he wanted prestige roles at that point in his career. He didn't realize that he would never work again."

It was the national interest in hypnotism, centering on the famous Bridey Murphy case, that sparked a production that Gordon cites as among his favorites. "I liked **The She-Creature**," he said, "mainly because I was able to use so many old-timers in that. I had Chester Morris, Tom Conway, Ron Randell and Frank Jenks. And playing small parts or working as extras I had people like Stuart Holmes, Frieda Inescort, El Brendel,

---

"1400 pounds of frozen fury that moves like a man!" Half Human

Jack Mulhall and Luana Walters. I had a lot of fun on that."

Though Gordon remembers the picture fondly, he recalls its genesis as being anything but smooth. "Originally, I had wanted Peter Lorre and Edward Arnold, who'd appeared together in Josef von Sternberg's **Crime and Punishment** in 1935. Eddie Cahn, our director, had directed Edward Arnold in several pictures. So he called Edward Arnold, who said, 'Sure, I'll do it, even though it's a fast picture, I'm not doing anything.' Two days before the picture started, he died. We were in shock. He was such a nice guy and Eddie had looked forward to working with him again. Peter Lorre read the script and thought it was junk and absolutely refused to do it. But his agency had committed him to us for a week's work. We actually had a contract but he created such a big deal that he fired his agency and went to another agent. I think Peter Lorre is a very fine actor who'd had to do a lot of things that weren't worthy of his talent and I didn't altogether blame him if he didn't want to do a picture like that. So I tried to get John Carradine who was in a high and mighty mood, too. He'd just done **The Ten Commandments** for Cecil B. DeMille. He wasn't going to do any nine-day picture. He got so worked up about it that he got drunk at Lucy's restaurant and actually wrecked the place. I said to his agent, 'My God! Let him off the hook!'"

In the end, the part of Lombardi the hypnotist went to Chester Morris, who, according to Alex, loved the role. "He liked the idea of playing a hypnotist. He was a professional magician and belonged to all the big magicians' organizations and gave performances at the Magic Castle."

In the lead role of the lovely hypnotic subject, regressed to a monstrous prehistoric state, Gordon cast a promising young actress who came to be thought of as "American International's Elizabeth Taylor." As Alex recalled, "Marla English was a very nice actress. When her agent came to us, we made a multi-picture deal with her and she was very easy to work with. She was very good and always knew her lines. She didn't mind doing low-budget pictures. She actually wanted to do Westerns.

"She introduced me to Elvis Presley," Gordon says. "During our first picture together, we went to lunch at a little restaurant near the studio. She put some money in the jukebox and this awful voice came out singing 'Nothing But a Hound Dog.' I couldn't understand a single word the guy was singing. I said, 'Who is that? That's terrible!'" She said, 'Don't

"Super-sensational preview of tomorrow's space thrills!" **The Lost Planet**

you know Elvis?' Later, when I was at Allied Artists shooting **The Atomic Submarine**, he was shooting on another set. When they finished the picture, they threw a little party on his set and he invited us, as we were sort of neighbors. He was so nice and so polite, just a wonderful person. Later, when we were at Paramount shooting **The Bounty Killer**, he was there shooting a picture for Hal Wallis. On the day we had Bronco Billy Anderson as a guest star, Elvis got so excited that he came down from his set to have his picture taken with Bronco Billy."

Sadly, the promising career of Marla English was short-lived. "She was never all that keen on having a movie career," Gordon said. "She saw beyond that. It wasn't life or death to her. It was her mother who really pushed her very hard into a movie career. She didn't mind at all when she retired. Arkoff and Nicholson told me to sign her for another six pictures. I met with her and her agent but she said she didn't want to do that." Gordon eventually lost touch with the actress, remembering that "for a long time she was a recluse. She refused to give any interviews, she refused to see anyone who wanted to talk about her screen career. For a long time I tried to find out where she was but we could never locate her. I heard several years after the fact that she'd died. There was never any obituary in the newspapers or the trade papers."

Having handily navigated every pitfall of the picture business, with a list of the best-loved programmers in cult-movie history to his credit, Alex nonetheless recognized rising production costs and the encroachment of television on the drive-in market as the writing on the wall. "I had been with Arkoff and Nicholson at AIP, then Allied Artists and Columbia and Embassy. Then 20th Century-Fox for 10 years and film restoration work. Finally, I just couldn't raise anymore money. It was the same thing with my brother. It became too difficult to raise money independently for these smaller pictures with television [taking our audience] and costs going up and up and up. It just became too

FILMS PRODUCED BY ALEX GORDON

The Bounty Killer
1965
Requiem for a Gunfighter
1965
The Underwater City
1962
The Atomic Submarine
1959
Jet Attack
1958
Submarine Seahawk
1958
Flesh and the Spur
1957
Motorcycle Gang
1957
Dragstrip Girl
1957
Voodoo Woman
1957
Girls in Prison
1956
Runaway Daughters
1956
Shake, Rattle and Rock
1956
The She-Creature
1956
Oklahoma Woman
1956
Day the World Ended
1956
Apache Woman
1955
The Lawless Rider
1954

"It kills ... but cannot be killed!" X ... The Unknown

difficult to finance these things. So after I left Fox, Gene Autry offered me this full-time job and, of course, I jumped at it."

The death of Gene Autry was a sad milestone in Hollywood history. The legendary cowboy, Alex's idol and friend, had only recently passed away when Alex and I had our first conversation. Alex himself, possessed of boundless energy, an entertaining anecdote about the old days always at the ready, continued until his own passing in June 2003, to work in the Autry offices, promoting and preserving the movies he loved.

"Attacked by a creature from hell!" Day the World Ended

BIG AS LIFE AND TWICE AS UGLY Leo GORDON MEETS THE B MONSTER

The above phrase is Leo Gordon's self-descriptive way of introducing himself. Midway through a lengthy interview he sneers, "What are you gonna do with this stuff?" He seems surprised that anyone would be interested in the career of one of the screen's most recognizable and

intimidating tough guys. When informed that there are many devoted fans who want to know what Leo

"A spine-tingling motion picture only the atom age could produce!" Atom Age Vampire

Gordon is up to these days, he quips, "No good, as usual." For years, Leo was one of the most believably imposing bad guys on the Hollywood scene, inciting a big house rebellion in **Riot in Cell Block 11** or engendering the wrath of John Wayne in films like **Hondo** and **McLintock!** Few Hollywood heavies have credits that match Gordon's gallery of toughs, a string of solid performances too numerous for the actor himself to recall. "Somebody sent me a list of credits, and there are things on there I have not the faintest remembrance of. It's ridiculous, really."

Leo Gordon is also an accomplished writer with dozens of screenplays to his credit — from modest Westerns such as **Black Patch**, to big-budget adventure films like **Tobruk**. The series of low-budget shockers and teen films he scripted in the 1950s for producer/director Roger Corman are fondly remembered by genre-film fans; **Attack of the Giant Leeches, The Wasp Woman** and **The Cry Baby Killer** were devised with genuine ingenuity and retain an unspecifiable charm some 40 years later.

Leo is a nice man with a sense of humor drier than the Mojave. But he can be evasive — even shy — particularly when it comes to discussing his collaborations with Corman. His answers were always short and not necessarily sweet. The gruff exterior was not a pretense. And underneath there was a gruff INTERIOR. Honestly, if he'd pretended to be anything else I would have been sorely disappointed.

B MONSTER: How did you get into show business?

LEO GORDON: Like most people, just by circumstance; I stumbled into it. I was in New York after the war with a friend of mine, standing in front of Carnegie Hall one day watching all the girls with their pony tails bounce in. I said, "How's your G.I. Bill?" — "I haven't used it yet" — "Neither have I" — "Well, let's find out what the hell's goin' on here." We went in and signed up for dramatic school on the G.I. Bill. The government had what they call a 52-20 Program. They paid you 20 bucks a week to go to school for 52 weeks.

Q: You'd never considered acting before that?

LEO: No.

"Yesterday, a teenage rebel ... today, a mad-dog slayer!" **The Cry Baby Killer**

Q: Not long afterwards you appeared in the London company of **Mister Roberts**. Who was in that?

LEO: Jackie Cooper played Ensign Pulver. Russell Collins played Doc and Ty Power played Mister Roberts.

Q: That's a heck of a cast.

LEO: Yeah. All amateurs. I came back and toured with the road company for another eight months. Then I went back to New York where I ran into Jack Palance. I said, "What the hell you doin'?" He said, "I'm in this play with Claude Rains and I'm gonna kill the little son of a bitch." He said, "I got a call from the Coast. They want me to do a picture with Joan Crawford but I can't go." Sidney Kingsley had him tied up in a run-of-the-play contract for **Darkness at Noon**. He said, "I got an idea. Why don't you go up and see Kingsley? You'd make a hell of a replacement for me." I went up and read for Kingsley's sister. She took me over to the theater. I met Eddie Robinson and Kingsley. They had me read and signed me.

Q: How did that lead to your first film appearance in **City of Bad Men**?

LEO: I got a call from Hollywood. They asked me could I ride a horse. I said, "Yes. If I can't ride it, I'll carry it." So I came out to Hollywood. They put me on a horse and I was on a horse for 35 years.

Q: Soon after, you were working with John Wayne in **Hondo** and later **The Conqueror** and **McLintock!** How was that experience?

SELECTED FILMS FEATURING LEO GORDON

Maverick
1994
Mob Boss
1990
Big Top Pee-wee
1988
Rage
1980
You Can't Win 'Em All
1970
The St. Valentine's Day Massacre
1967
Tobruk
1967
Beau Geste
1966
The Night of the Grizzly
1966
Kitten with a Whip
1964
The Haunted Palace
1963
McLintock!
1963
The Terror
1963
Tarzan Goes to India
1962
The Intruder
1961
The Cry Baby Killer
1958
Escort West
1958
Quantrill's Raiders
1958
Ride a Crooked Trail
1958
Black Patch
1957
The Conqueror
1956
Johnny Concho
1956
Soldier of Fortune
1955
Ten Wanted Men
1955
Riot in Cell Block 11
1954
Sign of the Pagan
1954
Gun Fury
1953
Hondo
1953
City of Bad Men
1953

"Takes you to the bowels of the earth for thrills and chills!" The Devil's Messenger

> "I GOT A CALL FROM HOLLYWOOD. THEY ASKED ME COULD I RIDE A HORSE. I SAID, 'YES. AND IF I CAN'T RIDE IT, I'LL CARRY IT.'"

LEO: Well, it was novel. I'd been out of circulation with the military and the CCC. I really didn't know that Wayne was as important an individual as he was. I never went to see Westerns, I was a New Yorker. Actually I was impressed with him. There's no question about that. He was unique.

Q: Was he friendly?

LEO: Not overly friendly, I wouldn't say. He was cordial. He was interested in getting performances out of people. He wasn't the buddy-buddy type but I liked him.

Q: Is it more fun to play bad guys?

LEO: Oh, much better. You get more recognition, I think, as a bad guy than a lot of these guys who've played heroes on long-running television shows.

Q: Is that how you want to be remembered?

LEO: Absolutely. I was walking down the street in Morocco when a little kid steps out of the alley and looks at me. He runs a few feet ahead of me — turns around and looks again — he puts his hands down like he's drawing two pistols. He goes "bip bip bip!" Y'know? Like he's shooting. You figure, here you are, a world away from anything you're familiar with, and some little kid in an alley in Morocco recognizes you? Once, coming down the street in Madrid with my wife [ed. Gordon and actress Lynn Cartwright have been married since 1950], a car slides up and these guys jump out. They were a couple of photographers from the Spanish press. They spent the whole afternoon with us.

And I got the Golden Boot Award just recently. It was quite a to-do at the Century Plaza

Hotel. 1,200 people at 175 bucks a pop. Anybody you can name of any stature in the Western field has that award. From Wayne to Clint Walker to Bob Urich. But I have a good foundation and Western background. I was born in the same hometown as Billy the Kid ... Brooklyn.

Q: Do you have a favorite among the Westerns you've appeared in?

LEO: **Night of the Grizzly** with Clint Walker and Jack Elam. It just had a quality to it. It was something that Disney might have done. Basically a clean story with no rotten nastiness about it.

Q: You've worked with an amazing variety of performers. Any that you remember especially fondly?

LEO: I liked Jim Garner. I thought he was an honest guy. The brief encounter I did have with Mel Gibson on **Maverick** — he seems to be cut from the same cloth as Garner. A nice, warm, regular guy. Clint Walker's another one. He's about as clean-cut and homespun as you can get in every good sense of the word. I've been pretty lucky. Most of the people I've worked with have been pretty good. I was never impressed by star status when I started out. To me, they were just feeding me the lines. Now, it's a funny thing. You're sitting down at a table looking across at another actor [in this case Mel Gibson] knowing you're getting $1,000 a day and he's getting $15 million for six weeks. I don't know about you, but I can't conceive of getting that kind of money. I've been working for close to 50 f——g years and haven't made a third of what this guy is making on one picture.

Q: Tell me how you hooked up with Roger Corman.

LEO: I sold a script to George Montgomery. Gene Corman, Roger's brother, was representing him. The script was a Western called **Black Patch**. Montgomery wanted the script and Gene Corman negotiated the deal. That's how I came in contact with Gene. I wrote three scripts for him and then two for Roger. One day I got a call from Roger. He asked me if I had anything with a castle in it. I said no. He said, "That's too bad. I've got this set over at Producers Studio — an interior of a medieval castle. I have it for a week and I've got Boris Karloff for a week but I have nothing to shoot." So, over the weekend,

"It might snap your mind!" **The Monster and the Stripper**

> "Corman has a book out, 'How I Made 100 Pictures in Hollywood and Never Lost a Dime.' I know why he never lost a dime. He never spent a dime."

I wrote [**The Terror**], 50-some pages of interiors in screenplay form. He was shooting it the following week. Corman has a book out, **How I Made 100 Pictures in Hollywood and Never Lost a Dime**. I know why he never lost a dime. He never spent a dime. I wouldn't say Roger is cheap. Let's just say he's frugal. But he put a lot of people in business.

Q: On the six pictures you made with Corman, were you called upon to do more than just scripting?

LEO: For Nicholson's first picture, **The Cry Baby Killer**, we were shooting at this drive-in trying to get a crowd reaction shot. There were all these kids who were involved. Roger says, "Leo, can you get in there? We need some bodies to fill in." So I get in. He said "Can you say something — a line as the camera pans?" So out of left field I come up with, "Teenagers. Lucky we didn't have 'em when I was a kid." What an inane f———g line."

Q: Do you have a preference — script writing or acting?

LEO: Oh, acting is much easier.

Q: Which is more rewarding?

LEO: The writing, I guess. But I was up for one recently — a picture called **The Edge** with Anthony Hopkins. They called me over for that — and they called me back on it. At that time I was seeing a doctor for a swelling I had under the sternum. It was an aneurism. They cut the damn thing out of me and I couldn't take the part. It was a great goddamn part — the best thing I've had in 30 years. That hurts, y'know? It's nice to go out with a good one.

Q: You wrote 21 episodes of **Adam-12**. How did you become involved with the show?

LEO: They hired me as an actor on one episode and I went to [producer] Herman Saunders later and said, "I've go an idea for one of these." He said, "Don't tell me. Rough it out and then give it to me." I did three. Herman went though them and said, "Okay, go to work." I said, "On which one?" He said, "The three of them." So I got three assignments in one afternoon. I wrote one called **The Buff**. This guy wanted to be a cop in the worst way. He was fairly wealthy. He was always coming up and bugging Malloy and Reed about police procedure and he'd go to police seminars. I wrote the story, wrote the teleplay. I played **The Buff**. My wife played a shoplifter. They used my car and my car radio. They used my gun. They also used my house. Everything except the dog. That was called Leo Gordon festival week.

Q: You didn't write a part for the dog?

LEO: No, I left him out. He really pouted for a month.

Q: How did your approach to scripting **Adam-12** differ from your movie work. In a case like **Giant Leeches** or **Wasp Woman** — did you just pitch the idea, or did somebody ask for a script about a giant wasp?

FILMS WRITTEN BY LEO GORDON

You Can't Win 'Em All
1970
All the Loving Couples
1969
Adam-12 (TV series)
1968
Tobruk
1967
The Bounty Killer
1965
The Terror
1963
Tower of London
1962
The Cat Burglar
1961
Valley of the Redwoods
1960)
The Wasp Woman
1960
Attack of the Giant Leeches
1959
Bonanza (TV series)
1959
Escort West
1958
The Cry Baby Killer
1958
Hot Car Girl
1958
Maverick (TV series)
1957
Colt .45 (TV series)
1957
Black Patch
1957
Cheyenne (TV series)
1955

"Their arms could kill ... or caress!" **Prehistoric Women**

LEO: They'd come up to me and ask, "You got anything?" And if I didn't have something, I'd go whip something up. You know that **Attack of the Giant Leeches** had some tender moments. Like when [Bruno VeSota] is talking about his wife. That was NOT shabby dialogue.

Q: What can you tell me about some of the actors who worked on those Corman pictures?

LEO: Bruno was a nice guy. Is Bruno still alive? That's the thing that bothers me now and then. I see a film that I've done, and everybody that was in it is gone. **Tobruk** is an example.

Q: What do you remember about the making of **Tobruk**?

LEO: We were shooting in Almira, Spain. Some other film company had had difficulty with the Spaniards who confiscated all their negatives. Universal got a little hinky about that and decided we should shoot down near Tucson out in the dunes. It was good. It was a stature picture. Arthur Hiller directed.

Q: Is that a favorite among your films?

LEO: Actually, there was one I liked better than that — though the director, Peter Collinson kind of screwed it up. **You Can't Win 'Em All** with Charlie Bronson and Tony Curtis.

Q: **You Can't Win 'Em All** reminded me of a picture called **Vera Cruz**.

LEO: Yeah. Strange, isn't it?

Q: So, that was intentional?

LEO: Well, no. It's just that, basically, that damn plotline involving somebody transporting something of value works whether it's an armored car or a chariot. The basic premise always works.

Q: Are you still writing?

LEO: No. I've given that up quite recently. To add insult to injury, I lost the sight in my left eye and the right one isn't too good. So I can't see what the hell I'm typing.

Q: Would you rather be remembered for your Western roles than for writing the Corman pictures?

LEO: Yeah, 'cause nobody believes I'm a writer anyway. I look like a heavy. I'm 6-2, 200 pounds. Got a craggy-ass face. And I should be 5 feet 8, 142 pounds, and wear leather patches on my elbows and jackets and horn-rimmed glasses and smoke a pipe. That's a writer.

Q: What lies ahead for Leo Gordon?

LEO: Well, I've been trying to convince myself that I feel good and I'm going to tell my agent to get his ass in gear and get me some interviews.

Leo Gordon answered my questions with the minimum of exposition, snarling his responses, grousing and growling, just like the Leo I saw on the big screen. A few days after we spoke, the "meanest man in the movies" sent me a "thank you" note. Leo Gordon passed away in December 2000.

*Though Leo Gordon's screenwriting talents were employed in films of all genres, as well as such TV series as **Bonanza, Cheyenne** and **Adam-12**, he is best-remembered today for a handful of drive-in classics made under the auspices of producer Roger Corman:*

ATTACK OF THE GIANT LEECHES (1959)

Leo wrote some genuinely poignant dialogue for this cheap, effective shocker. The leeches — extras wrapped in what appear to be Hefty bags — are more distracting than frightening. The main attractions are the film's sultry bayou setting and the interplay of sad, sweaty Bruno VeSota and his tantalizing tart of a wife Yvette Vickers.

"The fire-spitting monster predicted in the Bible!" The Giant Behemoth

The Wasp Woman (1959)

A honey-based youth serum makes a werewasp of Susan Cabot, who is quite convincing in spite of the ridiculous wasp head her role requires. One of the most enjoyable Roger Corman quickies with one of the great exploitation titles of all time. Unfortunately, the title conjures a mental image no film depiction could live up to.

The Terror (1963)

An atmospheric (considering the very modest budget) but strangely muted film. Karloff's performance and Gordon's literate script are just fine but the film is curiously ambiguous and therefore unengaging. A young Jack Nicholson's hesitant method acting is a distraction, and he's clearly uncomfortable in Napoleonic costume.

The Cry Baby Killer (1958)

Nicholson, in his first screen appearance, plays the Cry Baby. In many regards, Leo's story was ahead of its time, as Nicholson's character is bullied by local toughs into seeking revenge, a phenomenon that's garnered much press attention in recent years. Leo's better half, Lynn Cartwright (who you may recognize as the older Geena Davis in **A League of Their Own**), appears as a carhop.

"The management of this theater disclaims any responsibility for heart attacks or damage to nerves!" The Blob

GIVING BIRTH TO SPIDER BABY
jack HILL
MEETS THE B MONSTER

Jack Hill's uncompleted UCLA student film had languished on a shelf in his garage since 1961. Now, through the auspices of one of Hollywood's brashest young turks, Quentin Tarantino, the finishing touches are being applied after nearly 40 years. Tarantino, a

profile

longtime Jack Hill fan, recognized the short film's historical significance — Jack and classmate Francis Coppola had worked on

"A walking corpse lusts for revenge!" *Scream of the Demon Lover*

each other's school projects and a portion of Hill's film served as the inspiration for **Apocalypse Now**. Tarantino, overseeing the release of Hill's cult film **Switchblade Sisters** on laser disc, insisted it be included.

The re-release is the latest example of Hill's growing reputation in the eyes of young cult film aficionados. "All of a sudden I discovered that I was this legendary cult movie director," laughs Hill. "People have been inviting me to film festivals and all that kind of stuff — so let's see what happens." Certainly, Tarantino has the highest profile of all of Hill's boosters. "They were having a retrospective of AIP films at a theater that does that kind of thing in Santa Monica," Hill recalls. "I was going to come down and introduce **Coffy**. He came up to me in the lobby. When I was introduced to him, he had posters and soundtrack albums from **Coffy, Foxy Brown** and other movies. He was quoting lines of dialogue from the picture. I was quite impressed because the particular lines of dialogue he quoted were ones I'd given a lot of very careful thought to. An ordinary person wouldn't even notice them as being important. We've been friends ever since. How could you not like a guy like that?"

Jack Hill comes by his enthusiasm for film honestly and impressively. "My father was a set designer starting in 1925 at First National Studios and he stayed with them after they became Warner Bros. He ended up at Disney where he did all the interiors for Captain Nemo's submarine for **20,000 Leagues Under the Sea**. For Disneyland, he designed the Disneyland Castle and Tom Sawyer's Island." Young Hill's early exposure to such movie magic was significant, and he began lensing his own 8mm movies as a kid.

Remarkably, Hill didn't set out to become a film director. "Basically I was a musician," he says. "My mother was a music teacher. I decided to go back to UCLA to get my degree in music. I wanted to score films. I also took a writing course and they encouraged me to do more and I ended up directing a student film." The very same film that was recently completed through Tarantino's intervention. "I worked as a cameraman, a sound recordist, a writer and an editor before I got my first chance to do a little directing with Roger Corman."

Through Corman, Jack developed an aptitude for producing low-budget exploitation films at a rapid pace. One of the most fondly remembered is a 1960s kar kulture curio

"Caged, boy-hungry wildcats gone mad!" Reform School Girl

called **Pit Stop**. Set in and around the tracks and wrecking yards of southern California, it proved to be one of veteran Brian Donlevy's last film appearances. "Here's one of the tricks I learned from Roger Corman," Hill reveals. "You hire an actor and get a low price because he only works three days. Then you write the script in such a way that he appears throughout the whole movie."

> "AIP WAS NOT A FUN PLACE TO WORK, LET ME TELL YOU. THE PEOPLE THERE HAD NOTHING BUT CONTEMPT FOR THE AUDIENCE THEY WERE MAKING THE BLACK PICTURES FOR."

Switchblade Sisters, recognized in certain elite circles as a lesbian cult classic, was released originally as **The Jezebels**. "Theater owners thought the title was no good," Hill laughs, "because people thought it was a Bette Davis movie." (Hill points out with a chuckle that the film's writer, Fran Mayer, now edits Catholic periodicals for the Archbishop of Denmark). Surprisingly, despite its very exploitable premise, it was the only film of Hill's to lose money.

Hill's greatest successes, financially at least, were **Coffy** and **Foxy Brown**, his pioneering blaxploitation films starring Pam Grier. But the circumstances surrounding production were far from satisfying. "AIP was not a fun place to work, let me tell you," Hill says. "The people there had nothing but contempt for the audience they were making the black pictures for. They didn't understand the black audience. They thought the picture should look bad and rough and just full of violence from wall-to-wall. But [producer] Larry Gordon was very nice to work with and fortunately I worked one-on-one with him — I didn't have to deal with these other people very much."

"Slave girls sacrificed at the whim of a ruthless king!" Goliath, King of the Slaves

Disillusioned by the film industry, Hill and his wife turned to spiritualism, in particular, meditation master Swami Muktananda. "I had lost interest in trying to do films any more," he recalls. Once more, Roger Corman entered the picture. "He said he wanted to make a sword and sorcery movie. He said he was going to spend the money and make the picture look really, really big. That's what I felt at that time I needed to do — have a picture that looked really big and expensive after being famous for making pictures on such small money."

But the video boom of the early '80s exacted a financial toll on Corman's production company, and the producer began cutting costs unsparingly. "Instead of spending the money on the effects as he promised to do, he did it real cheap — flopped in music from an old movie, dubbed in voices using secretaries from the office — sound effects were missing — he took over the picture and I took my name off of it. I was really heartbroken by what happened." But, Hill adds with a grin, "in spite of it all, the picture went out and made money."

The film for which director Jack Hill is arguably best known is *inarguably* a cult classic, one whose success Hill attributes to serendipity, as much as anything. "I worked as a cameraman, a sound recordist, a writer and an editor before I got my first chance to do a little directing with Roger Corman," says Hill, summarizing his career matter-of-factly. "Then I just fell into this thing that turned out to be **Spider Baby**."

Though not nearly the financial success his blaxploitation features were, it is **Spider Baby**, the unique story of a murderous band of siblings who regress mentally as they age physically, which endures as a cult film benchmark. "I suppose **Coffy** is one of my best-known films. **Coffy** was a huge success — the No. 11 grosser of the year. **Spider Baby**, a much smaller film, had a much more limited release. But it's kind of a growing cult phenomena."

One of the film's obvious assets is its quirky casting, which Hill attributes to "one of those miracles of good luck. Of course, Lon Chaney was an obvious choice. And the name Carol Ohmart came up as being somebody who had a little bit of a name and was the kind of person who would be interested in doing it. The others were just people that somebody I knew happened to know." Gangling, wild-eyed and entirely convincing is Sid Haig as the psycho at the film's center. Haig was recommended by no less than

"A beautiful temptress from the sea — intent upon loving, consuming and killing!" **Night Tide**

pioneering female director Dorothy Arzner, who'd known Haig through his work at the Pasadena Playhouse.

Comic actor Mantan Moreland was nearing the end of a long show business career when **Spider Baby** came along. "Mantan was kind of sad," Hill recalls. "He was having a hard time because the civil rights movement had virtually destroyed his career. He played the kind of humor that he felt — and the black audience felt — was not demeaning. But he was lumped together with the Stepin Fetchits and those kind of people. When you're typecast and they eliminate the type, you're out of luck."

> "CHANEY JUST LOVED THE SCRIPT SO MUCH, HE WANTED SO BADLY TO DO A GOOD JOB THAT HE WAS ON THE WAGON DURING THE 12 DAYS OF THE SHOOT."

Chaney was in the twilight of an erratic, troubled career, but Hill enthusiastically asserts that he was "wonderful" to work with. "He was an alcoholic at that time," Hill remembers. "That was close to the last movie he did and he could hardly stand up. But he just loved the script so much, he wanted so badly to do a good job that he was on the wagon during the 12 days of the shoot."

The circuitous path that led to the production of **Spider Baby** began with Hill's previous film, coincidentally his directorial debut. "The first feature type film that I did any directing on was a film known as **Blood Bath** and later as **Track of the Vampire**. That's when the people who eventually financed **Spider Baby** came across me. An actor I had used in **Blood Bath**, who had worked in Francis Coppola's nudie, **Tonight For Sure** — he was working at that time as a private detective. He was working for these two guys who were in the real estate development business. In the course of conversation they mentioned that they were very interested in producing movies and they wanted to

---

"It'll scare the laughs out of you!" What A Carve Up!

start off with a low-budget horror movie — which was a good way to start off in those days. They had been reading a lot of scripts and hadn't found anything they liked. I had just written this story — which later became **Spider Baby** — the kind of thing that comes to you in a flash for no particular reason at all. They liked the story so much (it was so different from anything they had seen), they commissioned me to write the script, direct and edit the picture."

Much in the way that he admired Lon Chaney's personal tenacity, so did Hill respect the determination of Boris Karloff. Hill recalls with some chagrin the circumstances that led to their brief collaboration. "I was under contract to Universal, which became a kind of Kafkaesque situation," he laughs. "I knew my option period was up. I came to work one day and somebody else's name was on the door. Somebody else was lying on my couch." Hill took the hint; he was forced to seek gainful filmic employment elsewhere. "There was an attorney that I knew who was the attorney for all the Mexican film companies," he recalls. "He told me that a Mexican producer had engaged Boris Karloff to do four pictures, back-to-back — which was a totally insane idea. Roger Corman used to do two movies back-to-back and that was a struggle."

FILMS DIRECTED BY JACK HILL

Sorceress
1983
Switchblade Sisters
1975
Foxy Brown
1974
The Swinging Cheerleaders
1974
Coffy
1973
The Big Bird Cage
1972
The Big Doll House
1971
Ich, ein Groupie
1970
Pit Stop
1969
The Fear Chamber
1968
House of Evil
1968
The Incredible Invasion
1968
Isle of the Snake People
1968
Blood Bath
1966
Portrait in Terror
1965
Spider Baby
1964
The Terror
1963

In order to secure the assignment, Hill had to develop four scripts virtually overnight. His ideas were approved but, almost immediately, seemingly insurmountable caveats began to appear. "Boris Karloff's doctors would not let him go to Mexico. He had emphysema and was dying," Hill says bluntly. "I had to write the scripts in such a way that all his scenes could be shot in Hollywood, with the minimum of actors brought from Mexico, with sets that wouldn't have to be duplicated in Mexico. We'd shoot all his scenes in Hollywood and finish the rest of the picture in Mexico. It was a disaster right from the beginning."

The frantic shooting schedule was the least of Hill's worries. "The actors who came to

"How much shock can the human brain endure before it cracks?" Crypt of Horror

the set were not the ones I'd cast [in Mexico]. They were never on time. The producer's wife wanted to go to Disneyland — so he was off at Disneyland when he should have been on the set where he had to make decisions. The production ended up costing him a lot more money. I was supposed to go to Mexico to finish the picture but he just took off — disappeared and I never heard anymore about it. Eventually, he had a heart attack and died trying to scrape up the rest of the financing. I didn't find out until many years later that the pictures had in fact been finished. I finally saw one on tape and it just broke my heart to see what they'd done to it in Mexico."

But the experience didn't diminish Hill's affection for Karloff. "He was a great guy. I loved working with him but I never got to know him very well. Basically, he flew in from London to shoot the pictures and then went back to tend his roses. He said he liked working, even though he was in a wheelchair breathing oxygen. 'I want to go out in a harness,' he said. 'As long as somebody's willing to pay me to work, I'll do it.'"

His collaborations with the likes of Karloff, Chaney and Corman have served to pigeonhole Hill, perhaps unfairly, as a cult-horror filmmaker, even though his output spans diverse genres, and several of his non-horror pictures have turned enormous profits. Like **Spider Baby**, he defies easy categorization, so, like the film, he's simply labeled "cult." At one point in his career, he was so dismayed that he found temporary solace in philosophical writing. "I turned my attention to a series of very ambitious literary novels — which I recently put on the shelf because of all the interest in me doing pictures again." Excited once more about a proposed film venture, Hill seems quite prepared to capitalize on his "rediscovery." "I've got a project that looks like it's coming together. Something I've always wanted to do. It's a sophisticated, kind of winsome comedy." Once again, Quentin Tarantino figures in the mix, helping Hill pull the project together, serving as both admirer and mentor. Hill acknowledges his good fortune in having collaborators who happen to be devoted fans. But, after all, how could they not like a guy like Jack Hill?

"The film that defies every taboo!" I Spit On Your Grave

"A monstrous, terrifying story of black madness!" *The Terror of Dr. Hichcock*

SCI-FI FAIRY TALE jimmy HUNT MEETS THE B MONSTER

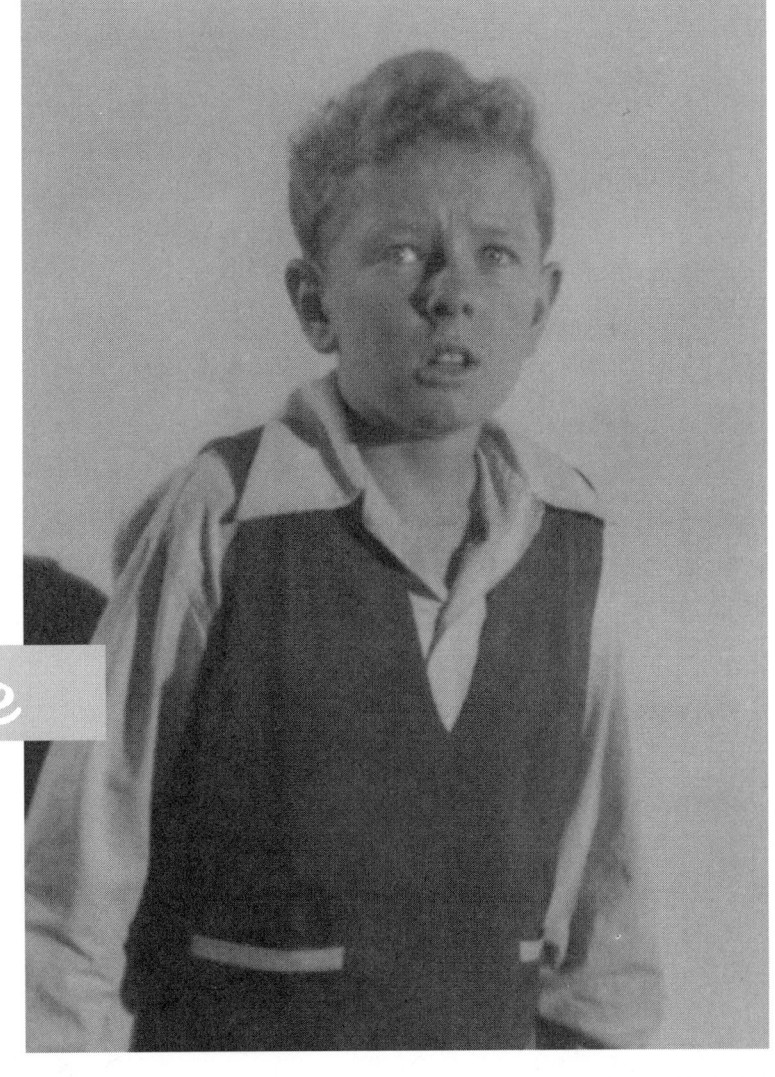

Throughout the late '40s and early '50s, when casting directors put out the call for a cute, precocious kid, slightly irascible, always endearing, very often Jimmy Hunt was among the first to be considered. "I guess I have the distinction of having the most movie parents of any child

profile

star," Hunt laughs. Scarcely a baby boomer escaped the spell of the storybook sci-fi classic **Invaders From Mars**, in which Hunt starred

"No girl was safe as long as this head-hunting thing roamed the land!" *Night of the Blood Beast*

137

as a pint-sized Martian fighter.

You might be surprised to learn that the little freckled fellow who helped stymie that Martian invasion is now a youthful-looking great-grandfather. 50 years after its filming, Jimmy Hunt is gratified by the influence **Invaders From Mars** has had. He's often approached to attend sci-fi conventions. He's been told by astronomers that the film was a decisive factor in their choice of career. A sales representative for an industrial tool supply house with a quiet home in California's Simi Valley, he recalls the making of a film that has yet to loosen its nostalgic hold on 30- and 40-somethings.

B MONSTER: Are you surprised that you're remembered for **Invaders From Mars** after all these years?

JIMMY HUNT: I always thought that [films] like **Lone Hand** and **Cheaper By the Dozen** and all those movies were much better than **Invaders From Mars**. Of course those movies, they come and go, but **Invaders From Mars** goes on and on and on.

Q: Do you have a particular favorite among the actors you've worked with?

JIMMY: Joel McCrea because of the fact that it was a Western movie [**Lone Hand**]. He had his own horse to ride. And all the wranglers that would handle the animals, all these guys would chew tobacco. And I thought, "Wow these are cool guys." He'd bring me little squares of licorice. They'd look just like a chaw of tobacco. I don't know where he got this stuff. I'd chew that and spit it. It was black. I felt like one of the guys. He was really the nicest man you could ever meet. I spoke to him about a year before he died. He was just a great guy. He was my favorite because of the fact that he just treated me like his son. He invited me out to his ranch. I live about 10 miles from where his ranch was.

Q: Any that weren't particular favorites?

JIMMY: Bob Hope and Bing Crosby. I can't say they weren't nice. They were just Bob Hope and Bing Crosby. They were up there, you know. They didn't relate too much to kids.

Q: According to your **Invaders From Mars** co-star, Janine Perreau, Van Heflin threatened her at knife point for scene stealing on the set of **Weekend With Father**.

JIMMY: It could have happened, who knows. The man broke my arm in that movie. Not for scene stealing. We were in a scene where we were in a sack race. The adult was in the front, the child was in the back and we hopped. Instead of hopping out of the sack like we should have, we tried to hop backwards and we lost our balance. He fell down on top of me and I put my arm out to try to break the fall and broke my arm. So if you watch the movie you'll see I always hold my left arm close to my side. Tommy Rettig of **Lassie** fame was in that with me. He got to do some of my other scenes. No, [Heflin] was good, and Patricia Neal was particularly nice.

Q: What would you say was your favorite of the films you appeared in?

JIMMY: I would say **Cheaper By the Dozen** was a lot of fun to make because it had so many kids in it. We just messed around all the time. And **Belles on Their Toes** was another one. We got in trouble all the time. They had the assistant director follow us around all the time. Those were good movies. I enjoyed **Lone Hand**. We got to go on location to Colorado. I got to ride the horses and things like that.

Q: How did you get started in the movie business?

JIMMY: I can remember coming home with my second grade teacher. My mom thought I was sick or something. She said, "the talent scouts from MGM were here and they're going to be contacting you regarding Jimmy being in a picture." [I read for them] and I guess I did okay because I got the part. I went to a school about five or six blocks from MGM. I went to school with Roddy McDowall and Elizabeth Taylor.

Q: Did you enjoy making films?

JIMMY: At that point in time I was playing sports in school and my mom would come and get me and take me away. Man, I hated that. I'd go and I didn't care if I got the part or not. I wasn't uptight in my interview because I didn't care. If I got the part, it was okay. If I didn't, it was still okay. Probably better.

Q: As a child actor, how were you treated by casts and crews?

"She's hell on wheels ... fired up for any thrill!" Hot Car Girl

JIMMY: They were all very good to me. All the guys, the camera guys. The only guy that every little kid disliked was the property man because they never let you play with any of the props. When the scene was over, he took all that stuff away so it didn't get busted.

Q: Why did you stop making movies?

> "I WOULD HAVE TRADED ALL MY MOVIE EXPERIENCES TO BECOME A PROFESSIONAL ATHLETE EXCEPT FOR ONE THING, MY BODY DIDN'T LET ME DO THAT."

JIMMY: I got to be the age of about almost 14, playing sports. I wanted to do that. I mean I would have traded all my movie experiences to become a professional athlete except for one thing, my body didn't let me do that. I was okay but I was never that great. I played football and baseball in high school. I just wanted to do that and didn't want to make movies any more. I just wanted to kind of have a summer vacation of my own instead of working. So eventually, I just told my mom and dad, "Look, I don't really want to do this any more." They said, "Are you sure?" And I said "Yeah." So they called my agent and said "That's it." I think they argued the point a little bit because they knew exactly what it meant. The fact that I could make, in those days, okay money. Of course, I didn't see any of it so it didn't make any difference to me.

Q: Is **Invaders From Mars** a particular favorite among your films?

JIMMY HUNT: No, it wasn't my favorite because it was made in a short period of time — like three and a half weeks. And I was the central focus of the whole movie. I mean, I was in every scene. You'd like to have a few minutes to yourself. But there wasn't any time for that. It was like I was either in school or I was on the set. It was tough. They

"Millions gasped when they read about it in Life, Time and Argosy magazines!" Snow Creature

expected a lot more out of you as you got older.

Q: Any particular memories of the making of the film?

JIMMY: The way the sets were, it was as though it was from a child's perspective and everything was bigger. When you'd go through a door instead of the door being 6' 8" or something like that, a door was now nine feet tall. So everything was stretched. And if you remember in the picture, the trees never had leaves on them. The whole thing had a stark look. They had the halftracks and the tanks and all that stuff. I got to play on them and that was cool. Of course, I always wanted to carry a gun but they never let you as a kid.

Q: Did you find the Martians scary at that time?

JIMMY: No, not like a lot of people think it was scary, because I knew everything about it. I could see the guys when they put the monster uniforms on. They were just big, big guys that put these green outfits on. So it was not scary. To me, it was more — kind of exciting. I saw how they built those tunnels. That's what I thought was so neat.

Q: What do you remember about director William Cameron Menzies?

JIMMY: I don't know if somebody tried to zap this picture right from the start, but he had all these storyboards. He had them all blown up and ready to go, and they disappeared. They had to start putting this thing together as we went. You don't know that much about someone when you're in there working, especially as a kid. I never realized just how much of, I guess, a genius he really was. He was very good. He knew what he wanted out of us. He knew the feeling he wanted out of us and I think he did a good job of getting us to portray that.

Q: **Invaders From Mar**s had the quintessential B movie cast.

JIMMY: When you think about it you've got Morris Ankrum and you've got the mom and dad, Hillary Brooke and Leif Erickson. And there was Arthur Franz and Helena Carter.

"Edgar Allan Poe probes new depths of terror!" Cry of the Banshee

Q: Were any of them particularly helpful?

JIMMY: All of them because we were all together. We were just all there, all the time working, you know? Milburn Stone, he was cool. Of course Morris Ankrum had already been is so many movies at that point in his life, in probably every science fiction film at the time. He was typecast as the general. He was going to go out and kill the Martians.

Q: What do you recall of Luce Potter who played the Martian "head"?

JIMMY: They put this makeup all over her and they put this round thing with the tentacles all around her — they had a box and they had the plastic globe around her and she sat in there and did her thing with the eyes moving and the tentacles. I don't know how they did that. She was a midget. My mom had known her husband in high school. In those days, they used a lot of midgets for stand-ins. In other words, what they would do was, while you were going to school, they'd have the midget come over there and be your stand-in. He would walk through the scenes and they would light the scenes. They'd have it all ready when you came in. You'd do one walk-through so you'd get all your marks and everything. And then they'd shoot the scene. When that was done and they were going to shoot the scene from a different angle, then you'd go back to school and they'd relight that one and the midget would go through and do his thing. I worked with a whole bunch of those guys. Billy Curtis was one of my first stand-ins. I remember we were walking to lunch — there was a picture taken of my mom, Billy Curtis and myself. Billy Curtis and I were the same size only Billy Curtis had this big cigar that was like a mile long. I knew Billy very well and went over to his house. There were a couple

FILMS FEATURING JIMMY HUNT

Invaders from Mars
1986
Lone Hand
1953
Invaders from Mars
1953
All-American
1953
She Couldn't Say No
1952
Belles on Their Toes
1952
The Mating Season
1951
Weekend with Father
1951
Katie Did It
1951
Her First Romance
1951
Louisa
1950
Capture
1950
Shadow on the Wall
1950
Cheaper by the Dozen
1950
Saddle Tramp
1950
Rock Island Trail
1950
Top o' the Morning
1949
Rusty's Birthday
1949
Special Agent
1949
Sorry, Wrong Number
1948
The Sainted Sisters
1948
The Mating of Millie
1948
Pitfall
1948
The Fuller Brush Man
1948
Family Honeymoon
1948
Song of Love
1947
High Barbaree
1947

"The screen's first story of space islands in the sky!" Spaceways

others that I knew then and I went over to their house and my sister and I thought it was so cool because they had little furniture that we could sit in because it was like kid's furniture.

Q: You appeared in the **Invaders From Mars** remake. What's your opinion of that film?

JIMMY: What should have been the all-time cool picture turned out to be terrible. The only film I ever got residuals from and that's the one that bombed.

Q: What do you think made it bad?

JIMMY: It was so phony and everybody's acting was bad.

Q: Did you enjoy working with director Tobe Hooper?

JIMMY: Tobe was different. He was a nice man. I mean, hey - he was the one who asked me to be in his movie, so I can't say anything bad about the man. I just think that he put everything into the **Texas Chainsaw Massacre** and that was his career. He didn't do a very good job of directing this one. It came out really bad. Let me put it this way: If you can make Louise Fletcher have a bad performance, what type of director are you? Those monsters should have been just terrifying, but they looked like the hind quarters of a horse. They were not scary at all.

Q: Who approached you about being in the film?

"The most loathsome peril the universe has ever known!" Cosmic Monsters

JIMMY: A [client of mine] at Lockheed started bugging the studio. I think that what happened was, just to get him off their backs, they had me come down. I met Tobe Hooper and he asked, "Can you be my sheriff or chief of police?" And I said, "Yeah, I can do that." It was a piece of cake.

Alien brains bent on controlling the human species are a time-honored sci-fi ploy. Probes, pods, implants, brainwashing; it seems there's nothing extra-terrestrials won't try in their attempts to master our minds. You will view the following remarkable examples ... You will view the following remarkable examples ... You will ...

The Brain Eaters (1958)
Based loosely on Robert Heinlein's *The Puppet Masters*, the gray matter gluttons of the film's title burrow upward from the Earth's core. Produced by star Ed Nelson and directed by character actor Bruno VeSota, its special effects are less than convincing, but the cast compensates. Watch for Leonard Nimoy in a smallish role.

Invasion of the Body Snatchers (1956)
Much has been written of this film's socio-political undercurrents. Whatever! Director Don Siegel's trendsetting, tension-wracked film is a crackling good shocker about seed pods plotting to make obedient vegetables of the whole human race. And it's still scary 50 years after it was made.

Invisible Invaders (1959)
Some contend that, visually at least, this cheapie anticipated George Romero's **Night of the Living Dead**. Alien interlopers revive human cadavers to do their fighting for them — a contrivance put to amusing use in **Plan 9 From Outer Space**. With John Agar, John Carradine and Robert Hutton. Creaky plot, hammy acting, terrific fun!

The Space Children (1958)
Jack Arnold directed this rather somber fable of a benevolent alien globule holed-up in a cave near a government rocket testing base. The big glowy brain seeks to manipulate the children of the facility's scientific staff into foiling an upcoming missile launch.

"Too awesome to describe. Too terrifying to escape. Too powerful to stop!" Monster From Green Hell

BUZZ CORRY'S PERSONAL SPACE *ed* KEMMER MEETS THE B MONSTER

Unlike a lot of the celluloid heroes and heroines we profile, Ed Kemmer is the real deal. He distinguished himself in 47 missions as a World War II fighter pilot before being shot down and captured. He later escaped from the German prisoner of war camp that served as the

inspiration for **The Great Escape**. In civilian life, he delivered his own daughter in the back seat of a police cruiser

"New horrors! Mad science spawning evil fiends!" Fiend Without a Face

that didn't quite make it to the hospital in time. Who better to serve as one of TV's first heroic role models?

At the start of the 1950s, television was poised to sweep the national imagination. A contagious creative spirit gripped the handful of writers, producers and actors drawn to the new medium. Emerging from TV's "anything goes" atmosphere were pioneering sci fi programs such as **Captain Video, Rocky Jones** and **Space Cadet**. Leading this spirited pack was Commander Buzz Corry of **Space Patrol**. Edward Kemmer, a struggling actor possessed of homegrown good looks and earnest demeanor, portrayed Buzz Corry, and is remembered fondly by fans of the show more than 50 years later. "When I started the show I didn't even own a TV set," Kemmer laughs. "Someone did a survey that showed we had more adults watching than kids. Of course in those days of early TV, most people would watch anything."

Ed Kemmer was honing his survival instincts before his acting career ever got under way. "I was in World War II," he recalls. "I was a fighter pilot shot down on my 47th mission. I became a prisoner of war. I went from 180 pounds to 135. I escaped, and was recaptured after almost two weeks. When I returned home after the war, I attended the College of Theater Arts at the Pasadena Playhouse, living on the G.I. Bill. I was notified that if you had been a prisoner of war, there was a bonus of a dollar a day. So I got over 300 bucks back pay. Shortly after that, I got a bill from the IRS." It seems the

> "SOMEONE DID A SURVEY THAT SHOWED WE HAD MORE ADULTS WATCHING THAN KIDS. OF COURSE IN THOSE DAYS OF EARLY TV, MOST PEOPLE WOULD WATCH ANYTHING."

"They grow — know — walk — talk — stalk — and kill!" **Day of the Triffids**

government wanted to tax Kemmer's salary for the time he'd spent in a Nazi POW camp. $186 were due in back taxes. Kemmer's accountant was certain that the debt would be forgiven, as he'd certainly received no government benefits while detained in Germany. Threatening to attach his meager weekly income, Ed was allowed to pay off the government in $15 installments. "The TV columns picked up the story," Kemmer recalls. "I made no bones about it. I was going to sing all I could about it. It made a lot of columns at the time, how I had to pay income tax while in prison starving to death."

It was future castmate Lyn Osborn who contacted Kemmer about auditioning for the part of Buzz Corry. Kemmer easily won over the show's producers. You might think that landing the part of the nation's leading space hero would bring him financial security, but as Commander Buzz Corry, star of a national television program, Kemmer pulled down a whopping $8.00 per show. Osborn, as Kemmer's comic sidekick, Happy, received the same. The remaining cast got $5.00. A raise was imminent after the show was picked up by ABC, but Kemmer and his castmates earned every penny of their salaries. Ed gladly acknowledges, however, that the experience of live television was invaluable. "You start by memorizing the script and it takes forever, it seems, and you're still not sure you'll get it. But after a few years of that, a child could do it. It's just a matter of doing it enough. It becomes second nature. In the beginning it took eight hours to learn a script. Later on, two readings was enough with my wife cueing me."

Kemmer points out one advantage of memorizing entire scripts that saved many broadcasts in those early days. "You would remember everyone else's lines, too. In live TV, that's a big thing. You might look at someone's face when it was their turn to speak, and you knew they couldn't tell you their own name. So you would take their line, adapt it, and try to get them back into the scene. Most of the time it worked." Ed leaves little doubt that live TV separated the men from the boys. "You'd work with people who did a lot of stage and a lot of movies," he remembers. "They'd come and do **Space Patrol**, and they would walk off swearing and sweating with blood in their boots saying, 'Never! Never again will I do a live show!' 'Well,' I'd always say, 'the first 500 shows are the toughest.'"

When Buzz Corry touched down for the last time, Kemmer moved into motion picture acting. A quick study, he hustled through an entertaining array of programmers. "There was an independent film released by Paramount called **The Hot Angel**," he recalls. "I

"Man-made monster with every human emotion!" Tobor the Great

did my own flying in that. I had a commercial license. I flew down into the Grand Canyon. That was a lot of fun."

Following notable turns in a number of Bs such as **Calypso Joe** and **Sierra Stranger**, Kemmer secured supporting parts in various "A" productions including **The Crowded Sky**. "It wasn't a big part, but it was fun to do. I had a couple of really nice scenes with Efrem Zimbalist and Rhonda Fleming. I played a mean guy. In most shows I played nice guys, which gets boring." He also appeared in **Too Much, Too Soon**, which featured Errol Flynn as John Barrymore. "It was fun to watch Flynn work," Kemmer laughs. "He was a delight. He'd worked for Warners for many years and earned them millions upon millions. But they didn't pay him what he thought they should. So they'd have him in a closeup and he'd blow line after line intentionally. He'd say, 'Sorry, old boy,' and start again. He'd go up to 20 or 25 takes. He was running them over and costing them money. I think he did it deliberately because he didn't like them."

Many die-hard fans of **Space Patrol** are surprised to learn of Kemmer's 20-year stint acting in the major television soap operas of the 1960s and '70s. "I think there's more recognition from soaps than there is from **Space Patrol** because of the age difference of the viewers involved." He'd appeared for two seasons on a Hollywood-based soap called **Clear Horizon** when **The Edge of Night**, a New York-based program, came West looking for actors. Ed returned to New York to appear on the show and stayed. "I met my wife [actress Fran Sharon] on **Edge of Night**. We married on the show shortly before I was 'murdered.' I was stabbed in the back and killed by Connie Ford, who played a jealous lover. I lay on the floor for a couple of days." Kemmer and Sharon later tied the knot in real life, and Ed worked steadily in the medium for two decades. "Every time I was ready to leave one show, another one came along," he laughs. "I did 20 solid years of soaps, which were very good. But 20 years is enough."

Having starred in a string of memorable B movies, grueling live television programs and innumerable soap opera episodes, Kemmer knows firsthand the money-saving secrets employed by B-movie impresarios. "I did many a script where the writer came on stage and apologized, saying, 'They only paid for a first draft.' Writers weren't paid to polish a script," Kemmer points out. "A first draft can be terrible, while a fourth draft can be great. A lot of first drafts were filmed."

"The undead awakened after 200 years!" The Vampire

Horror film fans will recall Kemmer from a pair of the decade's more vivid, low-budget shockers. One late show staple that was cheap, atmospheric and regarded by many fans with great affection, is **Giant From the Unknown**. "Now *that's* low budget," Kemmer laughs. In it, Ed does battle with a gigantic Spanish conquistador (former pro wrestler Buddy Baer), re-animated after 500 years by a blast of lightning. "It was pretty corny, but fun to do. We were up in the mountains shooting on location." The production, already hampered by its shoestring budget, was further impaired by weather that made post-production a nightmare. "Toward the end of shooting it started to snow," Kemmer chuckles. "Well, try to match scenes! That really hung everyone up. With a little bit of rewriting and some careful shooting, we got by with it. But it was out of left field. You don't shoot in sequence. When it started to snow, that changed a lot of things. You'd have to shoot outside and try to match anything you shot before."

> "A FIRST DRAFT CAN BE TERRIBLE, WHILE A FOURTH DRAFT CAN BE GREAT. A LOT OF FIRST DRAFTS WERE FILMED."

Kemmer is quick to acknowledge that the film fell short in many areas. "The snow wasn't the worst thing about it," he wisecracks. "The effects at that time weren't what they are today. The effects, like those on **Space Patrol**, were done live with miniatures and guys pulling strings, hoping everything turns out all right. There was nothing computerized about it. Today it's so totally different."

Kemmer admits frankly that he remembers little about director Richard Cunha. "With all of the problems, I didn't see much of him. He was trying to work out a script where it snowed and then didn't snow. All I can say is, I don't remember anything bad about him. He just did his job." On the other hand, Ed bonded easily with fellow cast members. "Bob Steele was a great fellow," he recalls of the former Western hero. "We chatted quite a bit." Fans of the film have commented on the chalky white makeup Steele wears throughout the film. Director Cunha states that Steele insisted on the pancake to make him look younger. Kemmer is of another opinion. "I think that probably he wasn't wearing any makeup. If you don't wear makeup, you can look very pallid. I think I would have noticed if he wore white makeup. He probably thought he had enough tan to cover it. But a tan won't take away that sheen. Compared to the other actors, it can look pretty ridiculous."

Another fast friendship was formed with B-movie stalwart Morris Ankrum. "We lived near each other in California. He was a dear old fellow. A really dear man and a joy to be around." Likewise, Kemmer found costar Sally Fraser to be affable. "She played the same roles over and over again. The really nice, sweet wife with no faults. She must have been so bored to death doing those roles. She was a very sweet gal."

Kemmer recalls the making of a second cult classic, Bert I. Gordon's **Earth vs the Spider**, as another enjoyable, low-budget experience. "The fellow who bought all the rights to **Space Patrol** sent me a lobby card from Italy where it was called **Vengeance of the Black Spider**. I have it framed in my bathroom."

Gordon virtually cornered the market on movie gigantism, enlarging everything from lizards (**King Dinosaur**) to grasshoppers (**Beginning of the End**) to men (**The Amazing Colossal Man**), even managing to shrink a few things (**Attack of the Puppet People**). "He was a very pleasant guy," Kemmer recalls. "In those kind of low-budget situations, you shoot very fast. The object is to stay within your budget. But he never pushed. I have only nice memories of him. And I helped him a lot. After **Space Patrol** I was a fast study. So while you were in makeup, they could bring you two pages of changes. I could do that with no problem. They'd say they had to cut a few minutes and I was so used to cutting on **Space Patrol** that it was a big help to them." Kemmer remembers the film's teen heroine, June Kenney, fondly, regarding her as "just a kid at the time, but sweet to work with."

Ed soon moved into series television, turning up regularly on programs as diverse as **Lassie, Perry Mason, The Rebel, The Twilight Zone** (that's Ed as the even-tempered airman who tries to calm William Shatner after he claims to have seen a man on the wing of the plane) and many others, while maintaining his schedule of B movie appearances. "Most directors treated me very well so I have very few complaints," he says, while

"Hideous, fiendish, terrifying nightmares come to life!" **Dracula vs. Frankenstein**

"YOU LOOK AT THE SCRIPT AND SAY, 'THIS IS SHIT! WELL, LET'S MAKE IT THE BEST SHIT WE CAN!'"

asserting that valuable lessons about respect were learned along the way. "Directors sometimes need a whipping boy and they'll pick on someone," he says. "You go through the whole show knowing he'll keep picking on the same person — and that person will allow it! That's one of the first things I learned. You don't allow that." Kemmer recalls shooting a popular daytime series for NBC. "Victor Jory was on an episode that I did. Vic had directed me in a play, and we'd appeared together in a play called **Command Decision**. Well, we were on the stage rehearsing, and the director said something to him in kind of a snide way. Victor Jory reached up and got hold of the mike boom and pulled it down and did he tell that director off. 'Come on down here,' he said. 'We'll discuss it!' He was no one to fool with, believe me. That director just talked the wrong way to the wrong guy."

Ed Kemmer admits that it was difficult to be choosy about scripts when consistent employment was the objective. Even stories about giant spiders and gargantuan Spaniards didn't seem outlandish. "It was work," he laughs, summarizing a philosophy that sustained him throughout his prolific career. "You look at the script and say, 'This is shit! Well, let's make it the best shit we can!' That's what you do. You've just got to play it the best you can."

*When **Space Patrol** was at the zenith of its popularity, Ed, Lyn Osborn and a vocal chorus recorded the show's theme song and the rousing **Up Ship and Away**. Ed transferred the 78 rpm disk to cassette and sent it to me. It's an exhilarating piece of nostalgia with Ed, his fine voice brimming with confidence, belting out the song's infectious, optimistic refrain: "Close ports, fire jets, up ship and away! We'll take it slow and only go a million miles today." Ed Kemmer passed away in November 2004.*

"A human bride, the enslaved victim of gargantuan horror!" The Bride and the Beast

"Super women who kissed and killed!" **Mesa of Lost Women**

HOW THE CREATURE FINALLY CAUGHT UP WITH HER
lori NELSON
MEETS THE B MONSTER

Lori Nelson may be best known to fans as one of three women beloved and pursued by the **Creature From the Black Lagoon** (Julie Adams and Leigh Snowden being the others). But her role opposite the Gill Man in **Revenge of the Creature**, the second film in the classic triad,

profile

came midway in the busy career of one of Universal Studios' most promising young starlets. Shortly after arriving in Hollywood,

---

"Diabolical murder monsters lusting for a death-duel!" Frankenstein Meets the Wolf Man

Lori had been placed under contract by the studio at the tender age of 16. Contract players at the time learned the rigors of their craft while appearing in a terrific variety of films. "**Ma and Pa Kettle at the Fair** was the very first movie I made after I was signed with Universal," Nelson recalls. The longstanding series of hillbilly-humor films proved to be a fertile training ground, and Nelson prospered from her exposure to character actors Percy Kilbride and Marjorie Main. "They were pretty much the same characters they played on the screen. He was a very intelligent man, however. Very quiet and sweet. Marjorie was rough and gruff and boisterous."

Nelson recalls **Pardners**, a raucous Western vehicle for Martin and Lewis, as the most fun she ever had on a picture. "Dean and Jerry were always playing jokes on the crew and on each other," she recalls. "Everybody had a good time. Dean was a very good-natured, sweet, nice guy. He loved to play jokes, but he was also a very serious actor."

Among the bigger-budgeted films in which she was cast, **Bend of the River** with James Stewart and **All I Desire** opposite Barbara Stanwyck hold a special place in Nelson's memory, due in large measure to the generosity of the stars. "They were really the first big stars I had ever worked with," Nelson remembers. "They were the ones I was most in awe of. [Stanwyck] was a lovely lady, and she was very helpful in the scenes I had to do with her. A very classy lady."

 Stewart and Stanwyck were two of the biggest stars on the planet and Lori was among Universal's most dedicated and promising contract players. So she was a trifle insulted when the studio asked her to appear opposite a scaly, six-foot, prehistoric amphibian. She was miffed at the time, but has since grown to love the Gill Man as much as the legion of fans that sustains his legend. "Little did I know," she laughs, "that it would be the one [film] I would be most remembered for."

At the time of her casting, science fiction and horror films were considered a step backward in a promising career. Nelson may have had second thoughts at the time, but any dubious notions concerning the genre have long-since vanished. "Science fiction is probably the most collectible genre today. I'm glad that I made [**Revenge of the Creature**] and a Roger Corman film [**Day the World Ended**]. But making a Roger Corman film, at the time, was the bottom of the barrel. You really felt like you were struggling to get work when you had to make a Roger Corman film. I think that almost

"Battling aqua-lung adventure!" **Manfish**

everybody in Hollywood felt the same way. You would only do a Roger Corman film if you couldn't get anything else. But you had to make a living."

Revenge of the Creature was filmed on location in Florida, as well as the Universal Studios backlot. A large measure of the film's dramatic success and lasting appeal is attributable to Nelson's solid performance as the lovely marine biologist who catches the Creature's eye. "I'm very proud that I did one of the three Creature pictures," she asserts. "**Revenge of the Creature** was a major studio production. It was very well done and had a semi-plausible story."

> "EVERYONE IN HOLLYWOOD HAS DONE A ROGER CORMAN PICTURE AT SOME POINT IN THEIR CAREER, IT SEEMS."

Significantly, throughout much of the film, that's actually Nelson, and not a stuntperson, being grabbed and pawed and dunked by the amorous Gill Man. "I did most of the diving in the tanks and some of the swimming in the [St. Johns] river where the scene on the buoy was. Some of the more extensive and more dangerous swimming they used a double for."

As it turned out, the experience was a happy one, and Nelson thought highly of her fellow performers. "John Agar couldn't have been a nicer man," she recalls, going on to admit that she harbored a crush on co-star John Bromfield. "It was only a crush," she laughs, "never to be realized. He was going with, I think, Corinne Calvet at the time, so it was just a silent crush."

Following her departure from Universal, Nelson began freelancing and appeared in a handful of low-budget pictures. Some of these B-grade curios have come to be regarded as classics of their kind, among them **Hot Rod Girl** ("Teenage terrorists tearing up the streets!") co-starring Chuck Connors, John Smith and Frank Gorshin.

"See maddened rhino killed by a woman!" Congorilla

Some fans of **Hot Rod Girl** have made note of the sporty, light-colored 1955 T-Bird Nelson drives as the title character. "That was my car. The film was so low-budget they asked me to drive my own car." The actress smiles while recalling how she came to acquire the classic convertible. "Debbie Reynolds and I were good friends in those days. She would go to New York to see Eddie [Fisher] and I would go with her. Whenever Debbie would go to see Eddie, she'd have to have a chaperone. We'd hang around together and double-date with Tab Hunter, who was a good friend of ours. We'd have parties at each other's houses — just general, wholesome, good fun. Eddie gave Debbie a red, full-length rabbit coat and a red T-Bird. So, then Tab Hunter got a white one shortly thereafter. Then Bill Campbell got a black one. I was the last hold out — I got a yellow one. As it turned out, the yellow one was the most rare. They didn't have them [when they first started making T-Birds]. There were only 500 yellow ones in California at the time."

The fate of that beautiful T-Bird reflects the direction Nelson's personal life was taking at the time of her first marriage to musician/composer Johnny Mann. "We moved to a place with a lot of acreage in Chatsworth, California," she recalls. "We lived up on a hill. We had my first daughter and a couple of dogs — German shepherds. We had to get a station wagon to haul the dogs and the trash cans up and down the hill. My little T-Bird was bought and paid for, but Johnny wouldn't let me keep it. He said it was foolish to have two cars."

Nelson's next excursion into sci-fi was the Alex Gordon-produced, Roger Corman-directed quickie, **Day the World Ended**. Says Nelson, "Everyone in Hollywood has done a Roger Corman picture at some point in their career, it seems." The film featured Paul Blaisdell in one of his sillier monster costumes. "The design of that Gill Man suit was beautiful," Lori offers, as though anticipating the next question. So how did it feel to go from appearing opposite one of cinema's best-looking monsters to, "one of the worst looking?" she laughs, completing the question. "I thought that it was very amateurish looking. I thought, 'Oh, no!' With those little wobbly horns on its head that kind of wiggled back and forth — and those wobbly claws it had on its hands. Paul Blaisdell was inside that thing and he had a really hard time maneuvering in it. It was kind of heavy and he was not a big man. One time he picked me up and fell forward, on top of me. We all laughed."

"Unfolding for the first time the emotional life of a cannibal girl!" Rama

> "PAUL BLAISDELL WAS INSIDE THAT THING AND HE HAD A REALLY HARD TIME MANEUVERING IN IT. ONE TIME HE PICKED ME UP AND FELL FORWARD, ON TOP OF ME."

Nelson recalls that Corman, ever the cost cutter, filmed much of the action at a notable eatery. "There's a restaurant out here in the San Fernando Valley called The Sportsman's Lodge," she remembers. "They have a lake over there. We did a lot of **Day the World Ended** at the Sportman's Lodge. We used that lake and that little garden area. That was our main location."

Lori recalls her castmates with affection, particularly leading man — and love interest — Richard Denning, who was a seasoned veteran of numerous films at that time. "They always cast older men with younger women. That's the complaint that women in Hollywood have always had. Men continue to work on up into their 50s, 60s and 70s. They cast them opposite young women instead of women their own age. That's why it's so difficult for women in films to work. Women, I mean — not girls. Past 35, a woman is going downhill as far as Hollywood is concerned."

Fortunately, **Day the World Ended** was not the film that ended Nelson's career, and in retrospect, she's happy to have appeared in it. "There's a Roger Corman cult out there," she says, noting that at conventions and personal appearances, it's one of the films she's asked about most.

In addition to the drive-in classic **Hot Rod Girl**, Nelson starred opposite Mamie Van Doren in another of the decade's best-known juvenile delinquent exploitation flicks, **Untamed Youth**. "That was neat because I really liked [director] Howard Koch a lot. He

"One day after a million years it came out of hiding to kill, kill, kill!!" Beast of Hollow Mountain

was then part of Koch/Schenck Productions. They were just a little production company starting out and he later on, of course, became a big producer in Hollywood and head of Paramount Pictures. We remained kind of distant friends down through the years.

"Mamie Van Doren was at Universal, too. We had both left Universal and were freelancing, and both of us wound up in this picture. Howard wanted to give her first billing because she was really a hot item about that time. She wouldn't do it unless she had star billing. I said, 'No. I'm a bigger star than she is.' And he begged and pleaded and begged and pleaded and finally he said, 'Look, I'll give you an extra bonus.' I said, 'No. I don't think so.' He said, 'I'll throw in a TV.' I said, 'Oh, Howard, if you want to that bad, go ahead and do it.' It really didn't make that much difference to me and I got some perks out of it."

There may have been trepidation about appearing in low-budget pictures at the time, but today Nelson has fond memories of the B films she made. "I just thought that they would go into obscurity," she laughs. "I did **Outlaw's Son, Hot Rod Girl, Untamed Youth** and **Day the World Ended** — those were my four forays into low-budget movies — they were all what they called 'B' movies. You really hated to do those pictures in those days because you were so afraid that they would hurt your career. Lots of times, they did. The major studios, if you were known for doing low-budget films, wouldn't hire you. They were very stuck up about it in those days. Isn't it interesting that, if you were a waitress during your lean times, they wouldn't hold it against you. But if you did a 'B' movie, or a television commercial — *that* they would hold against you."

There was a stigma attached to television at the time her film career got under way,

FILMS FEATURING LORI NELSON

Secret Sins of the Father
1994
How to Marry a Millionaire (TV series)
1958
The Pied Piper of Hamelin (TV)
1957
Outlaw's Son
1957
Untamed Youth
1957
Day the World Ended
1956
Hot Rod Girl
1956
Pardners
1956
Mohawk
1956
I Died a Thousand Times
1955
Revenge of the Creature
1955
Sincerely Yours
1955
Underwater!
1955
Ma and Pa Kettle at Waikiki
1955
Destry
1954
The All American
1953
All I Desire
1953
Tumbleweed
1953
Walking My Baby Back Home
1953
Bend of the River
1952
Francis Goes to West Point
1952
Ma and Pa Kettle at the Fair
1952

"Science baits the trap with a woman's beauty!" The Creature Walks Among Us

> "IF YOU WERE A WAITRESS DURING YOUR LEAN TIMES, THEY WOULDN'T HOLD IT AGAINST YOU. BUT IF YOU DID A 'B' MOVIE, THAT THEY WOULD HOLD AGAINST YOU."

but as the 1950s progressed, TV seemed like a natural move for a struggling actress. "I did the series **How To Marry A Millionaire** in 1957. I did 39 episodes." Nelson co-starred with Merry Anders and Barbara Eden in the sitcom based on the hit movie. But as her original commitment ended, Nelson answered the urge to move on. "I felt that I was the biggest of the three actresses in terms of star status, because I had been in the business for a long time. Merry Anders had been around, but she had never really gotten any good parts. And Barbara had just gotten a contract at Fox, and had come down here from San Francisco where she was a show girl, and this was really her first acting part. It behooved both of them to stay with the series, but I was in my late 20s and had started at Universal when I was only 16. I had done quite a bit of television before I did the series. I felt that I needed to move on. I didn't need to be stuck in that little series that was in syndication." Nelson was replaced by Lisa Gaye, but the program lasted just 13 more episodes.

But Lori wasn't finished with television by any means. She made the rounds of the top series in a variety of plum guest-starring roles. "I did guest appearances on practically every Western that was on at the time," Nelson laughs. "**Wagon Train, Gunsmoke, Have Gun Will Travel, The Rifleman, Sugarfoot** — you name 'em, I did 'em." In addition to her work in Westerns, Nelson points out that she appeared in the more prestigious dramatic showcases of the time, **20th Century-Fox Hour, Climax, Playhouse 90** and **GE Theatre**, among them.

"Clawing up from the earth's steaming depths!" *Them!*

Following the flurry of television roles, Nelson was separated and eventually divorced from her first husband, and decided to forego an acting career to concentrate on raising her children. "I was single for about 15 years — though I didn't face the same hardships that many single mothers do." Happily remarried to retired L.A. cop Joe Reiner, she takes on the occasional acting assignment and runs a thriving antiques business in southern California. In addition, there's an ongoing demand for personal appearances and autograph signings, affording her and Joe the opportunity to travel together. "People still ask," she laughs, "'Did you ever learn **How To Marry A Millionaire**?' I guess I didn't learn my lessons well, because I never ended up marrying one. Johnny Mann wasn't a millionaire and Joe Reiner certainly isn't a millionaire — but we do fine."

"THEM'S" THE BREAKS
Fess PARKER
MEETS THE B MONSTER

It doesn't surprise me that Fess Parker, an icon who once dominated international pop-culture, is one of the most modest and hospitable fellows I've ever met. You'd expect nothing less from Davy Crockett, the humble and heroic "king of the wild frontier."

It *does* surprise me to hear Fess compare **Them!**, the sci-fi classic that was the turning point in his career, to **My Big Fat Greek Wedding!**

"The fiend that walks lovers' beach!" Monster of Piedras Blancas

Parker's is among the most perfect Hollywood success stories. Plucked from the ranks of second-tier players, within months his face was on Davy Crockett toys, games, wallets, rifles, comics, coloring books, belts, badges, notepads and posters in countries around the globe. He pooled his earnings, invested in real estate — specifically acres and acres of land in the picturesque mountains above Santa Barbara — and, with his wife, children and grandchildren, established a thriving winery and resort hotel, ensuring financial security for the many generations of Parkers to follow. Fess and his people rolled out the red carpet for the B Monster, but it's evident from his establishment's attention to detail and hospitality that all people are special to this affable gentleman who supplanted the history-book Davy Crockett with his portrayal in the classic Disney series.

"I have a bone to pick with you," I tell Fess.

"Okay," he responds, pouring us each a glass of water.

"You finished shooting **Davy Crockett** before I was born. How is it you look younger than me?"

He smiles the same smile he employed in the first **Davy Crockett** episode in which he attempted to "grin down a b'ar." "I don't think I do," he laughs. "But, thank you." Fess is far too modest. He's stunningly fit for 78.

In the early 1970s, following a second successful run as a legendary frontiersman in the long-running **Daniel Boone** TV series, Fess reckoned that it might be time to slow down, take stock and parlay his acting career into something more. "Up to a certain point, your mind and your projects are not impeded by the fact that you may or may not have enough time to complete them. When you realize you [may not] have enough time ... "

According to Fess, this realization "turns life around. I've observed for 25 years now people who've attempted to retire and I've never seen anything about their lives in retirement that appealed to me. It's nice to go on a trip. But when you're reduced to a trip and a trip and a trip, or golf, golf and more golf ... I think I felt a little more acutely this [encroaching] 'sound barrier' than they do. All of a sudden you have to start doing an

"50 tons of creeping black horror!" **The Spider**

offense and a defense at the same time." Gradually, his thriving family business took shape and is today overseen by three generations of Parkers. In short, Fess found a way to live life to the fullest while simultaneously ensuring his family's security.

There's one question that has to be raised, one that might not seem so obvious seeing as how he's been a household name for nearly 50 years. "Fess? When you were breaking in, did anyone get stuck on the name? What kind of name is Fess?" "I'm a junior," Parker responds simply. "My father was Fess." He takes a drink of water. "And there was a rodeo clown named Fess Reynolds. I knew him. He was very big on the rodeo circuit."

Parker owes his initial success to some interesting chance encounters and his stubborn refusal to cave in to discouraging words. The towering Texan was studying Russian at the University of Texas when actor Adolphe Menjou came to narrate **Peter and the Wolf** with the San Antonio Symphony and to talk about his motion picture career. "I was a senior in 1949 and I was taking my second year of Russian. My professor, Dr. Arthur P. Coleman, was a very interesting man who founded the Slavonic language department." Before coming to Texas, Coleman had resigned a post at Columbia University over a political dispute with Dwight Eisenhower, who was then president of Columbia. According to Fess, it became "one of these cause célèbre things," generating much publicity, in the midst of which Coleman and Menjou became "political pen pals." "When Menjou came to Texas, I was sent by Dr. Coleman to pick him up at the train station because Coleman didn't have a car. So I drove Mr. Menjou to his hotel and then to meet Dr. Coleman. It was evident to me that they had no plans. It was either sit on a bench or go back to the hotel, so I suggested that I show them the town. After that, we went back to the fraternity house to have dinner, which was a big thrill for the boys in the fraternity and Menjou and Coleman enjoyed the food and the atmosphere." (Fess points out that "Morgan Woodward was a fraternity brother. I later introduced him to Disney casting for **The Great Locomotive Chase** and he never looked back. Excellent career. Fine actor.")

The following evening, Fess drove Menjou to the theater and arranged more entertainment for him following the performance, gathering several friends for drinks and discussion with the actor. The next morning, Parker drove Menjou to the train station. Just as the actor was boarding the train, he rather casually asked Fess if he'd like

"Space creatures snatch girls to mysterious planet!" Blood Beast From Outer Space

to appear in Western pictures. Apparently Parker had made an impression. At Menjou's urging he headed West. Menjou was about to begin shooting **Across the Wide Missouri** starring Clark Gable, and Fess looked forward to a meeting with director William Wellman.

Upon his arrival, Fess was undiplomatically passed down the food chain. "This casting director said, 'Fess? We can't send you in as Fess. Don't you have some other name you can use?' I said, "Well, I have an Uncle *John* Parker.' 'Great, we'll send you in as John Parker.'" At long last he did a screen test for an assistant director. "The fellow stopped me in the middle and said, 'Whatever you're doing, don't do it any more!'" Parker sought out Menjou for advice. The actor told Fess to finish his education before pursuing an acting career.

> "THIS CASTING DIRECTOR SAID, 'FESS? WE CAN'T SEND YOU IN AS FESS. DON'T YOU HAVE SOME OTHER NAME YOU CAN USE?'"

He may have been somewhat crestfallen, but Fess decided to stick it out in California, where he resolved to study drama. It wasn't long after his last meeting with Menjou that he and a buddy decided to hitchhike up to San Francisco. On a lonesome California highway in the middle of the night, they managed to thumb down a ride with a benevolent motorist. Fess and his pal climbed into the back of a long, fancy car. As they struck up a conversation, Fess realized that the man in the front seat was Walter Huston. He recalls that the celebrated actor was very friendly, so naturally Fess began pumping him for insights into the entertainment business. While some of the details of the encounter are lost to memory, Parker still recalls Huston's encouragement clearly.

As he was getting acquainted with Hollywood, Fess crossed the paths of many aspiring actors like himself. "I used to hang around the Monogram studios. A friend of

"He builds a bonfire of human souls!" The Mad Doctor

mine knew a secretary there who could get us in. We would go over and watch the Bowery Boys or Lash LaRue or Tex Ritter. There were some younger actors that were there who I got to know later on. One of the fellows was Jack Elam, who played in Westerns forever. He was in the accounting department at Monogram. He used to take all my money at Liar's Poker."

Fess also hit it off with up-and-coming leading man Don Castle. "He did a lot of pictures and then left to open a motel with his wife," Fess recalls. "We still see his wife Zeta from time to time. Don was unhappy with the way his career went and left the business. I think that sort of hastened his untimely exit." (ed. Castle was part owner with Jack Wrather of the 8mm Castle Films Co. After being seriously injured in a 1966 automobile accident, Castle died of a medication overdose.)

Eventually, the sometimes frustrating process of simply showing his face to the right people began to pay off. "In the summer of 1951 I finished a year of graduate study at USC and was just starting my thesis when I got a job with the national company of **Mister Roberts**. I was listed in the cast as 'seaman, fireman and others.' I was just atmosphere, really. I was put in the show by the famous director Joshua Logan and producer Leland Heyward. I spent that summer observing Henry Fonda up close. I used to stand in the wings and watch him do one particular scene. He would amaze me because he would approximate that scene every time. And I had a chance to talk with actors like Lee Van Cleef, Jack Klugman and Rance Howard, the father of Ronnie Howard.

"That show ran until September. And then I started calling agents. I got a book of agent's names. I started with the As. 'Hello, my name is Fess Parker. I just finished a run in the national Company of **Mister Roberts**. I'm thinking of staying on the West Coast and I'm seeking representation.' The response would be, 'Thank you, but we're not ...' I got to the Rs before anybody actually spoke to me. I went to see this agent named Wynn Rockamora. He was a successful agent. He had Francis Sullivan as a client, as I remember. He said that he might have to pass, but that 'my associates down the hallway might be interested.'

"So he took me down the hallway where I met a fellow named Bill Barnes. He was a retired postal worker who wanted to be an agent. He seemed like a nice guy. He was not

"All Hell broke loose when the mad monster escaped!" Son of Ingagi

very impressed with my possibilities, but he asked, 'Do you know how to get out to Warner Brothers?' I said, 'Sure, I'll find my way out there.' He said, 'I want you to meet Bill Tinsman in the casting office.' So I went out there to see Bill Tinsman about some small part in Michael Curtiz's picture **The Will Rogers Story**. Tinsman asked, 'Did you ever play baseball?' I said, 'Sure.' I'd already learned that the answer to every question was, 'Yes, of course.'

"'Hardball?'

"'Is there any other kind?'

"'What position did you play?'

"'I pitched a little and played outfield.'

"'I'm not going to send you over to see Mr. Curtiz. I'm going to send you to see a man named Brynie Foy.'

He gave me a pass and I walked over to Mr. Foy's office. 'Mr. Tinsman sent me to see Mr. Foy.'

"'Go right in.'

It was a big office and Mr. Foy was seated behind his desk. I walked in and he said, 'Jesus Christ, you look the part. Can you act?' I said, 'Yes sir!'

"'Well, tell me what you've done.'

"'I was in theater in high school and college.'

"'Well, what else have you done?'

"'Summer stock.' I was reaching for it. None of this was necessarily true.

"'Whereabouts?'

"'Southwest Summer Theater in Waco, Texas.' I'd never been there but I knew it was there.

"'He turned to these other fellows who were [in the office].' 'These two fellows are *from* Waco.' He asked them, 'Is that a good theater group?' They said, 'Oh, yeah. Charles Laughton has worked there.' Foy said, 'I'll tell you what, we're going to test you. Let's get the director in here.' He was a veteran director. He took one look at me and said [disparagingly] 'Holy moley. Well, Mr. Foy said we'd shoot a test. Look over this [script] and we'll call you in a couple of days.'

A day or two later I got a call. They said, 'We're not going to do the screen test. Sorry about that.'

"'I am, too.'

"'We're going to use somebody we have under contract.'

"'If you don't mind telling me, I'd be interested to know who you've chosen.'

"'Ronald Reagan.'"

Fess punctuates the story with a laugh. The picture was **The Winning Team**. The director was Lewis Seiler. In it, Reagan portrayed hall of fame pitcher Grover Cleveland Alexander. "I was together with [Reagan] at the 35th anniversary celebration of Disneyland and when we had the chance to swap stories, I told the President that story. He told me the real story of Grover Cleveland Alexander. How people thought he was an alcoholic when really he was suffering from epilepsy — which in Alexander's day was something to be feared, so he allowed the world to believe he was an alcoholic. Reagan had an uncanny memory for the details in the background of this character he'd played 40 years earlier."

Addressing his rather disappointing encounters with Foy, Tinsman and Barnes, Fess emphasizes that the important thing was, "I'd gotten the attention of the Warner Brothers casting office and then I did two pictures at Universal, then Warners' **Springfield Rifle** rolled around. I used to tell people that once you get started, you just go from picture to picture, but that wasn't true."

Maybe not, be it is interesting the way circumstances conspired to keep Parker visible. "I started **Untamed Frontier** with Joseph Cotten and Shelley Winters. We were on location, and Joseph Cotten was unfamiliar with cowboy boots, so in trying to put them on he threw his back out. So there was a two-week delay. We went back to the studio where they were making a picture with Tony Curtis and Piper Laurie called **No Room For the Groom**, so they gave me a part in that. I started to work on **Untamed Frontier** on Thanksgiving 1951. These projects carried over into 1952. Shortly after the New Year, I got a job with Andre deToth who was directing **Springfield Rifle** with Gary Cooper. Gary Cooper was such a super guy. It was a cast full of near-great actors like Paul Kelly, Alan Hale and Lon Chaney. There were old stunt men and guys like 'Big Boy' Williams who had been a star back in the days of Will Rogers. And Mark Dana, who I still see. He lives over in Santa Barbara. He and his wife had me over for lunch just the other day. It's amazing we've known each other for so long."

Fess kept working, learning, observing some of the best-known actors of the time. "I did about 15 movies in small parts, and some television leads — **My Little Margie, The Laraine Day Show, Dragnet, Tales of the Century, Annie Oakley.**"

There was one small but significant role he reluctantly undertook on the advice of Warner Brothers casting director Hoyt Bowers. "I'd worked in a number of Westerns with Randolph Scott and others, and by this time I was a 'featured player,' which meant that I got paid for a week even though I didn't have much of a part. One day Hoyt Bowers called. I was doing a film for the Navy about battle fatigue. He said, 'When you finish, come and see me. I have something for you. It's only a day's work and I know you don't want to do day work, but I really think this would be good for you.' I said, 'Hoyt, if you think so I'll do it.' So as soon as I could I met with the producer, David Weisbart, and he gave me the part." The picture was **Them!** "That was the picture that changed my life. Hoyt Bowers was absolutely correct."

In the sci-fi classic **Them!**, Fess portrays Alan Crotty, a rancher confined to the psychiatric ward owing to his claims that he'd been buzzed by a flock of giant ants. Federal agent James Arness and scientists Edmund Gwenn and Joan Weldon call on Crotty after hearing of his report. To his amazement, they believe his account. It was a rather small but pivotal role. A good piece of acting with Fess pacing, hand-wringing and excitedly relating the details of his encounter with the killer insects.

Fess recalls that he didn't even have the whole script for **Them!** He went in and did his scene cold. "The director, Gordon Douglas, was really a nice fellow who'd come up through the prop department. He directed a lot of interesting pictures. A very good director who enjoyed better opportunities than, say, William Witney and some others."

According to Fess, Jack Warner didn't much care for **Them!** Fess claims it was under-promoted, "just sort of dumped out there." Yet the film was a sensation both domestically and abroad (hence his rather apt comparison to **My Big Fat Greek Wedding** as a picture that beat the odds), and many fans of science fiction regard it as one of the best in the genre. Fess does realize that the film is very highly regarded today as an exemplary horror film ... doesn't he? He seems mildly surprised. "I did not know that," he says. His surprise is surprising. "I do know that it broke records in Great Britain when it opened." **Them!** played to huge audiences the world over, but one viewer in particular made all the difference in Parker's life.

Walt Disney was looking for someone to portray legendary frontiersman Davy Crockett in a series of television films. Someone had told him to take a look at James Arness. "Jim and I worked in a picture with John Wayne called **Island in the Sky**. It was a William Wellman picture and it had every tall guy in the world in it. Andrew McLaglen was the assistant director. He was 6' 10". Jim Arness was 6' 8". John Wayne? I never knew how tall he was. 6' 2" or 6' 3" — but he photographed like he was huge. It was billed as 'the tallest cast in motion picture history.'"

Disney was in the process of scouting James Arness when he screened **Them!** to see Arness in action. "It was just an accident that Disney saw that scene and said, 'Who's that?'" — indicating Fess, of course. And the story *isn't* apochryphal. There's a witness. "The one man in the room with Disney when he said 'Who's that?' is Peter Ellenshaw, Disney's Academy Award-winning matte artist."

It took a week or so for Disney to track Parker down. "They'd never seen me before. But Tom Blackburn, who wrote the script for **Crockett,** knew David Weisbart. That's how they got my name." Parker must have done something that distracted Walt's

---

"Bloodless: That's why he wants yours!" The Black Scorpion

attention from Arness. "The way I always thought of it," Fess says modestly, "is that Disney said, 'Well, Jim Arness' salary is this much, and this kid's salary is how much?'"

Salary may have been a part of Disney's reasoning, but according to Fess, music and his blossoming talent as a songster played an important part in his getting the job. "I had a little funny-looking guitar — which I'll probably end up giving to my grandson some day — that I'd gotten out of a pawn shop. I couldn't play very well. All the songs I could play were in the key of C. I tended to write songs that I could sing in the key of C. So when I went on my first interview with Walt Disney, for some reason I brought my guitar. We went into this little office, just a desk, two chairs, phone. I put the guitar down. Mr. Disney said, 'Tell me about yourself.' Well, that didn't take too long, so he said, 'I see you have a guitar. Do you want to play me something?' I said 'Sure. Here's a little song I wrote. It's a song about the lonely sound of the train whistle. 'I lost my pal, I lost my gal, I hear the train whistle ...' I didn't know it at the time, but Mr. Disney was an absolute train nut. He had a train in his backyard. When he got home, he got on his locomotive and took the kids for a ride. You know, the high point in his film career should have been **Fantasia, Snow White** or some of those other pictures, but the one he had the most fun with was **The Great Locomotive Chase**." (Fess starred opposite Jeffrey Hunter in this Civil War spy adventure directed by Francis D. Lyon. "We were working with honest-to-God antique trains from the narrow-gauge B&O Railroad Museum. Baltimore & Ohio rolling stock.")

So, Walt was quite taken with the train tune Fess plucked on his old guitar, but Parker

> "The WAY I ALWAYS THOUGHT OF IT IS THAT DISNEY SAID, 'WELL, JIM ARNESS' SALARY IS THIS MUCH, AND THIS KID'S SALARY IS HOW MUCH?'"

"The amazing new audience thrill that makes you part of the show!" *The Hypnotic Eye*

had no idea where that spur-of-the-moment serenade would lead. "Bear in mind that Disney had made a lot of pictures with some pretty interesting music and they had often been asked to get into the recording business. I've heard that they'd been considering it for 30 years, but Roy Disney never liked the idea." Something about Parker's plaintive train song must have changed Disney's mind.

"When I first reported to start work on **Davy Crockett**, I was told to bring my guitar to the stage. There I met George Bruns, who wrote the melody to **The Ballad of Davy Crockett**. There were three guitars, including mine, and a bass, which George played. A few days earlier they had given me the lyrics to **The Ballad of Davy Crockett**. I have framed that sheet of paper," Fess smiles. "They had spelled my name F-E-Z. Fez Parker."

As they ran through the song that day, it was decided that the lyrics needed just a bit of tweaking. "They decided at the last minute that they didn't like the last line as written, so they substituted 'king of the wild frontier.'" The line scribbled hastily onto that lyric sheet became a catch-phrase that resounded through America's pop culture.

"Anyway, Disney thought I was a singer," Fess laughs. "I wasn't a singer. I just sat around and plunked on my guitar, but **The Ballad of Davy Crockett** was released as a promotional record and it took off. Archie Bleyer of Cadence Records contacted Disney and said he'd like to lease the master. Disney said no. Bleyer said, 'Can I cover it?' Disney said yes. So they had Bill Hayes sing it. I came along later with my version on Columbia records and it was No. 1 for four months. It was nominated for an Academy Award but

FILMS FEATURING FESS PARKER

Climb an Angry Mountain
1972
Smoky
1966
Daniel Boone (TV series)
1964
Mr. Smith Goes to Washington (TV series)
1962
Hell Is for Heroes
1962
The Jayhawkers!
1959
Alias Jesse James
1959
The Hangman
1959
The Light in the Forest
1958
Old Yeller
1957
Westward Ho the Wagons!
1956
Along the Oregon Trail
1956
The Great Locomotive Chase
1956
Battle Cry
1955
Davy Crockett, King of the Wild Frontier
1954
The Bounty Hunter
1954
Them!
1954
Dragonfly Squadron
1954
Thunder Over the Plains
1953
Island in the Sky
1953
The Kid from Left Field
1953
Take Me to Town
1953
Untamed Frontier
1952
Springfield Rifle
1952
No Room for the Groom
1952

"Beware the stare that will paralyze the will of the world!" Village of the Damned

171

the writers got it thrown out because it was done for a television movie."

Fess sang Disney a song about a train and became **Davy Crockett** while the actor who lost the role became immortal as Marshal Matt Dillon of **Gunsmoke**. America gained *two* pop culture heroes thanks to that pawn shop guitar.

But many actors, in addition to Arness, were in the running. "I didn't know who else was in contention until I got the part," says Fess. Also up for the role of Davy was Buddy Ebsen. "They were pretty serious about Buddy. Walt liked him. What wasn't there to like about Buddy? But a lot of leading actors were up for it. [Producer] Bill Walsh once showed me a list of everyone they'd considered. George Montgomery, Sterling Hayden. The list they showed me was a whole page, single spaced, of people they'd looked at." Ebsen landed the role of Davy's crusty sidekick, Georgie Russel, who never tires of singing Davy's praises. "There was never any animosity between Buddy and I over casting. We stayed in touch, we've been lifelong friends and I owe much to Buddy for providing me a solid performance for a relatively inexperienced actor to bounce off of."

Tom Blackburn's scripts were fairly accurate, historically speaking, and broached topics like the mistreatment of Native Americans and abuse of political power. But more importantly, they were accessible, vigorous adventures filled with fighting, shooting and broad humor, snappily directed by Norman Foster, one of Disney's most reliable workmen. "There was one thing Disney did, that nobody else did," Fess points out, "and I saw it over and over again, I think to my detriment — he hired people who were extremely anxious to do what *he* wanted them to do. He did not want a John Ford or a Henry Hathaway or anybody with a large reputation to do his films. He wanted to do those stories as *he* wished." Which explains why Disney so often entrusted his projects to the same coterie of directors — Foster for TV projects, Robert Stevenson for features and such veterans as William Beaudine and Charles Haas for just about everything else.

"The show won an Emmy," says Fess, "and I was nominated for newcomer of the year, but Lawrence Welk and I lost out to George Gobel." Emmys and Oscars were rendered meaningless by the success of **Davy Crockett**. The phenomena's impact cannot be overstated. Crocket-mania swept America and then the world. Stores couldn't keep coonskin hats in stock. As Leonard Maltin relates in his introduction to the Crockett DVD collection, the Beatles, **Star Wars** — *nothing* compares to the cultural impact felt

"All new and more horrific than before!" **Return of the Fly**

when a nascent medium began pumping **Davy Crockett** into millions of homes. "Walt Disney personally gave me a 10% cut of all Davy Crockett merchandise. I did receive some moneys but there was some intervening event that put it in the category of most studio actor expectations. I never pushed it, whatever it was ..." But 10% of the Crockett franchise, even if the deal covered only two years, or one, or six months, must have been substantial.

I've brought to our interview a color shot of Fess as Davy. I found it on eBay — along with about a zillion other Crockett-related collectibles. This is one I could afford, however. I show it to Fess as if to say, "See how influential you were? Collectors spend small fortunes on this stuff." He is aware. I'm embarrassed, but the picture sparks a memory and Fess smiles. "This picture was taken on a day when Walt Disney and his wife and another couple visited the set in Cherokee, North Carolina. Pat Hogan, who played Red Stick, the Indian, was wearing me out. Oh, God, he was a tough guy." I'm amazed at his facility for recalling and relating such details. Clearly he had a ball becoming Davy Crockett and still relishes the trivia and the memories and the people.

I produce a snapshot given to me by a buddy from Hollywood. It's a black-and-white shot of my friend and his brother, both dressed in full Davy regalia, taken nearly 50 years ago at the height of the Crockett hysteria.

I ask, "How many times have you been shown pictures like this?"

"Quite a few ... and thankfully. I want to tell you, if you're remembered for anything 50 years later, that's pretty remarkable."

"So weird, so shocking, do you dare see it?!" **Nightmare Castle**

"Don't come before dinner!" Teenage Frankenstein

THE VOICE OF REASON rex
REASON
MEETS THE B MONSTER

This Island Earth endures as one of filmdom's most respected attempts at intelligent science fiction. Its primary bow to convention, a lobster-clawed insectoid mutant with a bulging, exposed brain, may have once seemed a conciliatory gesture to bloodthirsty monster lovers. But even the

profile

Metaluna Mutant can be seen today as integral to the film's overall success. Lush Technicolor and smart

"Scream as you ride the wake of a fiery meteor!" Rocketship X-M

dialogue also lend to its relative "high-brow" standing in the genre. Likewise, the casting of a storybook-handsome, 25-year-old actor as the film's central character, Dr. Cal Meacham, helped ensure its commercial potential. Rex Reason, audience surrogate for the eye-popping voyage to the planet Metaluna, brought suave conviction to a part that many aspiring actors might have looked down on at the time.

It's only recently that Reason has begun to appreciate the halo of nostalgia that surrounds the movie. "In the past year and a half I've gone to four autographing conventions," he says. "I was just overwhelmed by the people's reaction. This one guy came up to me. He had a funny shirt on that showed all his muscles. I asked, 'Were you born with that or do you work out?' He said, 'I'm here because of you, Mr. Reason. You so impressed me when I was young, I wanted to be big and strong and have a voice like yours. I'm working on the voice. I don't have that yet.' Things like that are just as exciting as can be for me."

This Island Earth is still held in high regard by genre fans, and it's interesting to note that the sarcastic cineastes of TV's **Mystery Science Theater 3000** risked alienating a portion of their fan base by skewering the film in their big-screen debut. Reason said at a recent convention that he'd been invited to a screening, which he attended, joking that he'd slapped **MST3K** producers with a lawsuit on his way out.

Reason, who has long since focused his energies on endeavors other than acting, conveys genuine surprise that his film work is remembered so affectionately. "I was 25 years old when I did **This Island Earth**. I'm a different guy, now. You grow up after so many years. I left the business when I was 33. All I can talk about now is man's relationship to his higher self. That's all that's in my mind. I have to dig through that and

FILMS FEATURING REX REASON

The Roaring 20s (TV series)
1960
The Sad Horse
1959
Miracle of the Hills
1959
Man Without a Gun (TV series)
1958
Thundering Jets
1958
Rawhide Trail
1958
Badlands of Montana
1957
Under Fire
1957
Band of Angels
1957
Raw Edge
1956
The Desperadoes Are in Town
1956
The Creature Walks Among Us
1956
Lady Godiva
1955
Smoke Signal
1955
Kiss of Fire
1955
This Island Earth
1955
Taza, Son of Cochise
1954
Salome
1953
China Venture
1953
Mission Over Korea
1953
Storm Over Tibet
1952

"Fantastic fury strikes from outer space!" Target Earth

go back to when I was 25 years old when I discuss the films."

As a young actor, he breezed through movies of all genres — Western, drama, space opera — at a breakneck pace, and Reason recalls his days as an aspiring matinee idol as something of a passing fancy.

"My whole career was fun," he laughs. "It was in and out. At 22 years of age I got a lead in a picture called **Storm Over Tibet**. We shot it in nine days. From then on I just went from one contract to another."

His only other fright film appearance was a supporting role in **The Creature Walks Among Us**, the closing chapter of the Black Lagoon saga. But it is **This Island Earth** for which he is undoubtedly remembered best. "It was my third picture with Universal," he recalls, noting that the subject matter didn't strike him as outlandish in the least. "I thought that **This Island Earth** sounded plausible — because I believe in science fiction."

> "I THOUGHT THAT 'THIS ISLAND EARTH' SOUNDED PLAUSIBLE — BECAUSE I BELIEVE IN SCIENCE FICTION."

Much has been written of the film's innovative premise — citizens of a dying planet trick Earth's most intelligent scientists into helping them wage a civil war in space — and its ambitious depiction of life on another world. But casting is central to the film's appeal, and Reason's credibility is pivotal. In large measure, his sonorous voice, an incredible baritone of reassuring authority, accounts for his arresting screen presence. "But because I was always thinking about the voice," he relates, "I wasn't free enough on the screen. And as I quit the business young, I didn't really have a chance to grow into what my capacity was."

"Bloated with the blood of its victims!" **The Blob**

Did having such a beautiful, too-smooth-to-be-true voice ever work to his disadvantage? "It stopped me from getting voice-overs, believe it or not," Reason laughs. "They'd say, 'Too stentorian, Rex. You're not the average guy down the road.'"

Ironically, it wasn't until stardom seemed imminent that Reason decided to bow out of his film career. "I'd kind of drifted through the business until I found that they were really planning to launch me," he recalls. "I realized that I didn't want to be an actor, so I left. I bought out of my Warner Bros. contract."

Prior to his current endeavors as a California land developer, Reason took an interest in the field of inspirational spoken-word recordings. "I tried with spoken word 30-some years ago. I recorded four albums of inspirational recordings. But the word 'inspirational' keeps people from even considering them — because that word, like God or the Supreme Being, is so misused. I went to Capitol Records with my recordings. They didn't have any use for them because it was so unfamiliar to people at that time."

Now in his 70s, his real estate business prospering, Reason relishes the nostalgia that attends his former career, enjoying the fact that people remember his work. "Every day," he laughs, "I jog around the block. The guy that lives three doors down the street stopped me the other day." Reason had apparently been the subject of a radio call-in show. "Hey, Rex!" the neighbor shouted. "The other morning on the radio somebody asked if Rex Reason was dead." The neighbor rushed to a phone and called the station. "No, he's not dead," he assured them. "He's in great shape."

"From time unborn, a hideous she-thing!" **Terror From the Year 5,000**

GEORGE PAL'S WORLD WAR WONDER ann ROBINSON MEETS THE B MONSTER

Ann Robinson, the first woman in films to help stave off a Martian onslaught, began her brief but memorable movie career as the youngest stunt woman in Hollywood. The 17 year old took on stunt and extra work in order to attain status in the Screen Actors Guild. "I

profile

was an extra on **A Place in the Sun**," she recalls. "Fortunately, one day George Stevens said, 'Who has a SAG card here?' and I raised my hand

"Fantastic sea-giant crushes city!" Beast From 20,000 Fathoms

immediately because a lot of the extras weren't interested. I was lucky enough to be standing near Mr. Stevens. He said, 'Okay, stand over here, and when Liz Taylor walks through the door, say 'Hello Angela.' That was my debut."

"My first featured part," Robinson remembers, "was in **Goodbye My Fancy** with Joan Crawford. I went on an interview for that part, did a screen test and got it." Ms. Crawford's stormy reputation for intimidation was well-earned, according to Ann. "Boy! She came up and stood right next to the camera and the director during my screen test! If you can get through that you can get through anything — and I did. She was pretty nice to me. She was quite pleasant. She had a reputation for being a bit much to people she didn't care for."

Seasoned science fiction fans will recognize Robinson from her string of appearances on the kid vid space opera **Rocky Jones, Space Ranger**. "Oh, it was terrific," she smiles. "I got to play twin sisters." It was some time before the actress felt comfortable with the primitive special effects, which were the norm in television's infancy, especially when required to play opposite herself. "We did all this stuff with electronics, so you were very limited. You were standing there speaking to nothing. Or they would have a girl with her back to the camera that was very similar to your stature. I did nine episodes — they were an hour-and-a-half. They wanted to make them feature-length movies so you did three episodes and they spliced them together to make a feature-length movie. It sort of ran as a serial." When asked about Rocky himself, Richard Crane, there is little hesitation. "Oh, he was a nice man. Charming man. Very sweet, quiet. Just a nice person."

But it is Ann Robinson's full-throated portrayal of Sylvia Van Buren in George Pal's trendsetting adaption of **The War of the Worlds** for which she is best known. Perhaps no other actress has so impressed fans of the genre by virtue of a single performance. Trading on its strength alone, Robinson is today engaged in a hectic schedule of convention appearances. "They're so much fun," she sighs. "I love them and I love the

FILMS FEATURING ANN ROBINSON

Midnight Movie Massacre
1988
Attack of the B-Movie Monster
1985
The Fantasy Film Worlds of George Pal
1985
Imitation of Life
1959
Damn Citizen
1958
Julie
1956
Dragnet
1954
Bad for Each Other
1953
The Glass Wall
1953
The War of the Worlds
1953

"Beware the beat of the cloth-wrapped feet!" The Mummy's Shroud

people. It still amazes you when people come over and are absolutely hysterical to meet you. They're so gracious. Sometimes it's fun to watch the expression on their face and it dawns upon them that they're looking at all your pictures and you're sitting there. There was a wonderful man down in Memphis and he said, 'Oh, you surely have been blessed.' I loved the way he said it. I mean, I was one lucky girl. When you think of how this has lasted. **Destination Moon** doesn't grab the attention like **War of the Worlds**." The incredulity in Robinson's voice is unmistakable. "I was so lucky," she says of landing the lead in the classic thriller at the age of 17.

Ann makes it clear that she never tires of the fans' questions and seems energized when citing a few of the most common: "What was it like to have the monster put his hand on my shoulder? How was it done and who did it? What was it made of? That sort of thing." She is perhaps remembered best for that one spine-tingling scene wherein she turns slowly, realizing a hideous Martian is right behind her, her lovely face frozen in a mask of terror. "Everybody loves it, you know. They say, 'That expression on your face! You looked so frightened you couldn't scream!' I have a lot of criticism about screaming too much. I've had a couple of people say, 'I thought you'd never shut up.'"

The maturity of her screen presence belies Robinson's actual age at the time. You'd never suspect she was a teenager, learning as she went. "[Gene Barry] was quite a bit older than I. I was surprised. I think he was 30 years old when the movie was made and I was just a couple of months shy of 18. I had just graduated in January from high school, we started [the film] in February and, in May, I turned 18. I thought it was Gene Barry's best performance," she offers. "He never looked more handsome."

Perhaps the confidence in Robinson's portrayal is attributable in part to the encouraging atmosphere that pervaded the production. Ann recalls cast and crew working in harmony and, of producer George Pal, the driving force behind a handful of science fiction's finest film offerings, she has only the happiest memories. "He was the nicest person in the whole world and what a loss to the world to have him gone. What a genius and what a nice man. Never too busy to talk. He would stop whatever he was doing; he was a perfect gentleman. [You could] come visit him in his office or call him on the phone any time."

With a nostalgic sigh tempered by wry self-deprecation, Ann Robinson recalls her

"Rondo Hatton as Moloch, the Brute!" **Jungle Captive**

> "HE WAS THE NICEST PERSON IN THE WHOLE WORLD AND WHAT A LOSS TO THE WORLD TO HAVE HIM GONE."

departure from motion pictures. "In 1957, I ran off with a bullfighter, got married and had two children. Lived in Mexico for ten years. I ruined my own career. Shot myself in the foot. Absolutely ruined my career. I was terribly young and stupid. I didn't understand that it was a business. That I had a job. Warner Brothers about had a stroke when I told them I was going to run off. They had such plans for me."

Robinson remains among the most sought-after guests currently attending film conventions. "The leading ladies seem to be the ones that everybody identifies with," she says, "because she was always so pathetic. She's lost, poor thing. The man has to look after her. Not any more — now, you've got Sigourney Weaver!"

In the 1950s, sci-fi cinema was crowded with beautiful screamers voicing their alarm. Ann Robinson's blood-curdling shriek is one of many still ringing in the B Monster's ears, as there was a bevy of "shrieking violets" with whom she had to compete:

This Island Earth (1955)
Faith Domergue as Dr. Ruth Adams is justifiably repelled by the site of the lobster-clawed Metaluna mutant. She was probably just plain tired, as well — that same year she tangled with Ray Harryhausen's overgrown octopus in **It Came From Beneath the Sea**. Heck, you'd scream, too!

The Screaming Skull (1958)
Peggy Webber gives the eponymous Skull a real run for his money in this horror cheapie

"The motion picture with the fear flasher and the horror horn!" Chamber of Horror

about a scheming husband (John Hudson) and his attempts to drive his lovely bride bonkers. Directed by actor Alex Nicol, who portrays the slow-witted groundskeeper, Mickey, **The Screaming Skull** is nothing to shout about.

I Married A Monster From Outer Space (1958)

Gloria Talbott has reason to shriek (just look at the title!). Her beloved hubby, Tom Tryon, is possessed by an alien lifeform. In fact, darned-near every male in their social circle is similarly inhabited. There are some genuinely affecting shots in this creepy little gem directed by Gene Fowler Jr.

House On Haunted Hill (1959)

In what is probably the B Monster's favorite William Castle film, Carolyn Craig cuts loose with some window-rattling screams upon being startled (understandably) by, among other things, a disembodied head and the creepy, witch-like housekeeper who sneaks up behind her in a pitch black room.

"Maddened mastodons wage warfare to the death!" Two Lost Worlds

"The candle of his lust burnt brightest in the shadow of the grave!" The Horrible Dr. Hichcock

HOW TO MAKE A MONSTER
herb STROCK
MEETS THE B MONSTER

Herb Strock directed some of the most memorable drive-in shockers of the 1950s and '60s, including **I Was A Teenage Frankenstein, The Crawling Hand** and **Blood of Dracula**. He broke into pictures shooting the Fox Movietone newsreels and soon began the arduous, educational

profile

climb through the editing departments of the major film and TV studios. His television work alone would

"Warning: Those easily nauseated approach with caution!" The Werewolf vs. Vampire Woman

require a discussion twice as long as the one that follows. Says Herb of his TV directorial career: "I did so many Westerns I pleaded to get out from under the manure."

B MONSTER: How did you find your way into the science fiction and horror film genres?

HERB STROCK: [Producer] Ivan Tors moved over to where I had been working, which was Hal Roach Studios, and was going to do a picture called **The Magnetic Monster**. So he hired me as associate producer and film editor. And I was editing the picture three days into production when Ivan and [director] Curt Siodmak had some kind of a falling out. I never knew what. And Ivan got me into the Directors Guild and insisted that I take over the picture.

Q: How much of **The Magnetic Monster** did you direct?

HERB: It was a great deal of stock from a German picture, called **Das Gelde**, and Ivan had written a science fiction story around the stock footage. And who knows the stock footage better than the editor? So I took over and actually did, I would say, 90% or 95% of the movie, though I did not get credit on the screen nor in the posters, much to my chagrin. Ivan must have had his reasons.

Q: It's been said that Curt Siodmak was rather bitter and jealous of his brother Robert's standing in the industry. Was this your experience?

HERB: I really don't know what was in Curt's mind. Curt was a strange, European type of guy who always felt picked on. I felt terrible having replaced him three times in my life. He's never talked to me since, although he says he doesn't blame me.

Q: Did you work closely with Richard Carlson on the direction of **Riders to the Stars**?

HERB: Because I had done such a good job on **The Magnetic Monster** — the day after we finished shooting I had it in a rough cut and they were shocked and said to go ahead and cut negative – apparently I had hit a home run with them. Because Carlson was part owner and Carlson was involved in **Riders to the Stars**, I was made editor. Then Dick suggested I come down and direct the scenes he was in because he knew I had directed

"See the terror! Feel the shock! Live the horror!" Blood Suckers/Blood Thirst

him in the other show and he couldn't stand back and look at himself while he was in the shots.

Q: Apparently Carlson was a formidable talent in many regards. Did you find this to be true?

HERB: This was a wonderful experience because I worked with people like Martha Hyer, Bill Lundigan, Herbert Marshall. It was just a pleasure, and Dick of course was a writer, producer, director, film editor – a brilliant guy and I liked him – we were very good friends. Due to my editorial expertise, I was able to get things back on budget and try to keep the film flowing along. As it was, Dick went slightly over budget on the film.

Q: You also worked with Lundigan on an early **Science Fiction Theater** episode. What memories of him?

HERB: At ZIV [TV], I worked with Ivan on the pilot of **Science Fiction Theater** which starred William Lundigan, who I thought was a marvelous personality and a wonderful actor and a real great guy.

Q: Was **Gog** your first screen credit as a feature director?

HERB: I got in trouble with the Directors Guild because I put on the screen "Directed and Edited by" and they didn't like that at the time. When Ivan offered me **Gog**, which was to be shot with two cameras, which was double the expense, he asked me to please watch the dollars and try to make up the over-budget that Carlson had gone. Which

> "WE WOULD JUST ALTER WALLS AND CHANGE DOORWAYS AND MOVE THINGS AROUND. WE BROUGHT THE PICTURE IN WAY, WAY UNDER BUDGET.

eventually did happen, only due to the fact that I had a marvelous art director by the name of William Ferrari whom I'd known at MGM. This man and I devised sets, colors and gimmicks in order to save the cost of building sets. We would just alter walls and change doorways and move things around. We brought the picture in way, way under budget.

Q: Why was the film shot in 3D but released flat?

HERB: The picture looked great in 3D. When that little robot shot the flame out at the audience, people screamed. Why UA [United Artists] released it flat I will never know. Maybe it was cost.

Q: Do you recall an unusual story pertaining to **Gog** about a monkey?

HERB: This monkey was supposed to be frozen as an experiment and then be brought back to life. Well, we put the monkey down and we sprayed him with frost but he wouldn't go to sleep. Well, the trainer, Tony, gave him a shot and it didn't take effect. So he gave him another shot and then the Humane Society said you couldn't give him another shot. So Tony disappeared for awhile and later on I found out he bonked the monkey on the head, knocked him semi-conscious, put him down, we shot the shot, the monkey went out like a light. I hope the SPCA doesn't find out.

Q: You made three films for producer Herman Cohen. Is it true that everything had to be done his way?

HERB: We had our problems on I was a **Teenage Frankenstein**. Herman was a very pontific type of producer, but he knew I always came in on budget and that's what he was looking for. After I did [**Teenage Frankenstein**] I never thought I'd worked for him again.

Q: What became of **Blood of Dracula** star, Sandra Harrison?

HERB: She came out here about three or four years ago, looked me up and we went to lunch and talked. I couldn't believe the woman. She became dumpy. I guess she's an entertainer with her sister. Never did another picture as far as I know. She was an oddball

"He was a country boy, but he played the wildest strings in this mad town." Wild Guitar

to start with and that's why I thought she'd be good for the picture.

Q: Did Whit Bissell give 100 percent, even on offbeat films like **Teenage Frankenstein** which some actors of his standing might consider beneath them?

HERB: I'm sorry about Whit Bissell. He passed away this year. He always gave more than 100%. He worked with you, he was always there. He reminded me so much of working with Boris Karloff. This was a man who was like a horse at the post. Ready to go, knew the lines, always on time, always ready, prepared, in the character. He was a dream to work with. Phyllis Coates also was darn good. She really worked hard, though I don't know whatever became of her.

> "WE DIDN'T PUT CORNY DIALOGUE IN IT, WE PUT SMARTASS DIALOGUE IN IT, WHICH WAS HERMAN'S IDEA."

Q: The film seemed to be leavened with intentionally corny dialogue. Was that your idea?

HERB: We didn't put corny dialogue in it, we put smartass dialogue in it, which was Herman's idea. Like, "Speak to me, you have a civil tongue in your head, I sewed it in there myself." Which people howled at.

Q: Just as in **Teenage Frankenstein**, the final scene of **How to Make a Monster** is in color. Was this difficult to achieve?

HERB: The color at the end of these pictures was [producer] Herman Cohen's gimmick and we always had to plan this as a separate reel. You can't intermix color and black and white because one would be out of focus while the other would be in focus. So we planned this very, very carefully. It was a lot of fun working with Herman. We got along fine.

Q: The cast of **The Crawling Hand** seemed to be a mixed bag of veterans and novices.

"Savage from shocking start to surprising end" The Wicked Go To Hell

Did this cause any problems?

HERB: **The Crawling Hand** was a strange experience. Joe Robertson went to a distributor with a screenplay he wanted to do. The screenplay was not that good. The distributor asked me to read it and I said no, I didn't think it would go. But I showed Joe a script I had been working on with some friends, called **The Crawling Hand**, and he fell in love with it. We were off and running with a $100,000, black-and-white movie. I knew in order to sell this picture we'd need some names. So I called on Arline Judge, Richard Arlen, Alan Hale. People I had worked with on **Science Fiction Theater**.

Q: Burt Reynolds read for a part in that film. Why didn't it work out?

HERB: I wanted Burt Reynolds, who came and read for me but he read so badly I thought I'd die. I gave him a second crack at it and he was no better. I told him he wasn't ready to be an actor, which he never forgave me for. I got suckered into Kent Taylor, a radio actor who was great, as long as he was reading. When it came time to do the show, he was never on time, he was always late; I don't know if he was drinking. But he wasn't there — his mind wasn't there. He didn't know the lines and he created tremendous editorial problems for me.

Q: You shot a nude scene for **The Crawling Hand** for foreign release only. Why?

HERB: I don't know how the hell you found out about this. Sirry Steffen was a very strange young lady. She was Miss Iceland and she was a cold tomato. But she had a body that had no ending. When I did this foreign version, I wanted one nude scene which they said you needed for a foreign picture which is a lot of baloney. She wouldn't let anybody be there except me and the cameraman and she allowed me and only me to put the body makeup on her. That's one for the books.

Q: Whose hand was **The Crawling Hand**?

HERB: There was a mechanical hand, which our special effects guy, Charlie Duncan, made, which had a motor in it and had little prongs on the fingertips and it would work great on the rug. But the minute it got to the floor, or crawling up the balcony, it had to be either the producer or me. So we used our hands and just put a sleeve on it. It [the

"His secret was a coffin named desire!" The Horrible Dr. Hichcock

mechanical hand] kept getting stuck, it kept slipping — drive ya nuts.

Q: TV's **Mystery Science Theater 3000** once featured **The Crawling Hand** as the butt of its special brand of acerbic commentary. Does this anger you, or do you have any reaction to it at all?

HERB: This doesn't anger me. I didn't see it. I don't care about it. It doesn't mean a thing. The picture stands up. In fact, parts of it were used in a foreign film a year ago, which was run at the Academy. I was shocked to see my hand making the motions on the beach with Sirry Steffen running in the background.

Q: The diversity of your television work is amazing. Which do you prefer, film or TV work?

HERB: It has been amazing, even to me. I do prefer film rather than TV because you have a greater chance to look at things in depth, to explain things, to go into backgrounds, to create more. In TV you're always running, especially on a half-hour show. And I did two half-hour shows a week, every week at ZIV for five years.

Q: What role did you play in developing the semi-documentary procedural format for **Dragnet**?

HERB: Joe Eisenger, who had written a show called **The Cases of Eddie Drake** which I had worked on, knew Jack and he recommended me. I met Jack and I met Homer Canfield, vice president of NBC, and they hired me to direct the pilot and edit it. Of course Jack, being the stubborn nut that he was, had to go through experiments with blue shirts and green makeup – different types of film, different types of lighting, which I had already been through in my television experience. But he wouldn't listen.

FILMS DIRECTED BY HERB STROCK

Monster
1979
Brother on the Run
1972
The Crawling Hand
1963
Rider on a Dead Horse
1962
The Devil's Messenger
1961
The Alaskans (TV Series)
1959
Men Into Space (TV Series)
1959
Bonanza (TV Series)
1959
77 Sunset Strip (TV Series)
1958
How to Make a Monster
1958
Sea Hunt (TV Series)
1958
Blood of Dracula
1957
I Was a Teenage Frankenstein
1957
Colt .45 (TV Series)
1957
Maverick (TV Series)
1957
The Man Called X (TV Series)
1956
Highway Patrol (TV Series)
1955
Battle Taxi
1955
Science Fiction Theater (TV Series)
1955
Gog
1954
Riders to the Stars
1954
The Magnetic Monster
1953
Sky King (TV Series)
1951

"Guts as hard as the steel of their 'hogs'!" **She-Devils on Wheels**

Q: The episodes of **Science Fiction Theater** directed by you are the most interesting and coherent in the series. Do you remember them fondly?

HERB: I loved doing **Science Fiction Theater** because those pictures used a better-caliber cast. We had better names, we had wonderful actors. We had better sets. We had a little more money. You could create. You could get angles. You could do things that other people didn't do. And I never went over budget. I always brought my pictures in on time or under time and under budget. Because I planned them. I'm a firm believer in pre-planning. Everything I do, even today, is planned out to the Nth detail.

Q: Do you have a favorite among your films?

HERB: When I did some of these horror pictures, my kids wouldn't talk to me ... and now they're cult films. I don't have a favorite, really. I don't really enjoy doing horror pictures. I don't enjoy doing science fiction pictures. I like doing something that says something. I like to do something with heart and humor.

Q: What keeps you busy these days?

HERB: I'm editing a movie which starts in a couple of weeks. It'll be shot in New York. I'm editing a short right now. I just finished editing two feature pictures. And I'm working with students from USC, UCLA and The American Film Institute. I'm writing a book, which is called **Everyone Has Two Businesses**, which is show business and their own. I hope to have it out within six months.

Q: What lies ahead for Herb Strock?

HERB: I'd love to direct a feature picture. I guess everybody looks at me like I'm one of the old dinosaurs. But I know I can do it faster and I know I can do it better than most people because I've had the experience.

"The most amazing picture of the year!" The Amazing Transparent man

HORROR OF PARTY BEACH: A SHORE THING
del TENNEY
MEETS THE B MONSTER

Del Tenney sounds like a contented man, warm and self-assured as he desribes his past life in the movie business, and his present life dabbling in theater and managing a solid real estate business. The man who put Stamford, Connecticut, on the B-movie map currently

profile

enjoys the comfort of several homes around the country, and speaks with good humor of his days as a director. He spins the story of his

"They turned a white hell red with enemy blood!" *Ski Troop Attack*

best-known film, **The Horror of Party Beach** with candor. The story of some rubber suits, a motorcycle gang and a group of friends who banded together to make a million dollars.

Tenney's story doesn't start in Connecticut, however. "I'm a California boy. Born in Iowa, actually. Mason City, Iowa. When I was 11, my mother and father took my brother and I out to California."

The stage interested Del early on. "I started acting in California. I went to Los Angeles City and State College, which was in those days — the '40s and '50s — the foremost theater acting school in California, even above and beyond Pasadena Playhouse. I was there with people like Alan Arkin, Bob Vaughn, Jim Coburn and Hugh O'Brian."

Tenney migrated east with several stock companies, playing on- and off-Broadway in some 300 productions. "Then my wife and I started a theater here in Stamford called the Harvest Theater."

Del broke into filmmaking as an assistant director on a handful of exploitation flicks with titles like **Orgy at Lil's House**. "I was assistant director on that and I was in it."

Next, Tenney tried his hand at directing an exploitation-horror quickie. Originally titled **Violent Midnight**, **Psychomania** was made for $42,000. It recouped this sum and made money, demonstrating Del's ability to produce an effective drive-in hit with a limited pocketbook. His talent for turning a profit on a limited investment impressed some big-time studio execs. "I did two films for 20th Century-Fox. They picked them up. **The Horror of Party Beach** and **The Curse of the Living Corps**e. I did **Curse** first, in two weeks. Both films cost me $120,000. I did both films, two weeks shooting with actors, then I did a lot of fill-in stuff. Did them here in Stamford, Connecticut, in the old Gutzon Borglum studios." (Borglum was the renowned sculptor, famed for his final project, Mount Rushmore.) "He had an estate out here and my father-in-law bought it. He developed the land and kept the studio. I did most of my films there, if not all of them."

Once more, with a very slim budget ever in mind, Tenney turning out an applaudably creepy, if threadbare B film. "We did **Curse** — which was not a bad little picture –

"Hideous, horrifying maniacs, psychos and fiends seek revenge!" **Nightmare Blood Bath**

certainly for two weeks' work. It starred Roy Scheider, and my wife, Margot, was in it." **Curse** was Scheider's screen debut. "I did some shows with him off-Broadway," says Tenney, "and you know, the theater business is quite small. That was his first film . . . and I always thought he was so right for that role, a kind of wonderful villain. And I had worked with Robert Milli who was also in it, who played the husband who got dragged by the horse. That was all shot in the Gutzon Borglum studio. I showed that to 20th Century-Fox. They were looking for something for drive-ins that summer. Summer of '64. They thought it was fine and I was already in pre-production for **Horror of Party Beach**. They said, 'Well, if it's anything like this one, we'll take them as a package.' What they meant was they were going to take them around to all those schlock drive-ins where they had to fill screens."

> "THE PRESIDENT OF 20TH CENTURY-FOX SCREAMED FROM THE BATHROOM, 'YOU SON OF A BITCH, TENNEY! I'M GONNA HAVE A HEART ATTACK!'"

Tenney remembers the unintentional comedy that accompanied one preview screening. "I finished **Horror of Party Beach** and the funniest thing happened. The day we screened it for the 20th Century-Fox executives, I had Robert Verberkmoes, our set designer, in the monster costume in the bathroom, the executive bathroom of 20th Century-Fox. We're all in the screening room just about to get started, and the president of 20th Century Fox screamed from the bathroom, 'You son of a bitch, Tenney! I'm gonna have a heart attack!' He'd come out in this costume, out of the booth, and scared the hell out of him. They all laughed. All the executives thought that was the funniest thing."

The importance of the drive-in theater to the success of filmmakers like Tenney cannot be overestimated. In fact, for many independent producers, the drive-in was an integral

---

"He comes to life to the sounds of rock & horror!" Teenage Dracula

part of their original pitch to distributors. As Del recalls, "[Fox] said 'Okay, we'll try it out in Houston and Dallas in back-to-back drive-ins.' On the other side of the screen was **Move Over Darling** and **PT 109**. That's about $15-to-$20 million worth of film. In those days that was big budget. And here's my little $110,000 wonders. What sold them was my associate producer Alan Iselin. The reason I got involved with him, he was a friend of the family. My wife's family came from Albany and he was from Albany and he had about 13 drive-in theaters up there and he was looking for product. He'd shown my **Psychomania** and it was quite successful. He said, 'I'd like to go into partnership with you,' so he came up with half the money. He developed a sales gimmick called a 'fright release.' Anybody who came to the theater had to sign a 'fright release,' a big deal that exonerated the company, and the drive-in, should anybody have a heart attack. To make a long story short, they played it on a weekend with **Move Over, Darling** and **PT 109** and we out-grossed them double."

> "ANYBODY WHO CAME TO THE THEATER HAD TO SIGN A 'FRIGHT RELEASE,' A BIG DEAL THAT EXONERATED THE COMPANY SHOULD ANYBODY HAVE A HEART ATTACK."

Tenney's twin features did land office business in their initial drive-in tryout. 20th Century-Fox was thrilled, and Stamford's favorite film son was on his way to cult-movie immortality. "I think they only had about a hundred prints printed at that point. I think they went up to 700 prints apiece. It was a big smash over the summer. And it closed the Paramount Theater the next year in Times Square. I have a picture of Alan and me standing in front of the marquee."

"Roaring guns against raging monster!" Jesse James Meets Frankenstein's Daughter

The Horror of Party Beach details the carousing of a band of toxically-bred algae zombies, the remains of sunken seafarers, reanimated by nuclear waste. Strangely, their appetites limit them to devouring only nubile young women. In the film's most notorious sequence, nearly a dozen are slain at a pajama party, albeit discreetly off screen. The sequence gave rise to something of a B movie urban legend concerning a bit of nudity that got by the censors. It never happened according to Tenney, but "I'm glad there's a myth," he hastens to add.

With the buffer of 35 years and an ongoing flow of residuals to comfort him, Del Tenney recalls the less-than-party atmosphere that dogged his best-known production. "There were a lot of incidents that happened. I got the flu during it. I was directing the thing from the bedroom, practically. Then there was an accident in the motorcycle-car race. We were using Charter Oaks [Motorcycle Club] as the bad boys of the motorcycle gang. I had gotten releases from everybody so if anything happened I would not be responsible either for their lives or for their motorbikes. This guy from the back of the pack thought he was going to be cute and speed up to the front. He clipped this guy's handlebars and over he went. The guy who was playing the lead of the motorcycle pack happened to be an actor who happened to like motorcycles. He went over and the bike went on top of him and we thought he had a broken back. I had to go ahead and change the whole shooting schedule. And on the way to the accident, the police car got into an accident. The mayor of Stamford said, 'Tenney, I don't think you'd better make any more films in Stamford.' That was the end of my Stamford shooting."

But the drafted cast of bikers wasn't quite through with Del Tenney. "We were filming in this room off the Gutzon Borglum studio — this is after the accident — and I hear this roar of motorcycles. There must have 20 of them. Huge, big Harleys out in the driveway coming to a stop, and I thought, 'Uh oh, they're after me. They're after me. I'm a dead duck.' So I get this sort of shy knock on this big door. So I go and they say, 'Del, could you please show us some of the rushes?' They sat there the whole night watching this gory mess of these guys poring into each other. They were going probably 50 mph. Flying all over the place, the whole pack of them. It put about five guys in the hospital. They wanted to see the accident so the editor kept running it over and over and over ... I said, 'Okay, that's enough,' after about an hour and a half, two hours."

Like a twanging Greek chorus, a surf-rock band called the Del-Aires keeps **Party**

"Blood hungry spawn of the world's most bestial fiend!" Daughter of Dr. Jekyll

Beach hopping, bracketing suspenseful scenes with beach ditties. "I think they were from Jersey, if I'm not mistaken," recalls Tenney. "They were a group that was pretty popular at the time. Actually, I think there was a record out of **Horror of Party Beach** music. I don't know whether it exists any more or not. I never got it but I understand there was." One doesn't soon forget **The Zombie Stomp**. ("You bring your foot down with an awful clomp!") or the sand and surf lament, **You Are Not a Summer Love**. "I don't know whatever became of them," muses Del. "People have asked me that before. I have no idea. I would assume that they broke up." [Ed. They did. But fans of the film and the group have tracked down band members and there is a Del-Aires Web site.]

The monster costumes were engaging and imaginative, if none too intimidating. An impromptu casting call determined who would wear them. "We had the assistant director. The fellow, Robert Verberkmoes, was my art director. He did a lot of the work. And whoever would happen to be around that it fit." The skulking sea-monsters weren't the only crew members doing double duty. Costumer Dina Harris is seen as one of an ill-fated trio of girls, and Tenney himself appears as a goofy gas station attendant. Del speculates as to the present whereabouts of his monstrous cast: "Bob is in Europe. Lenny De Munde the cameraman is out in California. I really can't tell you. I used a lot of people in a crew in Stamford. They're all grown up now, that's for sure. That was '63. That was 35 years ago. They're all my age."

When complimented, Tenney is modest. When told his film is recognized as a tidy, titillating B shocker that stands the test of time, Del laughs, "Oh. It's a terrible film! I did it as a camp and you know it. It was done off the cuff. Now it's a cult thing. The college kids are still going for it. I made my first million on those two pictures. Disney [has since] bought them, and they're on the Sci Fi Channel. Disney shows them down at Disneyworld in their restaurants. They gave me $10,000 a picture."

How many filmmakers go out on top? Del Tenney did. With a small fortune tucked in his belt, he quietly moved on to other, similarly profitable, enterprises. "Corman and Peter Cushing and all those people over at Hammer, they started making pictures in color and I was onto other things. I had to get more involved with the real estate business and I wanted to go back to the stage."

Tenney may be on to other things, but the world has not forgotten his budget-minded

"Man-monster from the slimy depths!" **The Monster of Piedras Blancas**

contributions to film history. "As a matter of fact, somebody's written a sequel to **Horror of Party Beach**. It's being passed around Hollywood right now by Castlerock and a subsidiary of Disney. I have the script somewhere and I okayed the script. What I would do is be executive producer on it. They would want their own director, which is fine. So that's being tossed around and there's a lot of people interested in it. It's a good script, actually."

Tenney doesn't live in the past, nor does he have any regrets about his career choices. And he still rubs shoulders with show biz pals now and then. "I bumped into Roy Scheider. He had a house down in Key West and I had a house in Marathon. I ran into Bob Vaughn. He lives near here in Westport." And what of Del's original band of beach partyers? "Those were buddies of mine. Actually, we're going out this weekend with [**Party Beach** star] Alice Lyon. She was my wife's roommate at Bennington. She was married to the brother of Jackie Kennedy."

Del is completely at peace with his place in B-movie history. "All my friends said 'How could you make those terrible films?' Easy! I laugh all the way to the bank." Label his tongue-in-cheek, beach party shocker "camp" and he won't be insulted. Del Tenney did the math and made exactly the film he set out to make. Go ahead and laugh. He made a million dollars.

Del Tenney's limited but lasting body of cult-film work is worth recounting as much for its economic ingenuity as for any intrinsic merit. With budgets pared to the bone, he delivered a handful of thrillers that are vividly recalled by those who saw them at an impressionable age:

VIOLENT MIDNIGHT AKA PSYCHOMANIA (1963)
Tenney and his wife Margot (who also starred) loosely based their screen treatment on the real-life murder of a Connecticut coed. Though tame by today's standards, this modest shocker was considered quite lurid at the time of its release.

"Doll dwarfs versus the giant crushing beasts!" **Attack of the Puppet People**

The Curse of the Living Corpse (1964)

Tenney transformed sculptor Gutzon Borglum's Connecticut spread into a Victorian estate for this shocker detailing the varied and grisly deaths of several members of a vindictive New England clan. A young Roy Scheider (his screen debut) and Candace **Carnival of Souls** Hilligoss star.

I Eat Your Skin aka Voodoo Blood Bath aka Zombie (1964)

Don't let the multiple titles confuse you. Tenney filmed this flimsy thriller on location near Miami, telling the locals it was a sophisticated spy romp called **Caribbean Adventure**. The film was later sold to another distributor who retitled the film **I Eat Your Skin** to co-bill with **I Drink Your Blood**.

"Was she one of the green blooded people?" Creation of the Humanoids

THE FIRST SEX KITTEN IN CYBERSPACE mamie VAN DOREN MEETS THE B MONSTER

This platinum queen of the drive-in screen resents being categorized with all the other buxom, blonde bombshells of the 1950s and '60s. The way she sees it, rock 'n' roll set her apart. Her proximity to the pioneers of the emerging rock music scene — Elvis, Eddie

profile

Cochran, Gene Vincent, et al. — gave her image a rebellious edge the others never aspired to. "I was always noted as an '**Untamed Youth**'

"Deep inside the earth, a lost civilization, a million years old!" The Mole People

type," Mamie says, referring to her cult-classic film of the same name. "I love that movie. That was my favorite. Even better than **Teacher's Pet** with Clark Gable." The Gable vehicle featured Mamie's corny, hip-swinging show-stopper **The Girl Who Invented Rock and Roll**, but the brassy night club number was a far cry from the rough and raucous music she loved best.

You've likely heard about the flings with Elvis and Eddie Cochran, Warren Beatty and Burt Reynolds; about bullet bras, see-through tops and **Playboy** centerfolds. Though she's banked on frankness and flamboyance throughout a near-50-year career (nipple-printed, autographed photos are available at her Web site), she still manages to surprise us with an outrage or two that she's held in reserve over the years. Even though her sensational autobiography **Playing the Field** (soon to be re-published with passages previously deemed too risque restored) broke new ground among tell-all books, there were stories left untold. "I want the fans to know that I'm not one of these so-called ex-glamour queens that's hibernating and is afraid to go out into the world and have anybody see them," she says. We're not about to temper the prose of this gracious and outgoing D-cup diva who relishes the opportunity to go on the record.

B MONSTER: You've often described yourself as ahead of your time. Now you're "The First Sex Kitten In Cyberspace." Whose idea was that?

MAMIE: We didn't just hire somebody. My husband and I did the Web site together. I've been into computers for a long time. When I wrote my book **Playing the Field** in '86 and '87, it was on a little teeny computer.

Q: What's the reaction been like?

MAMIE: There was an item in Liz Smith's column. She gave me a real good plug. **Entertainment Tonight** is going to do a story on me because of it. I asked my publicist, "Why are they doing it?" He said that they saw Liz Smith's column and they checked out the Web site. The e-mail is incredible. Don't even ask me how many. God, and I've got to answer them all. I'm surprised that I've only sold about six nipple prints and a couple dozen photographs [through the site]. But I'm not really counting on the site [to make money].

"The world's first horror movie made in hallucinogenic hypno-vision!" **The Maniacs Are Loose**

Q: Does it give you more control over you public image?

MAMIE: It's a way to reach your fans and the people who've followed you all their life. I want to get myself across to people because they're always reading about me through the eyes of someone else.

Q: The Vietnam section of the site contains details about the time you spent there that may be a revelation to many fans.

MAMIE: [Over the years] I would get notes from guys who would say, "Mamie, you really helped me get through that hell in Vietnam." Stuff like that would really make me feel good. I was rummaging through my garage and I ran across the spiral notebooks I would write in while I was in Vietnam. It started bringing back all these memories. So many kids who were over there are in their 50s now, and they're really into the computer world. On top of that, my husband and I have written a script called **Star in Eclipse** based on my adventures in Vietnam. It's about survival. It was 1968 when I went over — after Jayne Mansfield had gotten killed and Marilyn was gone — and I couldn't get a job. It was really bad. I just wanted to disappear. I thought the best place for that would be Vietnam. When I got over there, I hit every fire station. Bob Hope didn't have the balls to go to the places I went. He'd fly in and out to Bangkok and sleep. I slept right on the front line. If the North Vietnamese came close, the general had a helicopter waiting to take off in a hurry, and I would ask, "Do you have room for another person?" We had some real close calls. There were

> "I COULDN'T GET A JOB. IT WAS REALLY BAD. I JUST WANTED TO DISAPPEAR. I THOUGHT THE BEST PLACE FOR THAT WOULD BE VIETNAM."

different guys who I just knew by their first names, and I'm hoping I'll hear from them on the Internet.

Q: Tell me about the script.

MAMIE: It's been out there for about a year now. It's been close to a deal so many times. The story is all true, but I elaborate on certain issues. It's about an actress who goes to Vietnam because she wants to commit suicide. She's tried before. But then she goes over there and sees all these kids trying to survive. It was a lesson that made me the woman I am today. War up close is horrendous. When I first went over there, I thought we had a right to be there — but no way! No one seemed to care. It was a war that people got rich on. All that young blood was shed. Blood money.

Q: Who would you cast as Mamie Van Doren?

MAMIE: I tried to think of who could play me. The first one I thought of was Patricia Arquette. My manager sent her the script, and she said she wanted to play it. She was my first choice because she's a good actress. She's blonde and she's sexy and I just saw **Lost Highway** and I thought she was really great. She wants to do it. And Rebecca De Mornay wants to do it. I've got to find someone who's a good actress. But finding someone who has the glamour to go with it is very difficult. I sent the script to Madonna, not knowing whether she ever read scripts or not. Lo and behold, my manager called and said, "Madonna likes the script!" We were really close to a deal, when all of a sudden she got a new manager [who changed her mind]. Madonna sent me a really nice letter and told me that she really would have liked to have played it — but she was really into motherhood now, and she wanted to make a change to the groove that she was in now and forego the platinum blonde, glamour thing.

Q: You've appeared with everyone from Mickey Rooney to Francis, the Talking Mule. Who were the best to work with?

MAMIE: The nicest guys were Jeff Chandler and Clark Gable. But I had a hard time working with most men. I hate to talk about myself, but they don't want a sexy woman to play opposite them. They want a down-home kind of woman so it doesn't take away from them. But Gable liked anything that was sexy because he was sexy and he had

"World of women seeking male partners to carry on race!" **Fire Maidens From Outer Space**

confidence in himself. Even at his age — he was in his 60s when we did **Teacher's Pet** and I was 24. It didn't matter. He still had the confidence. He knew how to hold you in his arms, he knew how to kiss you. **Yankee Pasha** with Jeff Chandler was my second movie and I had to do a screen test. Jeff helped me get that role. He said, "I think you'd be perfect for it." But some of the guys I've dated want to die in their own arms, like Warren Beatty and Burt Reynolds.

Q: You're often thought of as one of the three great sex symbols of the '50s, Marilyn Monroe and Jayne Mansfield being the others.

MAMIE: You can't really compare me to Marilyn Monroe and Jayne Mansfield because I was so different. I was doing all those young movies. Marilyn was doing quite mature movies with mature men and Jayne was doing a caricature of Jayne. I was really into learning how to act. I had a wonderful acting coach, I took private lessons, I went to classes, I lived the role. I wanted to be a good actress. I didn't go out that much. I didn't go to premieres. And I've always felt that I was way ahead of my time. Hollywood is still conservative, as far as I'm concerned. If I wear a see-through top, it's like a big deal. I wanted to do that in the '50s.

Q: So, the comparison is unfair?

MAMIE: I just want people to recognize that I've always been different from the other girls — a maverick or a rebel — and that did stop me from doing a lot of things that I could have done. I guess I never went to bed with the right people. I went to bed with the ones I wanted to go to bed with.

Q: Did your love of rock 'n' roll make for any personal or professional problems?

MAMIE: I was married to an orchestra leader, Ray Anthony, at the time I did **Untamed Youth**, and he hated it because it was rock 'n' roll. The very thing that was making me successful was ruining his whole scene. He was into that Glenn Miller sound and I really wasn't into that.

Q: Who were some of your favorite recording artists at the time?

"It reaches from the grave to re-live the horror, the terror!" Frankenstein's Daughter

MAMIE: I liked Eddie Cochran and I liked Elvis Presley, who always came to see me when I was in Vegas. He'd just done **Love Me Tender**. He finished the movie and he came to see me at the Riviera where I was starring. It was kind of interesting. We went to see Sam Butera and Louis Prima at the Sahara. He was a fun date. But I couldn't continue because I was married and Ray would have killed me.

Q: Do you still listen to rock 'n' roll?

MAMIE: You're going to think I'm crazy, but I like Marilyn Manson. I think he's outrageous with all that devil stuff. I think he's very talented and artistic. I liked Madonna's **Ray of Light.** She's always been my favorite.

> "I WAS REALLY THE FIRST FEMALE TO DO ROCK 'N' ROLL ON THE SCREEN. ACTUALLY I WAS THE FIRST ANYBODY TO DO ROCK 'N' ROLL IN A GOOD MOVIE."

Q: Do you remember recording a novelty tune called **Bikini With No Top on the Top** with June "The Body" Wilkinson?

MAMIE: She didn't even sing on that. I did all the dubbing. I sang three times over my own voice. She was there trying to sing but I actually did all the singing.

Q: Why is **Untamed Youth** your favorite film?

MAMIE: I was really the first female to do rock 'n' roll on the screen. The very first. Actually I was the first anybody to do rock 'n' roll in a good movie. Eddie Cochran came up with the song **Ooh-Ba-La Baby** and Les Baxter did some of the songs — **Feel Like a Rolling Stone** and **Salamander**. I wanted to sing **You Ain't Gonna Make a Cotton Picker Outta Me**, but Eddie wouldn't give it to me. The music just came so natural to

"A mighty panorama of earth-shaking fury!" War of the Worlds

me. [Director] Howard Koch wasn't really into rock 'n' roll at that time. He said, "Mamie, do you know how to do rock 'n' roll?" I said, "Sure." I knew boogie woogie and I'd danced when I was a kid. I choreographed those numbers myself with the help of a dancer who was appearing in **Damn Yankees**. For a woman to do rock 'n' roll on the screen — it was unheard of. And I've never been given credit as the first one.

Q: The film was fairly controversial. What had everybody up-in-arms?

MAMIE: The script was great, from a paperback that was pretty successful. But everybody was putting it down. We couldn't get the Catholic Legion of Decency to approve it, and Warner Bros. was having a hell of a time. Cardinal Spellman was giving me a bad time. He just didn't like me because I'd done **Girls Town, Beat Generation** — all the movies with any cleavage featured Mamie Van Doren. He really f—ked me over, pardon the expression. He was gay, he'd turn his collar around and go out and raise hell, and then he'd put me down. That really pissed me off. The religious right was hot and heavy in those days. They still are.

Q: Any memories of the cast?

MAMIE: Lori Nelson and I had worked together in **All American** at Universal. She was always Miss Goody Two-Shoes and I was the bad girl. In real life, I was probably the Goody Two-Shoes. It's always the women that look pure who really know how to do it. Yvonne Lime, who played Baby, was dating Elvis Presley and went on to marry someone with a lot of money. Jeanne Carmen? No comment on her. No comment.

Q: You and Eddie Cochran were close?

MAMIE: Yeah, *real* close. He'd come to my house and we'd rehearse the songs. He'd come down to the rumpus room of our little two-story Spanish home. The pool table was there — let the imagination work.

Q: What do you recall about Al Zugsmith, producer of **Girls Town** and **The Beat Generation**?

MAMIE: When I first met Al Zugsmith at Universal Studios, I was at lunch in the

"Centuries of passion pent up in his savage heart!" **Creature From The Black Lagoon**

commissary, sitting with Rock Hudson and Tony Curtis. I'd heard about him — he'd just been signed to do X number of movies — and you always want to try and touch base with new producers, because if they have a script, they'll think of you. He came walking by and I said, "Hello, Mr. Smith." Tony said, "Why did you call him Mr. Smith? Why don't you call him by his first name?" I said, "I don't know him well enough to call him Zug." It was just a real dumb blonde remark. Rock and Tony fell off their chairs, and I didn't know what they were laughing about. That was the beginning of my relationship with Mr. Al Zugsmith. He was way ahead of his time. He wanted to do outlandish things and I was part of that whole scene. He hired Paul Anka and Jerry Lee Lewis — he was way out there. I never considered any of his movies "B." MGM and Warner Bros. put them out. But somewhere along the line somebody said that I was the Queen of B Movies.

Q: Any memories of filming **Girls Town**?

MAMIE: The one song I had in **Girls Town** was taken out. Paul Anka wrote it for me. Really a cute number sung in the shower. Nothing showed, I was just taking a shower and singing. But Cardinal Spellman wouldn't allow it to be put in, and Zugsmith had to go along with MGM. That was a hard movie for me to do because I had the flu. I was working with a 102 fever and I was burning up all the time. I had the responsibility of the entire movie on my back. I was the lead, and I was in every scene.

Q: There seems to be a growing cult of fans who love **The Girl In Black Stockings**.

SELECTED FILMS FEATURING MAMIE VAN DOREN

Free Ride
1986
The Arizona Kid
1971
Voyage to the Planet of Prehistoric Women
1968
Las Vegas Hillbillys
1966
The Navy vs. the Night Monsters
1966
3 Nuts in Search of a Bolt
1964
The Candidate
1964
The Blonde from Buenos Aires
1961
The Private Lives of Adam and Eve
1961
College Confidential
1960
Sex Kittens Go to College
1960
The Beat Generation
1959
The Big Operator
1959
Girls Town
1959
Guns, Girls, and Gangsters
1959
Vice Raid
1959
Teacher's Pet
1958
Born Reckless
1958
High School Confidential!
1958
The Girl in Black Stockings
1957
Jet Pilot
1957
Untamed Youth
1957
Star in the Dust
1956
Running Wild
1955
The Second Greatest Sex
1955
Francis Joins the Wacs
1954
The All American
1953

"With singin,' dancin' 'n geetar pickin'!" **Moonshine Mountain**

MAMIE: I had never played a dead person before. They had me up on an ironing board to try and get a better shot. Lex Barker and the sheriff (John Dehner) are leaning over me examining me and I've got this bullet bra on with breasts up in the air. I just burst out laughing. That was my hardest scene in the whole movie, trying to be dead *and* sexy.

Q: **Navy vs. the Night Monsters** was another late show staple that sci-fi fans remember you for.

MAMIE: I know of people that like that movie, more or less for the yellow sweater I had on. I had fun doing it — but I thought I should have been eaten by the monster. I was looking forward to being gobbled up. I just took my money and ran. Now that *was* a "B" movie!

Q: Which brings us to **Voyage to the Planet of Prehistoric Women**.

MAMIE: Everybody seems to remember that one. Peter Bogdanovich directed that one. It was a quickie — really fast. I really don't know why I did it. I guess I just wanted to work. I didn't have one bit of dialogue. Nothing! We just hummed. We'd go MMMMMMMMMMM! It was sort of like the **Planet of the Apes**. I thought, "Hell, if Charlton Heston can do it, I can do it." Peter was kind of an oddball. He was always sticking the camera up my rear end. I thought, "God, this guy is an amateur." In one scene, when he asked me to eat a raw fish I thought, "F—k you, you eat it!" I said, "No way!" So they had to get the prop guy to fix a dummy fish that I could eat the head off of. I had these shells over my boobs and they were killing me.

Q: Do you see many movies these days?

MAMIE: It's got to be really special before I'll go out and sit in a movie theater. I'll wait until it comes out on tape and spend my evening at home. I'm not much for sitting in a theater.

"The picture with the warning bell!" Cannibal Girls

"Creeping horror from the depths of time and space!" *Invasion of the Saucer Men*

LUST AMONG THE LEECHES
yvette VICKERS
MEETS THE B MONSTER

She had swagger down to a science and her sex appeal was employed to maximum advantage in several of the best known "Bs" of the '50s. With flashy roles in such films as **Attack of the Giant Leeches, I, Mobster, Juvenile Jungle** and, most notably, as the slatternly romantic rival

profile

of an outsized Allison Hayes in **Attack of the 50 Foot Woman**, Yvette Vickers delivered the sensual goods while simultaneously

"The horror of all mankind terrifies the screen!" The Werewolf

attempting to break free of the sex-bomb stereotype, and flesh out her resume with "A" movie roles.

"I did a myriad of TV shows," she recalls of this early period of struggle, "like **Dragnet**. Jack Webb became very, very supportive. Maybe he was flirting and I didn't even know it. I was so stupid. He used to get me coffee in the morning when I came on the set. I thought, 'Gosh, what a sweet guy.' I thought he did that for everybody. It was years later that I realized he didn't do that for everybody. I would have been much better off getting together with a solid guy like that than the ones I ended up with."

Her tumultuous romances placed her career — and her life — in jeopardy. Some relationships that seemed initially meaningful were fleeting. One in particular turned frighteningly abusive. "My first husband was a wonderful guy," she remembers. "He was a jazz musician who worked with the Bud Shank quartet, playing the bass. A very sweet guy. But I was just too young. I had no idea what the commitment really was. I must be truthful, my career was more important. When I started getting jobs, he was traveling a lot, and I couldn't go with him, so we were separated constantly. After four years, we both agreed we weren't able to go on like that. One or the other of us would have had to give up something they really wanted a lot."

A second, harrowing marriage, however, ended less amicably. "We both thought it was going to last forever," Vickers recalls of her second husband, a Hollywood-based writer. "But he turned out to be frightening and dangerous and very, very controlling. I had to leave town to get away from him. I was in fear for my life. I don't want to give his name because he may come looking for me."

Throughout these dark times, Vickers continued the struggle to advance her acting career. With a plum role in **Short Cut to Hell**, the only film directed by James Cagney, her success seemed assured. "I had three nice scenes in that," she asserts. "For a beginner, that was a good thing to be in a film with his name connected with it."

Working with the veteran actor proved to be a confidence-building experience for the starlet. "He was wonderful. He was an artist. He behaved in a way that made you both feel this was a very serious commitment, but it's also got to be fun. He had that magic in him. He knew how to lighten up a moment." **Short Cut to Hell** was a prestige picture

"Sights too weird to imagine. Destruction too monstrous to escape!" Devil Girl From Mars

that seemed certain to do big things for all involved. "Oh my God, we were treated like royalty," Vickers recalls. But somehow, the film didn't come together dramatically and, consequently, financially. Vickers submits that, as the film was a remake of **This Gun For Hire**, it lacked the charismatic central presence that Alan Ladd brought to the original film.

"It was right at that time that I was trying to bridge that gap from these little TV shows and B movies," Vickers remembers. "I was doing leading roles on television and in the theater, but I hadn't had that one lucky break in a movie. It was right at the time when it could have happened that I left town to get away from my husband. [My friend] Keir Dullea said to me later, that 'If you leave town when you're a hot property, even though you may have missed out on a few good parts, you'll get one if you stick with it.' But that's when I left to get away from this guy. I was still very young, 23 or 24. I went to New York where I was in a Broadway play. Then theater sort of dried up, too."

Feeling that it was safe at last to return to Hollywood, Vickers discovered that she'd been largely forgotten while she was away. The professional community was friendly enough, but the work just wasn't coming. "Everybody's saying how wonderful you are, but nobody will touch you with a 10-foot pole."

It was while appearing in a series of Grand Guignol horror plays in Los Angeles that Vickers fell into yet another tempestuous relationship. "That's when I met Jim Hutton," she remembers. "We had an on-and-off relationship for the next 14 years. The first seven years were pretty solid. We really thought we were going to stick together. But now my career was nowhere. I couldn't figure it out. I was trying so hard to recover, and Jimmy took up all my time, quite honestly. At a certain point, I should have let go of my career. I thought, 'Maybe this relationship is more important. Maybe we'll get married and have children.' I was very much in love with him and he was in love with me too. We were

FILMS FEATURING YVETTE VICKERS

Evil Spirits
1990
Vigilante Force
1976
The Dead Don't Die
1974
What's the Matter with Helen?
1971
Hud
1963
Beach Party
1963
Pressure Point
1962
Attack of the Giant Leeches
1959
The Saga of Hemp Brown
1958
Attack of the 50 Foot Woman
1958
I, Mobster
1958
Juvenile Jungle
1958
Reform School Girl
1957
The Sad Sack
1957
Short Cut to Hell
1957
Sunset Blvd.
1950

"Planet robber tramples the earth!" **Kronos**

going to get married. He called his mother and I called my mother. Then he made a second call to his ex-wife — the mother of Timothy Hutton. She said, 'Oh, it will kill the children. They will go mad! I'll have to take them to a psychiatrist. Timothy will never be normal if you do this!' She was so influential that he went back there to talk to her about it. I said, 'Jimmy, if she can do this to you, I don't think we're going to make it. If just a word from her can throw you off this much, maybe you ought to try to work it out.' He went back to her and he was miserable. I could never feel the same again if all it took was for her to say that it would drive the children crazy. We broke up, but we kept making up and going back and forth for years. I even married somebody else, got an annulment and went back to Jimmy. He married somebody else, got a divorce and came back to me. We did this over and over until the day he died. I was at the hospital and I said, 'Jimmy, what can I do to help?' He said, 'When I get out of here, I'm going to Malibu. I want you to come out and we'll have our time together. We'll do all the stuff that you always tried to get me to do.' Well, it didn't happen. He died, but at least the last words were good ones and the picture was beautiful."

Prior to her initial encounter with Hutton, Vickers enjoyed an abbreviated relationship that she describes today as "mystical." Referring to her liaison with Cary Grant, she says, "He was a special relationship because he was above and beyond every other one, just as he was as a movie star. It was a pure relationship. There were no hassles. There were no conflicts. There were no people tugging away at us saying, 'You shouldn't.' We simply liked each other."

"We met at Universal through [writer] Stanley Shapiro, a friend of my ex-husband's. We had lunch and laughed and had a hell of a good time. He said, 'Can you come over to dinner some night? I'd love it.' When I walked in, he was sitting at the piano playing Bix Biederbeck's **In A Mist**. My mother used to play that. It was mystical. How could he possibly know? Who knows Bix Biederbeck except music people? His music is extraordinary, and hard to play, and Cary was playing it beautifully. It was magic. I wasn't seeing anyone else and, as far as I know, he wasn't. He had been dating Dyan Cannon who was out on tour at the time. We talked about that and he said, 'I don't know what to do. When she gets back, I'll have to talk to her.' I said, 'If you have a commitment, I'm not asking you to change anything.' When she got back she told him she was pregnant and that was it. They got married.

"Re-created half beast, half woman!" She Demons

"It was right about that time that I met Jimmy. When he and Cary made their movie together [**Walk, Don't Run** in 1966], Cary told him that we'd had a love affair. Jimmy took it very well because he adored Cary. Jimmy said, 'If there's anybody in the world that I would be jealous of — and I am — it would be Cary Grant. It'll take a little time to get over, but we'll work it out.' And we did."

And what of the persistent rumors regarding Grant's bisexuality? "I know he liked women," Vickers says. "But I think a lot of men — and women too — especially actors, because they're a bit narcissistic, go through a period when they're attracted to both sexes. They're just able to express it without feeling guilty or ashamed about it. I think maybe that did happen with him early on, but at a certain point his preference went toward women."

Even while negotiating a series of trying relationships, Vickers was driven to succeed as a serious actress. Though significant roles in "A" productions such as **This Earth Is Mine** and **The Carpetbaggers** somehow slipped away, she remained focused. "I was always doing a play or a TV project or singing or writing," she recalls. "I was always trying to get another project going." Appearing in B movies and horror pictures allowed her to maintain visibility and bring in a paycheck.

> "PEOPLE THOUGHT I COULD ONLY PLAY FEMME FATALES AND SEX GODDESSES. THAT BECAME 'THE' ROLE FOR ME."

Typecasting can be a roadblock to stardom for an aspiring serious actress, as Vickers learned following her earthy performances as loose women in a pair of the 1950s best known Bs. At the time **Attack of the 50 Foot Woman** and **Attack of the Giant Leeches** first appeared, the cheesecake and boudoir publicity shots for which Vickers posed worked to her detriment. "That's something we were all blind-sided by," she says, referring to a coterie of actress

"Karloff dares you to see this holocaust of horror!" The Man They Could Not Hang

friends who posed similarly. "We all thought, 'Yeah, we can do this and then drop it. We can still go on and get the serious parts.' But it really doesn't work that way. People judge you very harshly. They say, 'Why did she show her figure if she's good?' Guys do it, God knows. You see them pumping up and you see their bodies and nobody seems to think there's anything too terrible about that. But women are judged quite harshly."

While fighting for more serious roles, Vickers was often forced to fall back on her image as a vamp to stay employed. "People thought I could only play femme fatales and sex goddesses," she remembers. "That became 'THE' role for me." The actress cites a salient example: "I did **One Step Beyond** with Mike Connors. [Producer] John Newland loved me and he loved my work. He loved the fact that I had this really hard edge — almost a Bette Davis-kind of delivery. I asked, 'Don't you think I should make the character a little more sympathetic?' He said, 'No! She's tough as nails, baby.' I had to accept his judgment."

Among the B films in which she consequently appeared, Vickers recalls the juvenile delinquent classic **Juvenile Jungle** opposite B-movie teen tough Richard Bakalyan as a happy experience. "I had fun on that. Dick Bakalyan was a buddy that I used to hang out with. I liked him a lot. Dick was a good friend. Corey Allen was a friend, too — and a very good actor."

In retrospect, typecasting might be recognized as a blessing in disguise, as Vickers is still beloved by B-movie fans for her role as the slatternly Liz in a steamy saga of marauding, swamp-water parasites. **Attack of the Giant Leeches** provided Yvette with a showy, dramatic role. There was just one hitch. "I'm afraid of water," she laughs. "I'd told all the divers and the leeches in their suits that if you see me gurgling or doing anything funny, grab me because I'm terrified. I almost drowned three times in my life. It's a fear you can't quite get over. But I would work in the water. And I have done other shows in the water. I even did one where I played an undersea diver. But only for the movies.

"Well, they were all watching me and, sure enough, I started gurgling and gargling and they pulled me out. Gene Corman was on the set and he had them pull me ashore. They bundled me up in an army blanket and gave me a shot of brandy. He said, 'You just take it easy. Don't worry about anything.' They were so kind. They didn't blow it off and say, 'Oh, she's a baby.' They really took care and I think they got some better shots because of it. I really tried a lot harder after that."

This incident was followed by another near-disaster. "We were at the old Charlie Chaplin studio on Highland," says Vickers, setting the scene. "The cave [where many scenes took place] was built on a set and the water was in a vinyl tub, five or six feet deep. As we were shooting a scene, I looked up to see the cameraman on his seat twirling and the camera spinning in circles and then — a rush of water. The tub that was holding that water had broken. I saw these big waves that looked like the ocean. The cameraman was swept away." Complete disaster was averted, thanks to a quick-thinking grip. "Some smart electrician pulled the plug. Otherwise we would have been electrocuted."

> "ROGER SAID, 'BRING UP YOUR CARS AND TURN ON YOUR HEADLIGHTS.' WE SHOT THE REST OF THE SCENES THAT NIGHT IN THE HEADLIGHTS."

Was it difficult to stay in character considering the less-than-convincing appearance of the leeches themselves? "I didn't really think about it," Vickers laughs. "I was so concentrated on what I was supposed to be doing — screaming, crying and moaning. I never saw such a long death scene in my life. I saw it again recently and thought, 'How long did I die in this movie?' They kept cutting back to the moaning and the groaning."

In describing the locations the film utilized, Vickers relates an example of Roger and Gene Corman's noted frugality. "We shot in the Arboretum in Pasadena where they did the Tarzan movies," she begins. "You've probably heard that the Corman brothers are a little thrifty. Well, they had to get a certain number of shots every day. We were running late, and we had no big lamps or studio lights. Roger said, 'Bring up your cars and turn on your headlights.'

"A picture from out of this world!" The Lady and the Monster

We shot the rest of the scenes that night in the headlights. The scene where Ken Clark finds me running in the bushes, that was filmed in the headlights."

The film's most credible scenes involve Vickers' character and her cuckolded husband, played by Bruno VeSota. "I respected him so much as an actor," Yvette recalls. "I thought our scenes worked really well. I really liked working with him. I should have kept in touch with him. He passed away so early on, and I had meant to keep in touch. He had other projects he wanted to work with me on. He was a very creative man."

One key player throughout this phase of Vickers' career was her agent, Jack Pomeroy, who coincidentally represented B filmdom's other reigning femme fatale, Allison Hayes. It was Pomeroy who secured Yvette parts in **Giant Leeches** and **50 Foot Woman**. "Jack knew I liked to work," says Vickers. "He knew I just wanted to keep working and I was up for several parts [that weren't coming through]. He said, 'Look, Allison does this stuff all the time. Nobody's even going to know you made it.' That's what we used to think about those B movies. 'I can do this stuff and no one will even see it.' Although I did do my best. I don't go into something and just walk through it. I do the best job I can. I wasn't ashamed to do it, exactly. I was up for all these big movies, but I didn't get them. But I could do this film, stay active, doing what I love to do and maybe next time, I'd get the big fish."

Though her role in **Attack of the 50 Foot Woman** as town hussie Honey Parker is regarded by B-film buffs today as one of her best, would she rather have played the towering titular female? "No, I loved my part," she says. "I loved playing Honey Parker because she was the vamp and the woman that got the man."

Like **Giant Leeches**, this low-budget shocker was not without its near-calamitous accidents. "There was a scary moment where I get killed when the 50 Foot Woman smashes a table with me under it," Vickers recalls. "All this stuff came tumbling down and it was very realistic. I thought, 'Gee, that must have looked good.' I started to move and one of the crew leaned over and said, 'Don't move.' They hadn't removed all of the nails from the boards [that were used] and one of these huge nails was right under my head. Any move the wrong way and it would have gone right into my brain."

Vickers struck up a friendship with Hayes, and the two socialized while maintaining

"It's the picture that has the whole town shivering!" Black Dragons

the struggle to advance their careers beyond the scope of B films. "She was dating Jack Palance at the time," Vickers remembers. "We both had this tendency to date actors. I had dated Ralph Meeker and Hugh O'Brian. Edd Byrnes was one of my boyfriends. The people I met, mostly, were actors. Because she and I had the same agent, we were kind of a package, and at that time she was living in the guest house of our agent's office."

Over time, both actresses came to realize that graduation to "A" productions was not in the cards. "I think Allison believed that she would make that transition as well. She was a glamorous woman. She had a wonderful presence."

Vickers lost contact with Hayes when she fled her abusive second husband. "We lost touch shortly after that because I went to New York. She got sick from a shot that her doctor gave her. It had too much lead in it and it eventually killed her. She was ill for many years and couldn't work and actually was housebound. All from lead poisoning. It was a frightening thing. I didn't hear about it until 1985. I had been trying to find her. I was at a St. Patrick's party with a guy who knew both of us. He said, 'Gee, Yvette. Didn't you know she died?' He told me how it happened. What a horrible thing to happen to anybody."

Today, Yvette Vickers maintains a schedule of personal appearances and autograph signings, where male fans of Liz and Honey Parker continue to flirt with her. In addition to the occasional stage role, she is also focusing on her singing career. In recalling her B-movie past, she is proud of the fact that the quality of her work never reflected the paucity of the budget. "All of the people on [those movies] were in the same creative mind-set. 'No cheating here. We're going to do everything we can to make the best movie we can make.' Who knew all these years later that this would be what I'm remembered for?"

"When the axe swings, the excitement begins!" Strait Jacket

"We urge you not to panic or bolt from your seats!" The Black Scorpion

THE LITTLE SHOP'S ORIGINAL PROPRIETOR *mel* WELLES
MEETS THE B MONSTER

profile

Just when you think you've got Mel Welles figured out, he tosses another surprise into the conversation. For instance: "I was a voice of the beatnik era," he declares. "I was definitely a beatnik, and proud to be. I get a kick out of it when young people today think they invented pot and dirty words." Welles fell into a thriving beat scene when he landed in Hollywood in the 1950s, and he eventually penned

"Nightmare thrills beyond belief!" Monster From Green Hell

several pieces for legendary hipster monologist Lord Buckley, including the classic **Hipsters, Flipsters and Finger-Poppin' Daddies**. But few fans today are familiar with this formative stage in the career of an actor best known for portraying the bellicose shopkeeper Gravis Mushnik in the original **The Little Shop of Horrors**.

The gruff and garrulous former beatnik, director, producer, psychologist and self-proclaimed Godfather of the voice-over industry ("I got into adapting and dubbing European films; I was one of the major voices [in the business] — I dubbed over 800 films") is widely recognized today for the handful of low-budget horror films he made with Roger Corman. "I have become, laughingly, an icon in the horror-film genre. If you look at my credits, only about six of my films even fall remotely into that category. I did over 65 films and 300 television shows and produced and directed 12 films. Of the 12 films I produced and directed, only two of them were horror films. But there's always a demand for stills and autographs at memorabilia shows."

> "I HAVE BECOME, LAUGHINGLY, AN ICON IN THE HORROR-FILM GENRE. IF YOU LOOK AT MY CREDITS, ONLY ABOUT SIX OF MY FILMS EVEN FALL REMOTELY INTO THAT CATEGORY."

What's on the mind of the typical Mel Welles fan? "It depends on their age and their contact with the Corman era of funk films. The baby boomer's first questions are always about [the Corman pictures]. Apparently, they were the first films that scared them. The younger fans, most of whom are half the age of the pictures, are interested in the genre as a whole."

"It chills as it thrills!" **Dr. Renault's Secret**

Welles is nostalgic regarding the ingenuity and "anything goes" attitude that attended the making of his best-known films. "In those days, the so-called horror film was more fun than it was scary. There was a warmth to those kind of pictures that does not exist today. Horror films were much more fun to make than to watch. **The Undead**, for instance, was originally written entirely in iambic pentameter — it was written in couplets. That would have been the classic of all time. But Roger lost his nerve. He had Chuck Griffith rewrite the script.

"Working with Roger was interesting because everybody did everything. Beech Dickerson was sometimes a sound guy. Another one of the actors would hold the boom. It was a collaborative effort. We could make suggestions. It was a fun time. Roger made a picture a month — a week to write the script, a week to prepare the picture, a week to shoot it and a week to finish it. There was always a Corman picture going on and, if you weren't working elsewhere, you could call him up and say, 'Roger, I need a job.'"

The low-rent shockers that Welles made with Corman stand today as classics in their category: **Attack of the Crab Monsters, The Undead** and, most notably, **Little Shop of Horrors**. The threadbare comic thriller, starring Welles as shop owner Gravis Mushnik, was very nearly not made. "Roger didn't like comedy. He didn't believe in it. He had tried with **A Bucket of Blood** and it failed. So he didn't want to do **Little Shop** at all. We had to beg him and cajole him. Ironically, it's his most famous picture. What sticks in his craw is that he had very little to do with it. All the exteriors were done by me and Chuck. We did 15 minutes of the picture for $1,100. We paid the extras in Skid Row 10 cents apiece. We got the entire Southern Pacific Railway yard for a night for two bottles of Scotch (the next day, 20th Century-Fox paid $10,000 for the same service). We got all those locations — the toilet yard, the tire yard and the mortuary — free. When Roger came on the set, the actors were already rehearsed, by me, for three weeks before we started."

Not surprisingly, Welles points to the film as among his favorites. "It has to be. The whole project was a love project. It's probably my favorite role because it was written for me by my best friend [Charles Griffith]. It was written around a character that I used to always do at parties. I used to do it for days at a time. Some people didn't know that I spoke without an accent. Mushnik was an outgrowth of a funny Jewish character I used to do. The only change for the film was that I made him Sephardic; the accent is more

"Slinking fiend! Skulking horror! Mad murder!" Behind the Mask

Sephardic than middle-European."

It took just two days and two nights to film **Little Shop of Horrors**. Total production cost: $27,500. A few years after it was seen in theaters, it began turning up the late, late show. Night owl channel flickers were fascinated for some reason, even though it clearly looked like a film that took two days and two nights to film and cost just $27,500. A cult began to grow.

More than 20 years after the film was released, **Little Shop** was transformed into a Broadway musical and, subsequently, a star-studded Hollywood production. "First of all, the remake was really *not* a remake," Welles clarifies. "The late, super-talented Howard Ashman and Martin Robinson saw the original film when they were 11 years old and each, independently, was obsessed with the idea of making a musical based on it. Years passed, and they met and created a musical with unprecedented success. I, personally, loved the play. I thought it was terrific fun!"

When it came to the Hollywood treatment of the **Little Shop** musical, some hard feelings were engendered among members of the original cast. "The movie was a disappointment, partly because, although I was paged for availability, when Frank Oz came on board as director, he decided that no one from the original movie could participate. Unfortunate, because I was probably the only member of the original cast who could have conceivably reprised his role, and, of course, I would have loved to play it."

Notwithstanding, Welles assessment of the "remake" is decidedly kind. "The movie was okay, but missed a

---

FILMS FEATURING MEL WELLES

Wizards of the Lost Kingdom II
1988
Commando Squad
1987
Invasion Earth: The Aliens Are Here
1987
Chopping Mall
1986
Homework
1982
The Last American Virgin
1982
Body and Soul
1981
Dr. Heckyl and Mr. Hype
1980
Joyride to Nowhere
1977
Revenge of the Blood Beast
1966
The Keeler Affair
1964
The Red Sheik
1962
The Little Shop of Horrors
1960
The Brothers Karamazov
1958
High School Confidential!
1958
The 27th Day
1957
Attack of the Crab Monsters
1957
Hell on Devil's Island
1957
Hold That Hypnotist
1957
The Undead
1957
Outside the Law
1956
Flight to Hong Kong
1956
The Big Knife
1955
Pirates of Tripoli
1955
Soldier of Fortune 1955
Abbott and Costello Meet the Mummy
1955
Fighting Chance
1955
Gun Fury
1953

"The place nobody knows except the girls nobody wants!" **Betrayed Women**

bit in soul. Ellen Greene was, as usual, brilliant. The whole Steve Martin-Bill Murray sequence was very funny and entertaining. Mushnik, sadly, had his songs and his "beytsum" cut. In case one gets the idea that Vince Gardenia's inability to sing was the reason for the cut, I'd like to point out that he has a beautiful voice and could have sung the hell out of the songs! I love Vinnie Gardenia's work, but I thought that one didn't care whether his character lost the shop or not. I think the ethnicity [missing from the musical] with which the role was created and played in the original version gave it real warmth.

"Also, there is one significant difference in the chemistry of the two films. In the $30,000,000 spectacular, the plant is positively Mephisthophelean, evil, a stone killer, whereas in the $27,500 funky little original, the plant was simply hungry."

Welles' identification with the Mushnik role (much of the time, his e-mail is signed simply Gravis) continues today, and recent events indicate that the character will survive well into the new Millennium. "In April, I will be playing Mushnik in the musical play at the Scott's Valley Performing Arts Theatre. I am looking forward to it and to singing the two songs they cut from the movie."

"Driven by a force he could not control!" **The Lady and the Monster**

KUBRICK AND THE CAT-WOMEN marie WINDSOR
MEETS THE B MONSTER

The first thing you notice is the eyes. Dark and glowering, you'd almost believe one glance could slice a guy in two. They saw Marie Windsor through some of the best B movies ever produced. Her image as the movie's quintessential sexy, tough broad is well-earned, but her *profile* versatility may be her most remarkable trait. In a 60-year career, she worked in every film genre, lending class to the lowly "Bs" and

"Human prey of giant gorilla on her wedding night!" *The Bride and the Beast*

outshining the stars of the "A" films in which she was featured. Few would argue that she'll survive film history as the definitive film noir dame, having appeared in three of the genre's finest offerings: **The Narrow Margin, The Killing** and **Force of Evil**.

Leaving her Utah origins behind, Marie found work in film land as a model for pinup legend Alberto Varga and as a cigarette girl at the Mocambo, Hollywood's legendary watering hole. Spotted there by producer Arthur Hornblow Jr., she landed her first film role and began learning the ropes in support of the major stars of the day.

Early films that showed her to good advantage include **Force of Evil, The Sniper, Hellfire** and **Double Deal**, a nifty little thriller co-starring Richard Denning. "A sweet man," Windsor recalls. "I think both he and his wife have passed away by now. His wife passed away — Evelyn Ankers — and then he remarried. I used to correspond with him when he was living in Hawaii."

> "I WASN'T THAT PARTICULAR, SHALL I SAY. I NEVER ASKED WHO THE COSTARS WERE OR ANYTHING LIKE THAT. I JUST ASKED WHEN IT WAS AND HOW MUCH MONEY."

The tenacious and talented Windsor worked hard and displayed an amazing range, eventually earning the unofficial crown as "Queen of the Bs" following a strange and diverse series of films. Her résumé is peppered with dramas, comedies, classics and camp. But to sci-fi film fans, she'll always be remembered for a movie she does her best to forget.

Marie is chagrined but affable when asked to recall the 3-D cult curio, **Cat-Women of the Moon**. "Oh gosh, it's almost embarrassing." Does an actress call upon untapped reserves of

"A new kind of terror to numb the nerves!" Monster That Challenged the World

good humor to survive an experience like **Cat-Women**? "Well, I've always been an actress," Windsor asserts, "I just wanted to work. And if they handed me almost anything — if I didn't have to strip — I would work. It had to be a fairly nice part."

With engaging humility, Windsor adds, "I wasn't that particular, shall I say. I never asked who the costars were or anything like that. I just asked when it was and how much money."

Is she still remembered by fans as a gun moll on the lam in producer-director Roger Corman's low-budget crime-thriller, **Swamp Women**? "Oh, yes," she laughs. "Yeah. I wish I wasn't. God. It's just such a corny picture." Yet again, Marie Windsor survived a trite script and adverse conditions with grace and good humor. "Well, we had such a rough location on it. In Louisiana," she recalls. "We were treading around in mud up to our waists. It looked like there was only about a foot of water and then you'd step down and just keep on going."

Windsor recalls young actors Beverly Garland and Mike Connors, for whom **Swamp Women** was something of a breakthrough. "Terrific. Darling people. We [still] exchange Christmas cards — and Beverly just called me a couple of days ago."

In 1952, the struggling actress landed a lead in what was to become one of the best examples of low-budget film noir ever made, **The Narrow Margin**. "My agent climbed through the window of the casting director with a test that I had made out at 20th Century-Fox — and that was it."

At the time of her casting in **The Narrow Margin**, Windsor knew little of Richard Fleischer, the young director helming the picture. "As I later figured out, I was lucky to have worked with him. I'm not too sure, but I think he would have preferred a big star in the role, which I certainly wasn't." Upon its release, the acknowledged crime-film classic garnered solid raves. "We certainly made a lot of noise with that picture. It ran with all the top pictures and we got all the reviews." It is still recalled by many as one of the very best B films ever made.

A great part of the film's success is due to the electric teaming of Windsor and gravel-voiced tough guy Charles McGraw. "He was a darling," Windsor says. "Everybody asks me 'Was he drinking on the set?' He wasn't," she asserts, recalling, however, that "he did have a problem with alcohol." Nonetheless she maintains, "He was wonderful to work with. We became very good friends. He had a beautiful wife and child. So we used to take turns at each other's houses."

Windsor exhibits mild surprise that **Narrow Margin** is still upheld as a film noir classic some 50 years after its release. "I didn't even realize what a film noir film was at that time."

For unfathomable reasons, **The Narrow Margin** failed to generate the opportunities that Windsor expected. She kept working, co-starring with Cat-Women, Swamp Women and Abbott & Costello. Learning her comic chops was part of the starlet's regimen. On the set of **Abbott and Costello Meet the Mummy**, costar Marie encountered two of the finest tutors imaginable. "Everybody wants to know about the two of them — how they were to work with, if they were fighting on the set, and that's supposed to be the time that they were — I wasn't aware of it."

What was Windsor's personal experience of the then fading, former box-office kings? "Costello frequently had cast and crew to his bungalow for lunch and I got invited once. I don't know if it was because of my bad table manners or what, but I wasn't invited anymore. Maybe he just gave everybody a one-time treat. But they were very, very nice to me, very helpful. And I did learn a lot about comedy timing from them."

In 1955, Marie was offered a part in Stanley Kubrick's classic crime film, **The Killing**. "I was very

SELECTED FILMS FEATURING MARIE WINDSOR

Supercarrier
1988
Commando Squad
1987
Salem's Lot
1979
Freaky Friday
197
Cahill: United States Marshal
1973
Support Your Local Gunfighter
1971
Chamber of Horrors
1966
Critic's Choice
1963
The Day Mars Invaded Earth
1962
The Girl in Black Stockings
1957
The Story of Mankind
1957
The Unholy Wife
1957
The Killing
1956
Abbott and Costello Meet the Mummy
1955
Swamp Women
1955
The Bounty Hunter
1954
Cat-Women of the Moon
1953
The Eddie Cantor Story
1953
Trouble Along the Way
1953
The Jungle
1952
The Narrow Margin
1952
The Sniper
1952
Double Deal
1950
The Fighting Kentuckian
1949
Hellfire
1949
Force of Evil
1948
The Three Musketeers
1948
The Hucksters
1947
Song of the Thin Man
1947

"The monster demands a mate" Bride of Frankenstein

impressed with Kubrick, and it was a wonderful role and I knew that he had seen me in **The Narrow Margin** and said to his producer, 'That's my Sherry.' "Kubrick went to great lengths to secure Windsor's services as tough broad Sherry Peatty. "He postponed starting his picture a couple of days so that I could [finish] **Swamp Women** [which] Roger Corman was making down in Louisiana. Corman was nice to let me go a couple of days early and Kubrick was willing to wait for me."

The young director, had just one picture to his credit, but nonetheless instilled great confidence in cast and crew. "From the minute we started to work, I was thoroughly impressed at how capable and knowledgeable he was about film," Windsor recalls, "so that made me feel like it might be a great success."

Marie points out that, even early in his career, Kubrick demonstrated his trademark eccentricities. "He was very funny about wearing these workman's pants all the time," Windsor recalls. "Even when we did something social like the opening of the picture in San Francisco or a party at our house, he always liked those comfortable pants."

Does the queen of film noir have a favorite leading man? "Oh, I could name several," she says, exhibiting some reticence. "Bill Elliott, Fred MacMurray ... as a matter of fact, it's very hard for me to answer a question like that."

But when it comes to favorite films, there is little hesitation. "First it was **Hellfire**, a Western with Bill Elliott, and then there was **The Killing** and **Narrow Margin**, they're all my favorites." Not surprisingly, she affirms that these also seem to be the films fans remember most fondly. "It's interesting that those pictures are replayed and replayed in England particularly. I get a lot of fan mail from England."

Marie Windsor, the sassy, sultry tough dame against whom all future movie molls should be measured, recalls co-workers with a sweetness that belies the screen persona for which she is recognized. "I really loved everybody I worked with," she says, surrounded by a backlog of year-old fan mail that she plans to answer.

Marie had been nearly incapacitated by a stroke just prior to our interview. I was deeply impressed that she took the time to speak with me. On and off the record, she was funny, brassy, acerbic and charming. She passed away in December 2000.

"Fiery, fearless, ferocious!" Cat Women of the Moon

"The newest thing in thrill-chill pictures!" Voodoo Man

3

Beware the Baby Boomer's Wrath!

A closing argument, for lack of a better term, that will hopefully incite the fans of classic horror in general, and "B" movies in particular, to condemn the mind-numbing sameness and unoriginality that have come to dominate the genre.

"Re-created half beast, half woman!" *She Demons*

"It came from another world!" *Giant From the Unknown*

Revenge of the boomer monsters!

WARNING: This might be construed as a "think piece." That's the dreaded phrase invoked to warn readers that a writer is about to ramble on about his personal feelings regarding some pop-culture phenomenon or other. That having been said ...

I begin with a seemingly incongruous question: Are you a jazz fan? Don't worry, it isn't a requirement, but it might help as we trudge through the following analogy (I beg you to be patient). There is a book called *Blue: The Murder of Jazz* (How's that for a grabber title?) by Eric Nisenson. The author's contention is that the development of this, arguably the most expressive and experimental music we have, has been stifled by its own commercial success. Only recently has it become acceptable to own up to liking jazz in the presence of your top-40 radio-reared friends. This is due in large measure to the media's crowning of Wynton Marsalis, a brilliant trumpet prodigy and eloquent spokesman, as the leading — heck, the ONLY — living authority on jazz. He is the jazz "go-to guy" for documentarians (most notably Ken Burns), talk show hosts, authors and radio programmers. The author of *Blue* contends that this practice has "murdered" jazz. No one in the jazz field can succeed now without the official sanction of Wynton Marsalis. Media wags will barely notice an emerging jazz talent without asking themselves if the artist has won the Marsalis stamp of approval. As a result, no one innovates, no one experiments, everyone falls into line, producing only what is expected and commercially acceptable.

The comic book and literary fields have their Marsalis counterparts, Scott McCloud, Kevin Smith and Michael Chabon among the latest to be installed. They're not to be blamed for availing themselves of the media's intense, myopic adherence to their opinions. We're to blame for accepting the stagnation it sanctions.

Which brings us to Stephen Sommers, the horror-film Marsalis. The success of his so-so **Mummy** picture surprised everyone, including Universal, the studio that produced it. His follow-up, **The Mummy Returns**, was uninspired, but did good business. **The Mummy** spawned a perfunctory spin-off called **The Scorpion King**, which performed respectably at the box office. Sommers' reward was to be handed the keys to the classic monster vault. The legendary creatures we baby boomers grew up watching were now his to maneuver like chess pieces (or mold into new and grotesque shapes if you prefer another power analogy). These mythic monsters, beloved by a generation, were his to "re-imagine" (to invoke a very tired phrase that Universal never tires of invoking). At a time when the studio desperately needed hits, Sommers delivered hits — albeit dumbed-

"A woman by day ... a monster by night!" Voodoo Woman

down, by-the-numbers, lowest common denominator hits, so he was given all the marbles, cart blanche, free reign, a clear field, an overstaffed, state-of-the-art workshop wherein to assemble the next money-making property. The result was **Van Helsing**.

I don't wish to belabor why **Van Helsing** is such a bad film (poorly acted, poorly scripted, excessive in every regard), because what the makers of **Van Helsing** DIDN'T do is just as informative. With these mythical, time-honored properties at their disposal, and some of Hollywood's finest craftsmen in their employ, did they innovate, did they experiment, did they break any new ground at all? The answer is "no." Far from "re-imagining," Sommers & Co. chose to "re-enshrine" the same hoary clichés already displayed ad nauseum in **Blade, Buffy, Angel, Lost Boys** and numerous similar extrapolations. They gave the public what it already had in a bigger, shinier package. And delivery of the package was preceded by all manner of ancillary products: everything from collectors cups to mini-monster trucks.

But the singular sin for which these filmmakers should be held accountable is the stripping away of the monsters' humanity. Humanity and monsters are reconcilable? Absolutely! It was the humanity of the classic monsters, more than any other quality, that made us love them. They were strong, ugly, fearsome to be sure, but the crux of their character was their desire to be human.

Dracula longed for mortality: "To die. To be really dead. That must be ... glorious." Lugosi delivered that line with pathetic and theatrical grandeur in the original **Dracula**. In **Van Helsing**, Dracula, his brides, his offspring, ALL vampires are bloodthirsty, kill-crazy, wholly evil things with no redeeming pathos whatsoever. In the incarnation I love, Frankenstein's monster yearned for acceptance, longed for the recognition of the man who created him. Few scenes in monster cinema — in any genre — equal the emotional punch of Karloff's child-like gesticulation toward the overhead light suddenly gone dark. In **Van Helsing**, the monster is a big, blubbering, victimized baby. We don't feel sorry for him (the script doesn't give us time), we just want him to shut up. **Van Helsing** gives the Wolf Man the shortest shrift of all, curious in that his predicament is the most pathetic and exploitable. The original Wolf Man was frantic to regain his humanity, tormented with each cycle of the moon as it slipped away. **Van Helsing** makes the faintest of attempts to invoke sympathy for the werewolf/brother of the heroine, but his appearances are fleeting, and we're given no chance to identify with his character or feel his pain. The film progresses like a soulless juggernaut, sparing no time to touch upon the humanity of any of its characters.

And you know what? Sommers isn't to be faulted. Given all those toys and all that

"Adventure into the unknown!" **Missile to the Moon**

freedom, I don't know that another contemporary director would have executed a better film. He turned out precisely the product he thought the guys in the front office wanted. Sommers' job is to sell popcorn, and he excels at it. To the bean counters, it just doesn't matter that his picture is all gloss and no gravity. So, who's responsible for this state of affairs? Who enables and sustains this cynical commercial mechanism? You and me, that's who, because we don't demand better.

A bit of history bears recounting: The classic monsters were neglected for years. They languished until, in the early days of television, they were tossed on the air merely to fill late-night broadcast slots. Their presenters ridiculed them. Hosts such as Zacherley, Vampira and their ilk are not blameless in this regard. (But hey, some of those oldies were less than inspiring.) No one gave two hoots about the classic monsters until we rediscovered them on the late show. The boomer generation fell in love with the monsters. The children of the boom identified with the childlike predicaments of the monsters, while simultaneously desiring to share their fearsome power. As the 1950s drew to a close, the monster boomers were gobbling up monster magazines, toys, games, forming clubs, building models. And then, we grew up.

But it didn't last. We were roused from the distractions of adulthood by the horrible realization that our mothers had trashed our monster memorabilia by the shovel-full. What could we do but go out and buy it all back again ... from mercenary collectors at 50 times the original price? Man, did they see us coming! How much should a piece of your past cost? That's the question that torments the majority of boomer monster fans who flock to conventions, seminars and autograph sessions. These sojourns in search of notions from a simpler time in our lives, the wistful, childish identification with the dilemma of the classic monsters, entitles you to a say in their legacy. Your memories (and money!) make them live.

The point of this diatribe? The monsters are YOURS! Only relatively recently did Universal honchos awake to the fact that there was money to be made from the moldering monster movies in their vaults. They roused from their snooze, noticed the nostalgia collectors, amateur modelers, growing throngs at film conventions and uttered a collective "holy s--t!" Soon, any studio or individual with even a tenuous tie to a monster film or actor sought out lawyers and accountants and set up shop. Lawsuits were filed, trademarks established and merchandising licenses issued. But none of this ever would have happened had you not kept the monsters alive in memory. So, why aren't you speaking your piece?

You can argue that, without **Van Helsing**, we wouldn't have **Monster Legacy**

"It reaches from the grave to re-live the horror, the terror!" Frankenstein's Daughter

Collections to enjoy today. But that's relinquishing too much of the credit YOU deserve. Because of fans like you and me, these monsters were on U.S. postage stamps — an impressive testament to their cultural standing — long before Stephen Sommers caught his big break.

The people who run the movie biz, the TV biz, the comic book biz — in short, the overlords of pop-culture — are monster boomers just like you. But they've grown cynical and lazy (and rich) and will keep recycling their same fantasies until you demand better. I once had occasion to speak with producer Avi Arad (**Spider-Man, Hulk**), Marvel Comics' man in Hollywood. His take on the movers and shakers, directors and producers currently at work on his pictures? "These guys are geeks who came from comics — who grew up with them — and now they have clout." My question to them: Why aren't you innovating, creating a new mythos, coming up with new ideas? Why should your children relive YOUR past? Why not create a wondrous present for them that they'll remember as fondly as you recall your past. And I don't mean dismal, dystopic junk like **The Matrix**; give them hope, for God's sake! Remind them of their humanity. You're talented people. Get busy!

"It'll make your skin crawl!" Bride of the Monster

About the author

Marty Baumann is an award-winning freelance artist with more than 20 years of experience in magazine, comic book, newspaper and children's book illustration and Web site design. His clients include HarperCollins, Johnson & Johnson, The Boy Scouts of America, Scholastic Books, Weekly Reader, McDonald's, Time-Warner and National Geographic. Samples of his work can be seen at www.martybaumann.com.

He is also an experienced journalist, having worked for six years at *USA Today* before co-creating the paper's Web site. He's since designed sites for Universal Studios, Time-Warner, The Sci Fi Channel, Turner Network Television, Woody Woodpecker and others.

Marty has written about film for The Sci Fi Channel, *Starlog, Sci Fi Universe, TNT's Roughcut, Script, Realms of Fantasy* and others. His love for science fiction, horror and fantasy films inspired his creation of *The Astounding B Monster.*

The popular search engine Excite named *B Monster* one of the "Top 10 Entertainment Sites of the Year" shortly after its 1996 debut. It is still listed among Yahoo's Top 10 most popular film Web sites, sharing the list with *Premier, Movieline* and *Boxoffice Magazine.*

Marty is also the creator of The Crater Kid (www.craterkid.com), a popular, all-ages sci-fi adventure comic strip with a devoted following.

Marty has been a rhythm and blues guitarist and singer for three decades and continues to perform at blues festivals with internationally known blues artists. He lives in Virginia with his wife and dog and he urges everyone to adopt a pet from their local shelter.

(In future editions, the remainder of this page will be filled with a list of awards, honorary degrees and doctorates bestowed upon Marty by peer groups and institutions of higher learning around the world.)

"Based on the authentic FACTS you've been reading about!" **The She-Creature**